The Great River Disclosure

By Larry Holcombe

Brandylane Publishers, Inc.

ISBN: 978-1-883911-88-1
Library of Congress Control Number: 2009930020

Brandylane Publishers, Inc.
Richmond, Virginia
brandylanepublishers.com

The Great River Disclosure

Carol
Hope you enjoy

My Best

*This novel is dedicated to Tiffany R. Cockrell,
my friend for forty years*

Acknowledgments

There are several people whose assistance in writing this novel deserves special thanks.

Stanton T. Friedman—Stan's help and suggestions to keep the plot in the mainstream of research into this fascinating subject was invaluable.

Colonel John Wilson (USAF-Ret.)—John spent many hours in the right hand seat of the Strategic Air Commands great F/B-111A. He was always willing to answer and explain my many technical questions, or on the rare occasion when he didn't know the answer, he would find it for me.

Alice Holcombe—My wife of forty-one years helped me overcome my woefully inadequate grammatical skills. Her encouragement, her enthusiasm, and her occasional nudge to get back to work kept me going when the doubts began to build.

I also want to thank Bobby and Ruby Albrite, Jake Russell, Marion Spurlin, and my son and daughter-in-law, Jeff and Lisa Holcombe; all who helped make it happen.

Special thanks goes to Robert Pruett who saw some worth in my writing and to Mary A. (Annie) Tobey whose editing skills were a source of great comfort.

While writing this novel Alice was diagnosed with breast cancer. During her treatment a good portion of work on the book took place sitting beside her bed for six or more hours as she received chemotherapy at the Rappahannock General Hospital's Cancer Center. The care and treatment she received there was nothing short of outstanding and I don't have the ability to properly communicate our gratitude to the entire staff.

Loving care combined with total professionalism is how I would best describe the Cancer Center staff. The RNs, Connie Deagle, Peggy Swann, Maggie Nickel, Fran Gaskins, Lorelle Perry, Laura Mills, Catherine Owens, Sharon Dunaway, and Hoppie Cockrell, are very special people, as is Terra Gaskins, PCT, and center secretary, Marian Harcum.

I would like to give special thanks to Dr. Thomas J. Smith and his staff from Virginia Commonwealth University's outstanding Massey Cancer

Center. Dr. Smith and his staff travels eighty miles from Richmond to Kilmarnock one day a week to treat RGH Cancer Center patients. His dedication and caring played a major role in helping us both through a most difficult time. Following chemo, surgery was performed by the capable hands of Dr. Barkley Zimmerman, a gentleman and gentle man who took the time to explain in whatever detail we wanted every aspect of the surgery. He's a terrific surgeon and a terrific man. Also, I would be negligent if I didn't mention the fine treatment she received from her radiation oncologist, Dr. Christopher Walsh and his staff at the Mid-Rivers Cancer Center.

Finally, but by no means last, is our family practitioner, Dr. Keith Cubbage at White Stone Family Practice. Dr. Cubbage was the first to diagnose Alice's condition, set up the medical team and closely follow her progress. Dr. Cubbage is special.

All indications are that Alice is now cancer-free. The prognosis for her recovery is excellent and is due in total to the efforts of all those named above. They all have our deepest gratitude.

"I do think it is of extraordinary importance for the future of this planet that we recognize we are NOT alone. We all on this planet do have something in common much as we hate to admit it. We all are Earthlings. It is time we started acting like it."

Stanton T. Friedman, MSc

PROLOGUE

April 16, 1986 – Somewhere in South America

They slipped from beneath the water, looking black and menacing like some otherworldly beings as they climbed a ladder to the top. They moved with fluid precision and took their assigned positions. No sounds, absolute quiet, eyes searching, senses razor sharp, flesh tingling.

It was all wrong, this wasn't the right place; he knew it the instant he reached the top. From the beginning Ted Carter had a bad feeling about this mission and now his senses were screaming to get out. His Navy SEAL fire team had made an underwater insertion to the base of a ladder that went to the top of a dock; now Ted had his eight-man team on the top side. It was too big. This dock was for oceangoing freighters. It was covered with steel shipping containers that looked like big rig trailer bodies. Intelligence said they would come in at a small dock about thirty feet long. He felt a cold shiver run through his body. They were in the wrong place; he needed to get his boats back in a hurry.

Ted grabbed the arm of his radioman. He was too late—lights, like the sun. Then automatic weapons fire from all directions. In his mind he was screaming, get down God damn it get down. Take cover. Oh God, they were being slaughtered. He saw his men falling; he had to take out the lights—now. Stepping into the open from behind a shipping container he took out one light as a round grazed the sleeve of his wetsuit, missing flesh. Grenades were going off. A man screamed—one of his guys got a bad guy, SEALs don't scream.

A rocket, it hit one of the containers and blew it apart, covering the dock in steel shrapnel. The automatic weapons fire was incessant and as the smoke from the rocket cleared he saw four of his men down. Maybe he was the only one left alive. Now rage took over. He rolled from behind the container and took out the second light, putting everything in the dark again. OK, you bastards, now the playing field just got a little more level. He heard more grenades landing all around him, then going off, and the fragments hitting the empty containers sounding like thousands of horribly out of tune bells. Then quiet, no more grenades, no more automatic weapons fire. You sons of bitches, you think you got me. Wrong, you're going to die; every fucking one of you is going to die.

He had night vision goggles and he eased down the backside of the container, saw nothing and moved to the next, where the ladder was located, then down the ladder and into the water. He saw them now, five of them, and he could see his men scattered and lying on the dock. He eased back up the ladder, staying behind the containers, and watched as the five started checking each of the men. The second man they checked was alive, one of the five grabbed his head and another started to cut his throat. Ted's rage was boiling. Fuck this, you son of a bitch. He stepped into the open and put a single round through the head of the man with the knife. His suppressed weapon just made a clicking sound from the action of the bolt and it took several seconds for the other four to realize what was happening. Their thought process took too long and was too late, as Ted squeezed off four more rounds into the respective heads of each man.

Going to each of his men, he found three injured but alive. There was an outboard runabout at the end of the dock and he quickly pulled it to the ladder. Through a superhuman effort he was able to get all three into the boat, but then he saw a light come on in a structure about one hundred yards from the dock. Coming from the structure were four more men with automatic weapons heading toward the dock. He motioned for his men to be quiet and then eased back up the ladder. He was in a state of calm now. SEAL training was guiding his every move—it could have been one hundred men and he would have been the same. Come on, you bastards, just a few more feet. It sounded like the click-click of a child's cricket toy, four times in rapid succession and the heads of the four men exploded.

Now he was acting on pure instinct without thought, just pure flowing mechanical action. He picked up another weapon and headed to the two-story frame building. Looking through the window he saw that three men had another team leader, Buck Meadows, tied to a chair and were taking turns smashing him in the face. His face was a bloody mess; then one of the men pulled out a knife and cut off Buck's right ear and waved it in his face. Click-click, click-click, click-click, three more heads exploded in a mass of blood, gray matter and bone that covered Buck.

Crashing through a door Ted picked up the knife and cut Buck free. Although bleeding profusely from the cut-off ear and cuts on his face, Buck was otherwise OK and Ted found a cloth for him to hold against his wounds. Spotting an assembled RPG-18 next to the front door, Ted picked it up as they left the house. Hurrying back to the dock, Ted directed Buck to the others waiting in the boat. He was proficient with the RPG and he now stopped, turned, put the weapon to his shoulder and fired at the structure.

The rocket struck between the first and second floor, exploding, taking out a section of wall and setting the building on fire.

Buck had the outboard running. Jumping in, Ted jammed the throttle forward and the twenty-foot runabout shot away from the dock. Ted still had the night vision goggles and he could follow the turns in the river as they headed back to the sea and their team. Then it happened, the explosion from the burning house. He had never experienced anything like it in all of his training. The flash was blinding, like ten suns, brilliant and white. He knew that a shock wave had to be coming. No explosion could that big without a massive shock wave. He turned and looked behind and saw it coming. The wall of superheated air looked like something out of a science fiction movie. On the high banks on either side of the river trees were snapping off from the force. Then he felt it, the searing heat and the force of the wind as the boat slewed sideways and almost heeled over. Please God, don't let us die now, not now, not after what we have been through. Ted was sobbing as he fought the wheel of the small boat. The adrenaline rush that had sustained him was gone. He was fighting for survival against something over which he had no power. The horror of what he had just been through was flashing through his mind. He didn't want to die.

September 2007 – US Army Dugway Proving Ground, Utah

It had been five days since Billy Smart or Mike Dunn had seen the light of day, but that was about to change quickly. Starting their fifth and final day of what was called MJ-12 indoctrination, it was discovered that the two men, two out of a class of sixteen, were there in error and were now being hustled away from this very secret MJ-12 facility. Both men had felt strangely out of place from the beginning but being totally loyal to and trusting in their employer, they had kept their mouths shut while learning the awesome secrets of the black government operation known as the MJ-12 Group.

Five days prior they had been met at the Salt Lake City International Airport by two Army MPs and driven seventy-five miles southwest to the Army's massive 800,000-acre Dugway Proving Ground facility. Entering the base, the unmarked Suburban traveled to a remote location and entered a hangar facility next to a runway that seemed to stretch to infinity. Inside the facility the vehicle proceeded to a circular ramp that descended several levels below grade and terminated in a garage type structure where the driver stopped and killed the engine. A massive steel door closed behind the Suburban as one in front opened, revealing a large, brightly lit service area containing several dozen civilian and military vehicles. The floor on which the Suburban rested started to move and carried the vehicle and its occupants to a parking slot at the back of the service area and in front of a glass partition.

Both Smart and Dunn were traveling on top-secret orders from their primary employer for whom they worked undercover, while taking vacation leave from the employer they used as a front for their activities. The men had only been told to take one week's vacation leave on a certain date, given round-trip first-class airfare to Salt Lake City, told they would be picked up at the airport, and that this was all to be handled as a top-secret operation, something they were well accustomed to doing. On the ride from the airport to Dugway both men had tried to question the two MPs but their questions were all answered with "Sorry, no comment, sir."

Now the MPs gathered the two men's luggage and escorted them through a doorway in the glass wall to a waiting tram where they were greeted by a smiling large man in khakis with no insignia, black boots, and a huge shaven head that glistened in the overhead lights.

"Mr. Smart and Mr. Dunn, welcome to Dugway Proving Ground, or Dugway underground as we like to call it. I'm Robert Ziegler—please call me Bob. Oh yes, I'm with the agency," which was a lie.

"It's a pleasure, Bob," said Smart. "Now we've got about..., oh let's see..., three thousand questions for you."

"I'm sure you do, and all in good time, but first let's get you both settled into your accommodations for the week, then you'll start to get some answers. Please jump on the tram and we'll go to the dorm area."

The two MPs had placed the men's luggage on the tram and they now popped the three men a quick salute and returned to the service area. The tram was like many airport trams, only this one had nicely upholstered leather seats and was extremely quiet as it flashed along at a speed that Smart estimated to be in excess of 60 mph.

Ziegler sat on a seat facing the two men. "Gentlemen, first the bad news: the indoctrination session you have been brought out here to attend covers the most highly classified matter in the country—in the history of mankind, for that matter. Because of this you will be escorted everywhere you go and you will be housed in locked quarters."

"I don't like the sound of that one bit, Bob. We're big boys and we play by the rules," said Dunn.

Ziegler ignored him. "You will stay in this facility for the five days. You are here until you return to Virginia at the end of the session. On the plus side, the accommodations and the food are excellent and we have superior exercise facilities. Also, I believe you will find the subject covered in these sessions to be fascinating and beyond anything you can imagine."

The tram slowed to a stop, where two more MPs waited on the platform to snatch the men's luggage as soon as the tram door opened. Ziegler then escorted the men through another glass partition into a reception area highlighted by marble and walnut. A smiling young lady at the reception desk handed each man an envelope with his name and room assignment on the front.

"Gentlemen, this is Ms. Stevens. She or one of her associates will be on hand twenty-four hours a day to assist you with your lodging or dining needs. You only need to pick up the blue phone in your suite to reach them with your requests and you will find their response to be prompt and friendly. Now, let's move on to your accommodations."

Ziegler motioned to a pair of doors across the room that opened into a wide and elegant hall that reminded the two men of the suite corridors in the five-star Great River Resort where they worked undercover. Reaching the assigned suites, Ziegler stopped as the MPs opened the entrances and placed the men's luggage in their respective suites.

"Gentlemen, I'll take my leave now as I'm sure you both would like to rest and order dinner. The envelopes you have contain instructions on our set-up here and how we accommodate your various needs. The first session is in the morning at 8:00 AM and the MPs will be at your door at a quarter to eight to take you both to the opening session, and that will also apply to all subsequent sessions. As I said, Ms. Stevens can handle any request and if you find it necessary to discuss something with me she can also arrange that. Once you have settled in, please turn on your TV to channel 3 to view a fifteen-minute briefing on the meeting and the facility, which should answer most of your questions. You also have HBO on channel 4, Fox News on channel 5, CNN on channel 6, and the Weather Channel on 7. Enjoy your stay."

With that said, Ziegler turned and quickly walked away. Each MP stood by the open door and motioned Smart and Dunn into their respective suites. The men entered and as the MPs closed the doors behind them they heard a faint electronic click that told them that they were now prisoners, but prisoners in a suite as fine as any five-star property anywhere in the world.

Smart pulled out a pack of Merits and the cheap butane lighter he had bought at the Richmond International Airport before leaving. He smoked a lot, chain smoked in fact, and he had been trying to quit but with little success. The wheel on the cheap lighter hurt his finger as he lit the smoke and he cursed the fact that he had misplaced his prized gold Dunhill lighter, a gift from the boys at the agency facility called "The Farm" near Williamsburg. It had been hours since he had had a smoke and the first drag caused his head to swim. Then it caught his eye, the window wall across the room. It looked out over the desert, but how? They were several stories below grade, he knew they were, but yet—the windows didn't open, of course, but the sun was in the right place. How the hell? It was an image, fake, but the best he had ever seen. It was perfect, and the same in the bedroom—what a place, what a suite. He glanced at the desk and saw a breakfast and dinner menu. The selections were superb and the room service was twenty-four hours. Unbelievable, he thought. Well, time for a shower and fresh clothes, then watch the briefing before ordering dinner.

He saw that the bath was large and marble as was the glass-enclosed shower. Soft towels hung on a heated towel rack along with a terry robe, even a damned bidet, for Christ sake. He thought about the lobster tail and filet as the hot water from five showerheads soothed his body. Hell, he could take being locked in here for a week, no big deal. Still, he was not totally relaxed. There was tension in the unknown. "The most highly classified matter in the history of mankind." What the hell was Ziegler talking about, what was he about to learn?

Smart dried off and slipped into the terry robe. There was a nice bottle of merlot on the wet bar. He opened it, poured a glass and started to cut on the TV, but something was strange. He walked to the fake window and it hit him. He couldn't believe it—the sun was going down, the goddamned sun was going down and the moon was starting to rise.

1

Ted Carter

September 2007 – Northumberland County, Virginia

H is mind was not on the sixty-something overweight man swinging the club; it was on the schooling rockfish just to his left in the mouth of Ball's Creek. He watched the water turn a frothy white as the feeding fish forced the small baitfish to skip and hop from the surface of the water like silver grasshoppers. His profession was golf, but his love was fishing, and he wanted to be down there, not up here with this two-time senior club champion with a swing flaw.

Ted Carter was the head pro at the Great River Resort and the adjoining Great River Yacht and Country Club, located in the Northern Neck of Virginia on the banks of the Great Wicomico River. He had enjoyed moderate success as a golf equipment salesman but had been persuaded to take the resort job by Great River owner and south Florida real estate developer, Bill Russell, one of his few friends. When he gave up his Navy career, a part of his life he concealed from everyone, Ted joined the old Nike Tour. He was playing on the tour when he met Russell. There was immediate chemistry between them and they became instant friends. When Russell decided to build the Great River Resort, he wanted Ted as director of golf and as club pro, and he pulled out all the stops to get him. Now forty-six, Ted bore a faint resemblance to his hero Arnold Palmer, whom he met while attending Wake Forest University on a golf scholarship.

Ted didn't care much for country club life and as a result he was not well liked by many of the Great River Country Club members. To compound this he charged $250.00 for a thirty-minute lesson, but he was good, so good in fact that one golf magazine called him the next Harvey Penick. The publicity appealed to the overblown egos of the club members so they put up with him.

"Notice anything yet?"

The sound of the question, asked through teeth clenched around the stub of a cheap cigar, diverted Ted's attention from the fish back to the fat man with the club. Two ice cold blue eyes locked onto the stare of the fat man, and with the flick of one finger of the hand holding a salt-rimmed tulip glass indicated that the man should return to the task of hitting balls with all due haste.

In fact, Ted had seen enough, and he wanted to get to the fish. His twenty-five foot Pro Line center console, a perk from Bill, was in a slip 100 yards away, and this was his last lesson of the day.

"Keep your left heel down, and shorten your backswing." Ted said to his somewhat startled student, while handing him a one hundred dollar bill to refund part of the shortened lesson. Stammering to ask a question that he knew would not be answered, he watched Ted walk off to the marina, step into his boat, fire off the 225 H.P. Yamaha, and ease away from the dock.

Ted's only close friend at the country club was the head of beverage services, an expatriated Cuban called "Mango." If Ted had a late afternoon lesson, Mango would send him a cooler that held a small carafe of his own margarita recipe, consisting primarily of Patron Reposado with a whisper of lime juice to, as Mango said, "take the warts off."

Mango grew up in pre-Castro Cuba and as a young boy had been taken under the wing of Ernest Hemingway as his gofer and fishing companion. Ted would sit with Mango in the men's grill for hours after closing, drinking margaritas and listening to Mango and his fish tales with "Papa" aboard *Pilar*. His favorite story, which got better every time it was told, was when Hemingway, aboard *Pilar*, tried to use a pistol to end the misery of a marlin, and shot himself in both calves.

Both Ted and Mango had cottages in the employee compound located on the resort property. There were twelve cottages, a twenty-four-unit condo, and a dorm for the hourly workers. Bill Russell made it mandatory that all management live on the property.

He said, "Nothing creates harmony among my senior staff like living together in the same neighborhood that you work in."

Actually, he knew the opposite was true, and he was only happy when his managers were trying to stab each other in the back. If they all came to him with their complaints, he felt he had complete control, and a direct pipeline as to what was going on with each. The dorm was primarily occupied by the Mexicans, and Bill didn't really care about their personal life, although he was there to help if any were in trouble. He just wanted them watched over as much as possible. His Mexican workers were loyal for the most part, sent most of their earnings to their family in Mexico, but under the influence of tequila could get in trouble. Several had auto accidents with some serious injuries.

Ted's cottage was the largest of the twelve and occupied a prime location facing east on a hill above Tippers Bridge at Glebe Point and the Great Wicomico River beyond. The great room had an enormous glass window that overlooked a brick patio and the river.

Most every evening Ted and his housekeeper, Ruth Bennett, could be found on his patio enjoying a cocktail and discussing the latest staff conflict. Ruth was an attractive forty-three-year-old divorcée from Richmond who moved to the Northern Neck with 1.5 million dollars of her former husband's money after finding him asleep in their Virginia Beach condo with his twenty-six-year-old secretary. Ruth had answered Ted's ad for a light housekeeper, not because she needed the money, but because she was tired of doing nothing. She loved to fish, played a little golf, hated country clubs, and she reminded Ted of his boyhood heartthrob, Ann-Margret. They hit it off from the start and within a month most of her clothes were in Ted's closet.

"What's up, big boy, cleaning supper?" Ruth asked Ted as she took two bags of groceries from her silver Crossfire. Ted had built a fish cleaning station just inside the cottage garage and was washing off four nice fillets.

"Yep, you got it, babe, fresh from the sea to you and me."

Ted wrapped each in wax paper, and followed Ruth into the house.

"How does dinner on the patio with one of your spinach salads and a bottle of Pouilly Fuisse sound?"

"Sounds good. When did you catch them?"

"About thirty minutes ago, and they cost me a hundred bucks. I had to give Baker a refund. I was giving him a lesson when I saw the fish working in the mouth of the creek and cut his lesson short by ten minutes. You should have been here, babe. We don't see these size rockfish up in the creek very often and they had the water boiling. The bait fish were jumping two feet in the air and the rockfish were right behind them."

"So you couldn't stand it, you handed him a hundred dollars and took off to your boat."

"Damn right. You don't get a chance like that very often and I certainly didn't want to waste it on Baker."

Ruth laughed and said, "I don't know why people around here put up with you."

Ted grinned. "It's my sparkling personality, babe, what else could it be."

Ruth stopped putting away groceries and cocked her head to one side with a puzzled look that Ted had come to know and love.

"Ted, you are the smartest, kindest, and most interesting man I've ever met. Why does this place bring out the dark side in you?"

Ted shook his head. "It's country clubs and country club life. I can't stand the pompous phonies and their witch wives. There are a few members who are good people, but most are just overfed rich jerks. Bill Russell knows this about me, which is why he gave so much to get me here. Oh, it's a beautiful place, the hotel guests are fine—they come and leave—the fishing is great, and Bill owns it, that's why I'm here."

Ruth smiled, and walked over and ran her hand through his sandy windswept hair and gave him a kiss on the cheek.

"Well, I'm glad you are, but go take a shower, you smell like fish."

Ted turned and looked out the large plate glass window.

"This place would be paradise to me if it weren't for all the government bureaucrats that retired and moved here, people who don't have a clue what it's like to have a real job or run a business. The only thing that keeps me sane is the locals, like Lawton over at the boatyard, a great guy who is one of the best...." Ted's voice trailed off.

"OK, I'm on my way to the shower. Fix us a couple of drinks and I'll meet you on the patio. I just got an e-mail from Bill and I can't wait to tell you about it."

Ted showered, shaved and slipped on a pair of khaki shorts, a polo shirt without any Great River logo, and his well-worn Rockport boat shoes. He joined Ruth on the patio. She had put Guy Clark on the Bose and he was singing about "boats to build."

"Sit down, big boy, and cool down. Tell me about the e-mail from Bill."

Ted picked up his drink and sat down beside Ruth on the rattan love seat. A large motor yacht was sliding under the high-rise section of the new Tippers Bridge.

"Well, Bill wanted to know if I had heard anything from Dieter, our German head chef, about a problem he was having with Billy Smart, the front desk manager. It seems that Dieter sent Bill an e-mail about Billy; you know how much Billy smokes, and he uses a gold-plated Dunhill lighter with his initials on it. Seems like Dieter stepped on it last night when he was getting into bed. He picked it up and asked Inga about it, and according to what Dieter told Bill, she turned as white as a bag of flour.

Ruth's eyes were as big as saucers. "Hell, Ted, Billy looks like Mortimer Snerd, and Inga is a Swedish bombshell...there's no way...I mean hell...no way."

Ted laughed. "Bill said that he hears ole Billy is hung like a horse, and Dieter is more interested in popovers than pussy."

Ruth threw back her head and laughed until tears started flowing.

"Anyway," Ted continued, "Bill said Dieter and Inga had it out, and he moved into another room. Billy has been away for a week, but Dieter told him that when Billy comes in tomorrow he was going to shove the lighter up his ass, and then he was going to—to use his exact words—cut the little fucker's dick off. Bill's flying in tonight so he can referee in the morning. He can get another Billy, and probably should, but it would be hard to replace Dieter."

Ruth had stopped laughing and was in thought. "Ted, I don't understand. The resort hotel has a general manager, and the club has a general manager and Dieter has food service authority at both. Why doesn't one or both of them handle the matter? Why does Bill have to fly in to get involved?"

"The answer is simple, babe," replied Ted. "Both of the managers have their own affairs going on and that would just inflame Dieter more, and Bill, well he just loves this crap."

Ruth picked up the two now-empty glasses and headed to the bar.

"Lover, this place is nothing but a hell hole of a Peyton Place!" She fixed the drinks and returned to the seat. "You know, Bill Russell is a great guy, and I like him a lot, but this side of him—he's an enigma to me. I really don't know much of his past, I mean before the resort and club was built. Tell me about him."

"OK, babe," replied Ted, "but let's fix dinner while I do. It's a long story."

2

Swamp King

Bill Russell was fifty-five years old, as was his wife, who was also his former high school sweetheart, but they both looked ten years younger. Bill and Bonnie were devoted to each other. They were best friends, business partners, and lovers. They had two sons: Bill Jr., who was a senior at the University of Miami, and James, who was a freshman at the University of Virginia. Bill's dad had owned an auto dealership in St. Louis, but sold it and retired to Naples, Florida when Bill was nineteen. Bill spent two years at the UVA School of Business, but he wanted to marry Bonnie and get on with his life. He left UVA at the end of his second year, much to the distress of his and Bonnie's parents, and went to St. Louis, married Bonnie in a huge wedding that neither wanted but was insisted on by Bonnie's bank president father and her mother. After a brief Virgin Island honeymoon, the young couple moved to Naples, took a small apartment in an upscale area downtown, and set up housekeeping. It was a happy time and they were very much in love. Soon Bonnie would be pregnant.

In 1977 Naples was still a small town on the southwest Florida gulf coast. There were just a few motels, and the Naples Beach Hotel and Golf Club. An upscale neighborhood on the south end of town was the winter home to industry movers and shakers from the north. Route 41 coming from Ft. Meyers to the north made a ninety-degree turn downtown heading east to Miami. Most development was on the west gulf side of Route 41 and going east several blocks put you in the undeveloped swamp and farmland of Collier County. Upscale shops, catering to the well-heeled from the North, dotted several attractive avenues just west of where 41 took its turn toward Miami. Keeping straight at its eastern bend took you to the Cove Inn and Marina on the Bay of Naples. The Cove Inn was a motel type condo that featured a Tiki bar overlooking the marina. The east side of the Inn was Tin City with several restaurants and shops, and just to the west was The Dock at Crayton Cove, a rustic informal bar and restaurant. It was in this area that most real estate deals were discussed and finalized over cocktails at lunch. Every day at lunch a young Bill Russell could be found, meeting people and forging friendships with the builders and developers of this still-small south Florida town. The ink on his real estate license was not dry when he entered into a deal with a local builder to develop a parcel of land a mile east of downtown. Within three years Bill and Bonnie were millionaires, and well on their way to toward building a south Florida real estate empire. They were a team—Bill handled the sales and Bonnie handled the finances—and together they changed the face of Naples forever.

In the early fall of 1987, Bonnie and Bill were cruising from Martha's Vineyard back to Naples aboard their seventy-six foot Broward, *Swamp King*. Heading down the Chesapeake Bay Bill decided to have a close look at Smith Point Light. As he circled the light his left engine shaft and propeller became tangled in a crab pot line, killing an engine. Checking his waterway guide, he found a listing for "Lawton Custom Yachts & Boatyard," located up the Great Wicomico River about a twelve-mile run from his present location. Bill didn't want to limp far on one engine so this seemed to be the best place to start. He placed a call through the Norfolk marine operator to the boatyard. Since it was 2:30 PM on a Saturday afternoon, the phone rang about ten times before being picked up.

"Lawton speaking, we're closed but how can I help you?" boomed through the earpiece.

"I'm on a boat off Smith Point, picked up a crab pot and need repairs," Bill replied.

"You're not on a goddamned sailboat, are you?" asked the voice on the phone.

"No, I'm on a '76 Broward," Bill shot back, shaking his head.

"OK, bring it up here, and tie up at the end of the dock. We should be able to get you going before the bay freezes over."

There was a click and the line went dead. Bill turned as he heard his wife Bonnie come up to the bridge.

"Any luck?" she asked with a trace of a worried look.

"Damned if I know. The guy said he was Lawton, and could get us away before the bay freezes. I guess that means in about three months. My rear end is getting raw already."

The trip up the Great Wicomico River was about five miles to the boatyard. Arriving at the dock, Bill struggled to lay the large vessel alongside with one engine. A man in about his mid-forties watched the struggle with some amusement from the end of the dock. Finally the man yelled to Bonnie.

"Pretty lady! Better throw me a spring line before you all run out of fuel."

Bonnie heaved the line, which he caught and then put a couple of turns around a piling.

"Come back on her, capt'n," yelled the man on the dock, who Bill and Bonnie now assumed was Mr. Lawton. Bill slipped the starboard engine into reverse and the big yacht nestled against the pilings. Bill shut the engine down as Mr. Lawton handled the lines.

Any boat owner can watch someone handle dock lines and instantly know how experienced that person is with boats. It was clear that Mr. Lawton was indeed "salty."

"You must be Mr. Lawton," Bill said with outstretched hand. "I'm Bill Russell and this is my wife, Bonnie."

"It's just 'Lawton,'" said the man. "Last name's 'Crockett.' What the hell were you doing in so close to the light in this rig?"

"Just wanted a close look at the light," replied Bill.

"Yep, those pots cover our yearly payroll." Lawton winked at Bonnie as Bill shook his head.

"Just kidding, Mr. Russell," said Lawton with a laugh. "If you stay around here very long you'll hear a lot of that stuff from everybody. Hell, we kid each other and we kid the customers just to keep from going nuts. That works here; that's just the way we do things."

Bill smiled and nodded. "It's Bill and Bonnie. When do you think you can take a look at the damage?"

"We'll get her in the travel lift first thing Monday, but let's take a look at the engine room now; I don't want you two standing in water when you hit the deck in the morning."

"May I fix you both a drink when you return from inspecting the Titanic?" asked Bonnie.

"I've never turned down a drink from a pretty sweet lady in my life," replied Lawton as he followed Bill to the engine room forward access.

"I'll bet that's the damn truth," muttered Bonnie under her breath.

With no apparent damage to the hull, the three settled in the main salon and began what turned into a fascinating and funny two-hour conversation covering boat building, family history, the Chesapeake Bay and other topics, with increasing laughter as the Jack Daniels flowed.

"Oh hell," said Lawton, "I should have put the crabs on an hour ago. My wife will think I've run off," he said as he rose from his chair. "Too late, here she comes now," he said.

An attractive petite lady was walking down the dock in the direction of the *Swamp King*. Bill stepped into the cockpit.

"Mrs. Crockett, your husband is aboard and has been entertaining us for the past two hours. Sorry if we held him up and ruined your dinner."

"Oh no," she chuckled, "sometimes we even eat Saturday dinner by midnight, and please call me June."

"Come aboard and let me fix you a drink."

"Well perhaps one, but I really need to get back to the house." She added, "If you are leaving your boat with us, our regular customers have learned to lock up their liquor before they leave."

"There is one thing they never seem to understand," shot Lawton. "I build these sons of bitches, and I sure as hell can take 'em apart!"

When the laughing stopped, the Russells were invited to a Chesapeake Bay treat, hard crabs and beer, which they gladly accepted.

As a full autumn moon rose to the east, reflecting off the now still waters of the Great Wicomico River, five miles from the Chesapeake Bay, laughter could be heard coming from the screened-in porch behind the Crockett home. Lawton was true to his word when he told Bill and Bonnie: "You never know who will show up for Saturday night hard crabs. A couple of drunks, the preacher and his wife, our banker, a few watermen, and one night we even had a hooker and her date from Baltimore who pulled in to the dock for gas and ended up spending the night."

Bill and Bonnie agreed when they returned to the *Swamp King* at midnight that that night was more fun than they could remember. It would be repeated many times over the next twenty years.

The Great Wicomico River is a gem of the bay: clean, deep, with miles of pristine shorelines. It was fertile breeding ground for all forms of seafood before the bay's troubled waters saw a demise of its beloved shellfish. The deep waters and many sheltered coves and points were prized stopovers for many boaters traveling north or south on the Intracoastal Waterway.

At 2:00 PM Sunday afternoon, Bill and Bonnie boarded Lawton's newest forty-six-foot sport fisherman for a sightseeing cruise on the river and bay. Before returning to the dock Lawton took them through the Tippers swing bridge and up pretty little Ball's Creek. Bill noticed a mile-long shoreline of pristine land with wonderful views. Lawton told him that he understood that the 350-acre parcel was owned by a group from Richmond and it had been on the market for about a year. Monday morning, while the *Swamp King* was in the travel lift, Bill was on the phone to his Naples office to get particulars on the property. The boat was repaired and ready to leave by the end of the day Monday, but Bill and Bonnie decided to stay a few days and look over the property. For two days they walked the hills and ravines of the property, looked at the views of the river, and an idea for a grand resort was born. By Thursday Bill had made an offer to buy the property for 1.7 million, a price that Lawton felt would drive local real estate prices "right through the roof of heaven," and it was accepted.

Developments of projects such as this are usually controversial, and this one was no exception. The planning fight was on the front page of the local weekly paper for six months. Most locals wanted it because of the jobs it would create and the added tax revenue to this very rural county. Some watermen were concerned about the impact of the marina on the river, their livelihood. But most felt the project was worth the risk. The "come here's" on the other hand fought it tooth and nail.

As one local put it, "Those damn people made a lot of money somewhere else, come here and build a house, and then want to slam the door on everybody else. Well, what about us, don't we deserve a good living?"

The fight was heated but finally approved with some modifications. Bill told Ted that the fight cost him $500,000.00, but he made it up. "All the come here's that fought it bought a club membership and I raised the initiation fee to cover the loss from the fight."

The final design of the project consisted of the resort having twenty two-story buildings with eight suites each. The main resort building had the reception area, dining rooms, meeting rooms, three bars and a large patio wrapping half of the main building. Also, the main building had 100 guest rooms with patios or lanais. The complete complex was situated around winding brick paths with plants, fountains and streams. There was a large swimming pool and poolside bar near the water with a wonderful river view. The eighteen-hole golf course was located on the west side of the resort with country club beyond and west of the course. The country club was private, except it offered privileges to the resort guests. The marina was centered between the hotel and club and served both.

A unique feature of the resort was a helipad located on a back remote area of the property protected with a security fence. A beautiful Polynesian inspired structure was located in a garden setting just off the helipad to welcome guests who chose to arrive by helicopter. Guests were picked up at the pad in a specially built electric car, taken to the reception building, welcomed with a bottle of Dom Perignon and then taken to the lower level where they would be whisked through underground tunnels to their suite.

The entire project, including the employee compound, was reported to cost $100 million. The grand opening was April of 2000, with both of Virginia's senators, congressmen, governor, and local officials in attendance.

3

Tip of the Iceberg

Ted was in the shower with his mind on his first lesson of the day. It was with an aging Hollywood star who was tired of looking like an idiot at the Pebble Beach Pro-Am. A 10 handicap from his home course was ridiculous, but the $10,000.00 for six lessons was real, so Ted took the job. He was deep in thought when Ruth jerked the shower door open and told him she heard screams in the compound. He jumped out of the shower, pulled on shorts and a shirt, and ran outside in the direction of the scream. He got to the young Mexican woman and saw Bill coming from the other direction. Ted had heard Bill's chopper land in the compound about 1:30 AM. The young woman seemed hysterical; she was screaming "Billy, Billy," waving her arms and pointing toward his cottage. Both men ran to the cottage, broke through the front door and stopped cold. Billy was lying face up across the kitchen table, his throat was slashed almost to the spine and his gold lighter poked from his mouth. The head was turned at a grotesque angle and blood covered the top of the table and pooled on the floor. Ted turned pale, and Bill started heaving up the club sandwich the hotel kitchen had left in his suite as a late snack.

The commotion brought people from the cottages into the cottage courtyard. Ted had shut the front door and was keeping everyone away while Bill stepped away to call 911 on his cell. Ruth, who had been trying to calm the young woman and the slain man's housekeeper, now ran up to Ted as he stood at the door.

"What's going on?" she asked.

"Billy's been murdered," he whispered.

"Oh my God! Dieter!" she said on impulse just as Dieter walked up to Ted.

"Oh my God Dieter what?" he asked with a quizzical look.

Ted thought, what the hell's he doing here, he just murdered a man? His mind started to race and his thoughts were confused. Maybe he didn't do it, but the lighter...shit!

Dieter asked again, this time more to Ruth, and with irritation.

"Dieter what? What's going on?" The German temper now rising: "God damn it, what is going on?"

Ted saw Bill approaching with two of his assistant pros.

"Dieter, give me a minute and I'll fill you in on what's going on. Just stay here with Bill while I talk to my boys."

Ted motioned to his two assistants to follow him as he hustled them back to the front door.

"Guys, don't ask questions, just listen. Billy is inside murdered. I want you both to stay right here, and keep anyone from going inside the cottage. Don't tell anybody anything. The sheriff is on his way. He told Bill he will be here in ten minutes. When he gets here tell him where we are and that I need to talk with him."

Ted turned to the crowd of gathered employees.

"I want all of you to return to your cottages or work now. That's not a request—it's a demand. Everyone will have an explanation of what's going on here shortly."

A voice to Ted's left, the club assistant manager, said, "I don't work for you, you don't have the authority to give me orders. I want to know what's going on in that cottage."

Bill's voice rang out loud over the group.

"The hell he doesn't! From now on, anything Ted says is the same as if I said it. If you or anyone else here wants to keep your job, do exactly what he said, and do it now. I'll notify all the managers of a meeting by e-mail shortly. Now get moving."

Everyone assembled slowly started to move away. Ted looked at his boys and then walked over to Bill and Dieter.

"Let's go to my cottage." He turned to Ruth and saw that she had found the young Mexican woman's husband and had put her in his care. Ted got Ruth's attention and motioned for her to follow.

Back at the cottage Ted told Dieter to take a seat in the great room, and looking at Bill he said, "Bill, I think this is your show."

Bill nodded agreement. "OK, Dieter here it is. Billy is inside his cottage murdered, and in view—" Dieter jumped to his feet, white and shaking, his heavy German accent almost unintelligible.

"You don't think I did it, my e-mail...I know...I was mad. Damn. How do you know murdered?"

"Sit down, Dieter," said Ted. It was more of an order than a request. He turned to Ruth in the kitchen.

"Ruth, would you put some whiskey in a glass for Dieter?" The faint sound of a siren could be heard as Bill continued.

"Dieter, you sent me an e-mail about Billy, and I'm going to have to tell the police about it. I will not put myself in the position of withholding evidence. Whether I think you did it is not important right now. The police will be here in a few minutes, and you must be able to account for your time over the last few days. The police will establish when Billy was murdered, and you will have to have to answer a lot of questions. Everybody around here will have to answer questions, so pull yourself together."

Dieter continued to mumble. "How do you know he was murdered?"

"Dieter, his throat was slashed," said Bill.

Ted had walked to the window and now stared out over the river, but he really looked at nothing. His mind was on two men he had seen in the compound that he didn't know. There was something wrong about the way they were dressed—they didn't fit. He knew they didn't work there, so why were they in the employees' compound and at that hour of the morning?

Bill had pulled up a chair in front of Dieter and when he told him about Billy's gold lighter sticking out of his mouth, Dieter moaned and dropped his glass of whiskey to the floor.

"Dieter, what did you do with the lighter after you sent me the e-mail?"

"I put it and a note on Billy's desk in his office last night before I left the hotel," Dieter replied, almost weeping.

"What did the note say?"

Dieter replied in a whisper, "It said, 'I found this on my bedroom floor and I want to see you this morning.'"

There was a loud knock on the back door and Ruth let in Sheriff Ronnie Stone and a deputy.

After everyone was introduced, Stone said, "OK, folks let's start at the beginning, all the details no matter how small."

The events were related in detail and the deputy took notes. Sheriff Stone asked several questions, and then turned to Dieter.

"Mr. Dieter—"

Dieter interrupted, "It's Rumstead, Dieter Rumstead."

"Sorry. Mr. Rumstead, ah, there is no denying that circumstances make you a suspect, perhaps I should say a prime suspect, but I'm not accusing you of this crime, not at this time anyway. I want you to return to your cottage and stay there until I get back in touch with you, which should be within several hours. If you do not do that, if you try to run, I'll find you and put you behind bars, do you understand?"

"Yes," replied Dieter.

"OK, you may leave now, and I'll be by before noon to talk with you and your wife." Stone then raised his hand to gesture Dieter out. Stone knew both Bill and Ted well, and once Dieter was gone he turned to both of them.

"Well guys, you've got a hell of a mess on your hands. I've called in the state police crime investigation unit and they'll be here shortly. I've got the house sealed as a crime scene and no one is to go in or near it. Bill, I'll want to talk with most if not all of your employees ASAP. I would appreciate it if you asked them to give me their full cooperation."

"Consider it done," replied Bill.

"I'll also need the names, addresses, and phone numbers of all employees, and highlight employees that live in the compound."

Bill replied, "You'll have it in an hour."

"Stay close," said Stone, and he left.

Ruth had made coffee, and she, Ted, and Bill moved to the patio. Ted made a quick call to his office to have an assistant call his morning lesson and put it off for an hour.

Bill said, "We need to keep this thing under wraps as far as the guests are concerned. I'm going to call a managers' meeting in thirty minutes, but there's no need for you to be there, Ted. You go ahead with your lesson, and let's meet back here at noon for lunch and plan how to handle this mess. Ruth, would you call the hotel and have sandwiches sent over?"

Ted was more involved in this lesson than usual. Two of his assistant pros watching from the pro shop were surprised at how attentive he was to the actor, and thought the boss must be star struck. The fact was, Ted did like this actor known for action films, but more than that, he was trying to clear his mind of the morning events, but it wasn't working. While he adjusted the actor's shoulder turn, he noticed the two men he had seen in the compound earlier. They were in the cockpit of a large motor yacht in the hotel marina just below the practice range. The lesson concluded, a session was set for the next morning, and the actor/student went off to play a round with one of the assistant pros. Ted returned to his office and set up a meeting with his staff for 2:30 that afternoon. After that, he went out the back entrance of the pro shop, down to the brick path to the dock master's office, and in to see Bert Riner, the dock master. Bert was on the marina's VHF radio giving a slip assignment to a yacht as it approached the marina. He signed off and waved Ted over.

"Bert, what do you know about the motor yacht at the end of the dock?"

"Funny you should ask, Mr. Carter. One of my guys was just asking me about them. They have been coming here for about two or three days at a time, leaving for several days and then back again. This has been going on for some time. There are only two people on the boat that I know of; they keep to themselves, don't talk much, but the one that seems to be in charge did tell me that they just wanted to cruise this part of the bay and use our marina as a home base."

Bert continued. "By the way, I was in the managers' meeting with Mr.

Russell, and this thing about Billy is just awful, but we are not supposed to talk about it, so I guess I should shut up."

"That's OK, Bert. Just don't let the talk get out of hand—rumors travel fast," replied Ted.

"You know, Mr. Carter, Billy could have given you some information about those guys on the boat. He and his assistant desk manager seemed to know them. In fact, they spent some time with them on the boat."

This statement startled Ted, and it showed.

"Mr. Carter, you don't think there is a connection with them and Billy's, uh, death, do you?"

"No, not at all, it just surprised me, I'm sure there's nothing to it. Well, got to run, see you, Bert."

Ted left the marina office, and slowly walked to the dock with the motor yacht at the end. He continued out on the dock and casually looked at the boats in each slip. When he reached the end of the dock, he could read the name of the motor yacht on the stern: "High Roller – Miami, FL." He looked the yacht over, and in the cockpit he saw dive tanks. On the upper deck above the cockpit was a davit attached to a Zodiac with outboard motor. The door to the salon from the cockpit slid open and one of the men he had seen this morning in the compound stepped out.

"May I help you?" he asked Ted.

"Oh, no," replied Ted, "just a break from work for some salt air. Good for the lungs I'm told. Nice boat."

The man looked at Ted for several seconds, nodded his head once, turned, and returned to the salon. Ted walked on to the end of the dock T where the bow of the yacht was tied, but he showed no more outward interest in the boat. He checked his watch. He saw it was almost noon, so he returned to his cottage to meet Ruth and Bill for lunch.

Bill had not arrived yet but Ruth had put up a patio umbrella in the center of the glass dining table and placed an assortment of sandwiches and a pitcher of iced tea on the table. Ted was in the process of telling Ruth about the men on the yacht when Bill arrived.

The three sat down, fixed plates, and Bill started to fill them in on his morning. He had just left the sheriff who told him the medical examiner had placed Billy's death around 3:00 AM this morning. The sheriff had also met with Dieter and his wife, and Dieter didn't have a solid alibi. Dieter and Inga were sleeping in separate bedrooms, Dieter went to bed around 11:00 PM and Inga around midnight. Inga could not say for sure that Dieter didn't leave after she went to bed, but she insisted that she was sure he didn't. Inga also had a small bruise on her left cheek that she said she got when she hit the edge of the car door.

Bill added, "In the managers' meeting three people told me about two men they felt were strange. These men are on a yacht in our marina, and were seen in the compound when we found Billy's body."

Ted stopped him, and told of his experience. They discussed this for a few minutes, but decided that because they seem strange didn't mean anything, although the fact that they were in the compound was troubling. On the other hand, they could have been taking an early morning walk, heard the commotion and come over. Bill did not want to involve a guest unless they had more to go on.

"Let's just keep an eye on them for now."

Bill took a bite of a sandwich and a sip of tea before continuing.

"Let's change the subject for now; there is another issue I want to discuss. Bonnie and I are selling out in Florida and moving here. We are going to build a home on the other side of the club. Until then we'll live on the boat. I've got more money than I could spend in three lifetimes, the boys are starting their own lives, and I want to be in a place they can come, bring their wives, and hopefully our grandchildren, and be away from the craziness of south Florida. I want to slow down, run this resort," and added, looking at Ted, "with you as my partner."

Ted almost choked. "Damn, Bill, I don't have that kind of money."

"Don't worry about it, we'll work that out. You've been a great friend, loyal, trustworthy, and I value your opinion. I need a partner. I don't want the full load, and you are my man. If you'll accept in principle, we can work out the details later. Think about it for twenty-four hours before you give me an answer. Also, I think there is someone else you'll want to talk this over with before you make your decision." He looked at Ruth and gave her a wink.

Bill's cell phone rang. He answered and listened for a few seconds.

"I understand. Keep me informed if you would, and I'll check it out on my end, thanks." He closed his phone and turned to Ted and Ruth. "That was Ronnie Stone. It seems that Billy's assistant manager, Mike Dunn, is missing."

4

The Second Shoe

Ted had the 2:30 meeting with his staff. He told them of the events of the day, but he did not go into specific detail. He admonished them not to discuss the matter with hotel guests and to stay away from rumors. He answered a number of questions, then went over greens crew reports, and set his schedule for the next day, a schedule he was sure he could not keep. On the way to his cottage he stopped by the hotel bar to see if Mango could come over to the cottage and join him and Ruth for a drink.

"Sure," Mango replied. "Want me to bring a blender of stuff?"

"Forget the blender, just bring the stuff—we may need more than one blender full."

Mango laughed. "OK, OK, see you in thirty minutes."

In a little less than thirty minutes Mango arrived at Ted's cottage. Jimmy Buffet was on the Bose and his happy music took the edge off the serious discussion of the day's events. Ted fixed drinks and the three went to the patio to enjoy the warm evening.

"Hell, Ted, you know as well as I do that Dieter didn't kill Billy. Dieter is a pain in the ass, but he ain't no murderer. Somebody set him up. I was in the kitchen about a week ago and one of the cooks cut his finger. Dieter got sick and had to go outside, he ain't cut no throat." Mango offered his opinion in his thick Cuban accent.

"I agree," said Ted, "if for nothing else, the way he looked and acted in the compound this morning; and later he asked Bill over and over why Bill thought Billy had been murdered. I just don't think he's that good of an actor. And now Mike's missing. I think we've got a problem that's way above Dieter, or at least that's my take on this right now."

Ted did not disclose to Mango what he had learned about the men on the boat, and the possible involvement of Billy and Mike.

Ruth asked, "By the way, where is Bill?"

"He's been having private interviews with the staff all afternoon, and he said they would go well into the night."

"Ted, why is he doing that? That's police work and he really shouldn't be involved, it could cause him some trouble. I was married to a lawyer, a son of a bitch but still a lawyer, and I've learned some things about police work and legal matters."

"Sweetheart, that's just the way Bill is—this is his place and he's going to do just what he wants; no one is going to stop him."

There was quiet around the patio table for a couple of minutes as all three were into their own thoughts.

"Ted, how the hell you get this beautiful place and I live in a dump?"

Ted knew Mango was trying to lighten the mood, so he just smiled and shook his head. The fact was, Mango had a very nice cottage with a reasonable view. He had even installed beautiful Spanish tiles throughout the cottage, like the ones from the buildings and homes in his beloved Havana.

"All you have to do, Mango, is become as big a prick as people around here think I am, and good things start to happen."

"On that note," said Ruth, "I think I'll start dinner."

Bill called Ted at 7:00 AM the next morning and told him he really didn't know anything new. Mike was still missing, the state police were involved in the investigation, and he couldn't get much out of Ronnie Stone except that the crime investigation unit had sent Billy's body to the state medical examiner in Richmond. He went on to say that he had a lot of fish to fry in Naples so he was heading back midmorning, and putting out an e-mail to all managers that in his absence Ted was to be considered executive director of both the resort and country club. This information was also given to Sheriff Stone.

"Ted, I told you to think over my proposal for twenty-four hours, but I need to get back to Naples now, so we can discuss this by phone in a day or two. In the meantime, we will consider this elevation temporary, but make no mistake: I want it to be permanent. Think it over carefully, I need you."

Ted hung up and stared out the window for a few seconds, then he turned to Ruth.

"I need to go fishing. I'm going to the office and clean up some things, and plan to leave around noon—want to go?"

"You bet. I'll pack a lunch."

At noon on the dot Ted eased out of the slip, and then out of the creek. Once away from the marina he shoved the throttle forward and the Pro

Line shot under Tippers Bridge and down the Great Wicomico River, around Haynie's Point, past the tip of Sandy Point, and into Ingram Bay and the Chesapeake Bay beyond. The one-foot following swells were just enough to make Ted and Ruth stand to better take the impact as the boat sliced into each swell, throwing a white sheet of spray to each side.

Ted leaned to Ruth's ear. "Let's run to Smith Point Light. They've been catching trout there for the last several days."

She didn't try to talk over the sound of the engine and wind, but just nodded in the direction of Smith Point, seven miles up the bay. Ted was in heaven, bounding up the bay at twenty-eight knots, holding on to the stainless steel windshield rail with one hand and the stainless steel wheel with the other. Ruth, on his right, was holding the rail with her right hand and Ted's arm with her left. At this moment they were a pair of happy explorers looking for fish. Ted took his hand from the wheel and pointed east across the bay to a 900-foot LNG ship, its bright red domed tanks glistening in the afternoon sun as it made its way up the bay to Cove Point, some forty-five miles ahead.

Ted dropped the anchor just south of the light so the southwest breeze would lay them just off the outside of the light structure. Ruth got the rods out as Ted went about cutting soft crabs into quarters for bait.

Looking up at Ruth he asked, "Babe, what's your favorite seafood?"

"Well, I guess it's lightly battered soft crab sautéed in butter."

After a couple of seconds she smiled.

"I know, I know, why use my favorite seafood as bait to catch some other seafood. Well old sport, it's the sport of it, now shut up and cut bait."

An hour and four nice gray trout later, Ted's cell phone rang. Ted looked at it for three rings then checked the caller ID and saw it was his office.

"Yeah.... I'm sure you do, what is it?"

Ted listened while looking at Ruth and rubbing his forehead with the fingers of his right hand.

"Oh, my God, I'll be there in forty-five minutes." He snapped the phone shut and looked at Ruth. "Mike Dunn is dead. Lawton was fishing this morning with a couple of friends and found him in a pound net off the mouth of the river.

Ronnie Stone met Ted and Ruth at the marina as Ted was tying up the boat.

"Could we talk in your office?"

Ted looked at Stone, who was accompanied by a young man in suit and tie.

"Sure, no problem. Babe, would you mind taking our stuff to the cottage?"

Ted motioned for the two men to have a seat as he closed his office door.

"Ted, this is Richard Dill. Richard, Ted Carter." The two men shook hands. "Ted, Richard is with the FBI, and he and his people have taken over the case."

The stunned look on Ted's face prompted Dill to speak before Ted had a chance to gather his thoughts.

"Mr. Carter, the state police found some data on Mr. Dunn's computer that makes this a federal matter, but I really can't say any more than that, not at this time anyway."

"Well, can I at least ask how Mike died?"

Stone looked at Dill and Dill nodded.

"Ted, Dunn's throat was cut, just like Billy's, and it appears he was in the water for some time."

Dill interrupted. "Mr. Carter, I understand that you are the person in overall charge of the resort and club. We would like to have access to all employee records and in particular the time cards or records of the employees for the last two weeks. It would also be helpful if you would give us a secure location on premises to go through these records."

"I can arrange all that you ask, and will do so quickly, but you must understand that this is a resort filled with guests and I need time to get an action plan together."

"Mr. Carter, please just take care of my request now, and I will give you your future action plan later."

Ted's face turned beet red as he stared at Dill.

"Mr. Dill, I don't care who you are, this is a private business, I'm in charge and—"

Dill raised his hand to cut Ted off.

"Mr. Carter, this is a matter far more serious and involved than you can imagine. I am asking for your cooperation. If I don't get it I will have this property under federal control in less than an hour, so sir, please do as I ask."

Ted looked at Stone, who averted his eyes, and then back at Dill.

"What about our guests? This can be disruptive—federal agents, and God knows what else. How can this be kept quiet?"

"Mr. Carter, your guests will be leaving, and each will be screened before they leave. You will not accept any new guests as of twelve noon tomorrow. I will have written instructions in your hand by 8:00 PM tonight. I need you to stay close, and if you would, make those records available at once."

Ted stared at the top of his desk for several seconds, and then picking up his phone he dialed the administration office extension.

"Becky, it's Ted Carter. I will be sending a Mr. Dill with the FBI to your office in a few minutes. Please give him anything he asks for in the way of personnel records; anything beyond that, call me."

As soon as both men left Ted's office he placed a call to Bill's cell number. The call went to Bill's voicemail and he left an urgent message for Bill to contact him at once. He slowly placed the receiver in the cradle, then he turned and looked out his office window at the practice range. Thoughts were racing through his head. He knew action was necessary, but what?

5

Fraternity Brothers

At almost the same time the cell call came through to Ted on his boat about Mike Dunn, American Airlines flight 361 was descending through 29,000 feet over the Salton Sea on its approach to San Diego's Lindbergh Field. Bill Russell sat in seat 3B in the first class section of the Super 80, pondering his afternoon meeting in this beautiful southern California city.

He had expected to be on his own Citation X, but a major electronic problem with the plane had forced him to use a commercial flight. After calling Ted he had checked in with his flight crew at Richmond International Airport's Executive Terminal, and since repairs were expected to be completed by 3:00 PM, he instructed them to fly to San Diego that afternoon. He then called Bonnie and told her that he had to attend a quickly called meeting with potential developers in Orlando, and would not be home until after midnight. His pilot dropped him off at the main terminal and he picked up a ticket in the name of Robert Bates, using very sophisticated forged credentials, for the 8:15 AM flight to Dallas-Ft. Worth with connection to San Diego.

If anyone had looked closely at him as the plane was on its final approach into San Diego, they would have noticed a trickle of sweat around each temple. William Madison Russell was in deep and troubled thought about a 3:00 PM meeting he had been directed to attend. The urgency in the directive had unnerved him and continued to do so now. In his mind he kept playing the call over and over. The gravity in the voice and the words, *affecting the lives of everyone on the planet*, reverberated inside his head.

Lindbergh Field is unusual in that it is located near the heart of downtown San Diego. Harbor Drive separates the airport property from the manmade Harbor Island and its hotels and marinas, and San Diego Bay beyond.

Bill Russell was met just beyond the airport security checkpoint by three men he didn't know, but who obviously knew him. He was quickly escorted to a waiting Suburban and taken from the airport, across Harbor Drive to Harbor Island, and to a marina just beyond the two-building Sheraton Hotel complex. He was escorted by the three men with great haste down a dock to a waiting thirty-six-foot sport fisherman. Once the men were aboard, the boat left the dock, circled out of the marina into San Diego Bay, and ran down the bay past the city docks and the city itself on the left, under the Coronado high-rise bridge and into a secluded dock at the San Diego Naval Base. Waiting at the dock was an idling Navy patrol vessel. All four men left the sport fisherman and boarded the patrol vessel. That boat then pulled away from the dock, turning right into the bay, and retraced the trip back past the city, past the marina they had just left, following the channel around the North Island Naval Air station and on toward Point Loma and the ocean beyond. Before reaching Point Loma the boat slowed and turned to starboard into the San Diego Naval sub base harbor. The boat eased into a berth at the sub base and all four men left the boat and walked to a small frame structure about 100 yards from the dock. Opening the door was a Navy rear admiral, who motioned Bill to a small office located in the rear of the building. The admiral opened the door to the well-appointed office and Bill was greeted by an old friend, Barry Cummings, director of the United States Secret Service.

"Bill, how the hell are you, my friend."

"Pretty fair, Barry, considering all the intrigue you've put me through in the last twelve hours. I've been sweating blood on the flight out here, and to make matters worse I couldn't use my own plane."

Cummings walked over to Bill and put his arm around his shoulder.

"How's Bonnie?"

"She's fine, unless she gets wind of my little lie about my plans and decides I'm running around on her."

The smile left Cummings's face.

"Bill, we have some serious issues to deal with, issues that could impact the stability of the entire world, and it seems that my old UVA fraternity brother is right in the middle."

"Yeah, I'm right in the middle because that's where you put me. Now are you going to tell me just what the hell is going on, or is this another 'if you told me you would have to kill me' bunch of crap?"

Cummings motioned to two leather chairs on either side of a coffee table with coffee and sandwiches.

"Sit down, Bill; I know you're uptight, so relax and I'll explain all that I can at this time."

They both took seats and Cummings leaned forward. "Now, when we backed your investment in the resort for allowing us to make some modifications, I told you that the time might come when you would be placed in an uncomfortable situation. Well, we now face such a time. The very secret little conference that the President is scheduled to host at your resort is much more than just a little conference with advisors. This conference is going to be with several Middle Eastern, European, and Asian leaders and involves a new plan to attack world terrorism. We've picked up some chatter that indicates word of this meeting has been leaked to some of our enemies. From what we have just been told by the FBI, it appears that the two murders at the resort are tied in to this matter. So what—"

Bill held up his hand.

"What do you mean, two murders?"

"When was the last time you talked with your people at the resort?"

"I talked with Ted Carter at 7:00 AM this morning, and I have an urgent call from him that I haven't had time to return as yet, so what else has happened?"

Cummings filled him in on Mike Dunn and told him to take a break and return Ted's call. Bill poured a mug of coffee and stepped outside to return Ted's call. Ted got the call just before 6:00 PM and related the events of the day, and in particular the FBI closing down the resort.

Numb and confused, Bill thought for a moment. "Ted, do whatever is asked of you; give the authorities your full cooperation; let me make some calls and I'll get back to you as soon as possible. Keep your cell phone on at all times." And he hung up.

"OK, Barry, I've got the story on Mike Dunn, and how the FBI is closing down the resort, so what—"

Cummings jumped from his chair. "What do you mean, the FBI is closing down the resort?"

Bill related the story just told to him by Ted. Without speaking, Cummings went to a secure phone in an adjacent room. He returned in about five minutes.

"Bill, I don't want your property closed. I don't want any more attention brought to this matter than necessary. I've relayed that message to the FBI and told them it was backed by the White House. I requested that the names and addresses of all guests at the hotel be given a background check, and any of a suspicious nature will be investigated in depth. Of course, this will be done as discreetly as possible."

Cummings thought for a moment before continuing.

"Before the service entered into our joint venture with you and modified the construction of your property, you were given a complete security check, allowing you to receive a top-secret security clearance as an undercover operative of the Secret Service. This security clearance allows you access to top-secret information on a need-to-know basis. So far this has only involved certain construction details of your property, and the knowledge of the President's conference a month from now. As far as the murders, they are not in your area of need-to-know; in fact, the FBI should not be running the case but assisting the Secret Service, as it involves the security of POTUS."

"POTUS?" asked Bill.

Cummings smiled. "Sorry, Bill, for the jargon. POTUS is how we refer to the President of the United States."

Bill acknowledged his understanding with a nod. "Barry, I don't know who should be running what and who should be assisting, and I don't care. And let me add that the rivalry between the intelligence branches never ceases to amaze me. It seems counter-productive, but that's not my concern. However, the operation of my resort is my concern, and in addition, I would think that you would at least want me to have some basic knowledge of what you know about this case that would allow me to possibly pick up bits of information from my people, information that your people may not get."

Cummings sat back in his chair and thought for a minute. "OK, Bill, I'll give you some background, but remember your trip here, this meeting, everything that's been said, is covered by your security clearance and the laws of the United States."

"Barry, I know all of that—it was hammered into me by your FBI friends when I got the clearance."

Cummings pulled open a drawer in the coffee table and took out some papers, looked them over and was quiet for a moment.

"The FBI found some classified data on the hard drive of Dunn's computer, stuff with the highest possible level of security classification, way above top secret. We don't know how he got it but we have reason to suspect that it has to do with the Presidential meeting."

"Barry, that's impossible. No one at the resort had or has any idea about the meeting. I have those dates blocked out for a to-be-named celebrity function and I hinted to reservations that it was a West Coast superstar who wanted one wing of the property. That covers the space your people said the government would need."

"Bill, we don't know if Dunn was a plant when you hired him or if he was recruited after he was employed, but in either case his knowledge of the meeting came from outside sources, or that's our best guess at this time. Now to continue the speculation, we think that your front desk manager somehow found out about Dunn's activities and he was murdered in a manner to frame your head chef. However, the murder of Dunn seems to blow that theory out of the water, on the surface anyway."

Bill looked puzzled at this statement.

"Look at it this way, Bill: the murderer or murderers went to some trouble to frame your chef. Within hours a second murder was committed in the same manner as the first; so it appears that both murders were committed by the same person or persons, and we have good reason to believe that the autopsy results will confirm this as fact. When the second murder was committed, the chef was all but under house arrest and being watched, so he couldn't have committed the second murder. Whoever murdered Dunn had to have known this, so committing the second murder in the same manner as the first, well, as you can see it destroys the frame-up and that's got us a bit confused."

Both men were quiet for a couple of minutes before Bill spoke.

"When you called me last night, you said it was critical that I meet you this afternoon on a matter of grave national emergency, and that I should travel undercover using my service alias. Barry, I'm not a spy and this stuff scares the hell out of me. So far we've only discussed Sherlock Holmes stuff, so what is the real reason for me being here?"

Cummings got up and walked to the other side of the room.

"We think that al-Qaeda is planning to hit the conference, and this is going to require some security measures that have never been seen before. The extent of these measures is still in the planning stages, but they will be unusual, they will be severe, and you will be involved."

"Barry, for God's sake, why not move the conference, or cancel it?"

"Bill, your property is the best place for a conference such as this, and you know why! As far as canceling the meeting, well, if I could I would, but the President won't, and it's the job of the Secret Service to protect him. That subject is a case closed, the President and the leaders he's meeting with are in agreement that they will not be intimidated by terrorist threats."

Bill stood up and walked to the door, head down, thinking.

"Do all the foreign leaders and their people know about the depth of the threat, and I assume it has more depth than just the average terrorist alert?"

"The answer to both of your questions is yes, at least I believe so. I am supposed to have the latest intelligence data and briefings, but keep in mind that is really the job of the CIA."

"I see. So what do you want me to do?"

"Nothing at this time, but there will be much for you to do in the coming week. When you return, one of my people will give you a secure method of communication with me. Keep it with you at all times. Four of my people will be your guests from now until after the end of the meeting. One week before, there will be more, and my guess is that for one week prior to the conference the entire wing, and perhaps more, will be occupied by federal agents and agents of other countries. This will be worked out with you by our people when you return tomorrow. This meeting was once a fixed plan; now it's in a state of flux and changing by the hour. In fact, we may need your whole hotel. I'm sure you'll work with us and of course extend your best government rate."

Bill smiled and shook his head at the last comment.

"This is a secret meeting," Cummings added, "no press of course, the delegations will be small, but their security forces will be large. Again, my people will get into the particulars when you arrive. And one final thing: everything I just told you is subject to, and probably will, change."

"OK, Barry, one final question before we wrap this up: can I discuss any of this with my new partner, or the person I hope will be my new partner? I can't carry the weight of this alone."

"I assume you're talking about Ted Carter based on your discussions with me on whether to bring him into the loop on our interest in the resort. Let me think about that and I'll have one of my people brief him on what he should know, tomorrow or the next day, in your presence." Cummings walked to Bill and shook his hand.

"Sorry to do this to you, old friend, but I guess you had an idea this may happen one day when you agreed to help Uncle Sam. Now let's get back to the real world, as ugly as it may be."

As they started to the door, Cummings stopped and looked at Bill.

"Bill, one final thing—I don't know how you'll staff the conference but, ahh, if this develops in some unexpected fashion, well, people could die. Keep that in mind."

Cummings watched Bill return to the boat. He hated lying to his friend, as almost the entire story was a fabrication. The trip here wasn't even necessary but only a method to instill the need for extreme secrecy. The meeting planned at the resort had nothing to do with world terrorism. Cummings knew that, but he didn't know the full story of the meeting. The President didn't even know the full story—at least he didn't know it yet. What Cummings did know was that the subject of the meeting was so startling that when revealed would shake the very foundation of human civilization.

6

The Mexican Connection

Dusk was settling on the small south Texas city of New Braunfels when two men, one tall and slender and of Middle Eastern heritage, and the other shorter of Spanish heritage, stood at the edge of the spring-fed Comal River that runs through the city's municipal park. At this time of day the park was all but deserted, yet they talked in hush tones.

"I shall be home with my family in Mexico tomorrow. I have been away a long time but your people have trained my people well, Omar."

"Yes, Felix," replied the taller man, "they will do well, but the task is difficult, and success will be elusive even though the plan is solid."

He started to add, "It's unfortunate that all of your men will die," but he held his tongue.

Felix said, "It's unfortunate that the training facilities that turned out such men like the ones that trained my people have been destroyed by the Americans. There could be so many more like them today."

Omar nodded. "Yes, the attack on America was unwise, too small in scope to do lasting damage, and now we are scattered so we must have the help of good friends like you. Sometimes a man can achieve such power that he loses his good judgment."

As he was speaking Omar handed Felix an envelope, which he placed in his inside coat pocket.

"We have the chance now to achieve a great victory and bring the enemy of my people to their knees. America is our enemy, we want to see the country crippled and impotent, but you make your money supplying drugs to people in America, so why do you help us take over your business?"

Felix smiled and touched his jacket where he had just placed the envelope.

"I was paid well for my assistance by your leader, more than I would make in two years running drugs on my own into this country. With this last payment I shall return home tomorrow and retire before my luck runs out and my children have no father."

The other man nodded. They stopped speaking as two young Mexicans in tattered clothes approached them. One of the ragged men had a cigarette in his mouth and asked for a light. Felix muttered something in Spanish and waved them off. At that instant a person yelled on the other side of the stream, and as both men looked in that direction they were struck on the back of their heads and crumpled to the ground. The young Mexicans quickly went through each of their victims' pockets as a large van slowly approached without lights.

7

Lawton

At 7:00 PM Ted Carter was getting ready to leave his office when Richard Dill tapped on his open office door.

"Come in. I'm sorry to say that your visit was expected. I guess you want to burn the damn place now."

"Mr. Carter, I really don't understand your attitude. There have been two murders committed to your employees in the last twenty-four hours, and I've told you this is a matter of national concern, and yet you continue to be abrasive."

"Mr. Dill, let's don't get into the psychology of my attitude as I really don't think you would understand. Just give me my orders."

"Your orders from me, Mr. Carter, are to forget all that I told you earlier, continue on as you were before we met. You will be contacted tomorrow by a member of the United States Secret Service and I'm sure they will give you your orders. However, I wouldn't repeat that little gem of knowledge to anyone if I were you."

Dill turned on his heels and walked out, leaving Ted with a dropped jaw. Ruth walked in just after Dill left.

"Hi, I see your new best friend just left." She paused. "What's the matter with you—you look like you've seen a ghost."

Ted shook his head. "Let's take a boat ride, if you don't have supper on."

"Sure, fine with me. I just stopped in to see what you wanted tonight, and what time you would be in, so let's go."

They idled out of the marina, out of the creek and under Tippers Bridge. This was not a ride for speed; it was for talk and clear thought. Ruth fixed a couple of drinks while Ted related the short meeting with Dill.

"Babe, I don't know what we're in the middle of but it's big, really big, and I think Bill knows more than he's telling me. In fact, I talked with him a short while ago and got the feeling he was not where he said he was. He didn't sound like himself."

Ruth kept quiet and let Ted talk.

"Sure, two murders are something big, but the FBI being involved, and now the Secret Service." Ted shook his head from side to side and sipped his drink. As they approached the docks at Lawton's boatyard Ted saw Lawton washing down his boat. He eased along the end of the dock, tied up, and he and Ruth walked over to Lawton's boat. Lawton didn't see or hear them approach, and when Ted spoke Lawton almost jumped over the bow rail.

"God damn! Oh, sorry, but I'm so nervous from this morning I feel like a dog." Then looking at Ruth, he added, "Well, you know what they say about a dog and peach seeds. Come aboard and let's have a drink."

Lawton gave Ruth a hand into the cockpit and Ted and Ruth went into the salon and took a seat while Lawton fixed the drinks.

"I'm not one to let much bother me but seeing that kid hung up in that trap line is something I don't want to ever see again, and I hope I can forget it. It's going to be a while before I eat hard crabs!"

That comment brought a very noticeable shudder from Ruth.

"I had three guys fishing with me and when we got back to the dock two guys from the FBI were waiting for us, and questioned us for over an hour. They talked like they thought we did the damn thing. I damn near slugged one of the pricks before they finally left. Then about 4:00 PM two men showed up and said they were with the Secret Service, and started asking a bunch of questions. Now get this: they wanted to know if they could lease my boat."

Ted asked, "What did you tell them?"

"I said sure, for $1,500 per hour, and I run her. I thought that would end the matter, but they said they would let me know when and for how long. Now I'm thinking I should have said $3,000 an hour. I don't know what's going on at your place but it sure looks to me like deep shit trouble. This used to be a quiet little village until Bill got the idea to turn it into Monaco West."

"Did they say why they wanted to use your boat?"

"I asked them but they just ignored my question, but they did want to know how fast she ran. The FBI guys had a real interest in Mongo; they pushed on him hard."

"Mongo was with you?" asked Ted.

"Yeah, we went out early. Mongo goes with me a lot since he doesn't start work until 1 PM."

Ted couldn't put his finger on it, but Mongo being with Lawton bothered him. However, there was no reason for it to do so, and that bothered him even more.

Lawton was in the galley area looking down the river.

"Yeah, it's been a hell of a day alright. Used to be such a quiet area, everybody knew everybody, in fact most all of us were related."

Lawton turned around and smiled at Ruth and Ted.

"You know, I dated for two years in high school before I met a girl I wasn't related to some way or another. After I married June we found out we were distant cousins, and that was a relief. We were afraid to check our backgrounds and maybe find out we were first cousins. Now you may not believe this, but one of my high school buddies married his aunt."

Ruth started laughing. "Come on, Lawton, you know better, nobody would marry their aunt."

"It's the truth, I swear it is, although it's really not as bad as it sounds. This boy's mom was killed in a boating accident when he was a baby. When his father was fifty-five he married a younger girl, about thirty, I believe. Now this girl had a younger sister about the age of my friend, and damned if they didn't fall in love and married. The two couples were almost inseparable, and no one around here even gave it a second thought. Like I said, it was a quiet and close community."

Lawton looked back out of the salon window.

"But you know something, those high rollers who stay at your fancy digs, well a lot of them come over here and look around. I guess they think of this business as sort of a tourist attraction. Anyway, I give 'em the full tour, show 'em how we build our boats, and if there is a good looking gal along I may give 'em a ride down the river."

Ruth laughed. "Now Lawton, I know you've sold some boats to resort guests."

"Well yes, I have, about $16,000,000 worth to date, but my accountant tells me that my cost to build them was $17,000,000.00. I told him, hell, I don't do this to make money, I do it because I love it. When I die, my ashes will be spread on the bay, and for a tombstone, well, they'll be running up and down the bay. What more could a man ask for?"

Ted looked at Lawton. "You know, my friend, sometimes I don't know when you're putting me on or when you're serious."

Lawton smiled. "It's not important that you know, Ted, it's only important that I know!"

Out of the corner of his eye Ted saw the Zodiac from the *High Roller* heading down the river. It turned into the restaurant about a mile below the boatyard.

"Lawton, do you know anything about the motor yacht *High Roller* that spends a lot of time at our Marina?"

"Yeah, they were in here several days ago with a vibration that turned out to be a bent wheel. Two men were on the boat, both strange ducks, very quiet and serious types. They paid for the repair in cash, over $3,000 as I remember, and they never let any of us go on the boat alone. They stood right beside me when I put her in the travel lift. I was damn glad to get them the hell away from here."

8

Friends for Life

Ted was in his office early the next morning putting details in order to move his office to the main building, and take over his new responsibilities as the resort executive director. There was a knock on his office door and in walked another suit, but this suit was smiling ear to ear and holding out his credentials for Ted to see.

"Ted Carter, I'm agent Roy Lee Steele, United States Secret Service," the suit said as he stood in Ted's doorway holding the ear-to-ear grin.

Ted cocked his head to the side. "Roy Lee Steele," he said, getting out of his chair.

"The same," said Steele as Ted approached and embraced the man in a bear hug.

"Lee, you don't know how often I think about you and I don't know why I haven't taken the time to look you up."

"Same with me, Ted. It's a damn shame, but life just moves too fast, I guess."

"How's your wife, Lee—Linda, if I remember correctly, and any children?"

"Well, Linda and I divorced about five years ago, the service is hard on marriages, and I, or we, have a sixteen-year-old daughter who is going on twenty-seven, I think."

Ted smiled and shook his head.

"Sorry about your marriage, but I understand. Sit down, and tell me why you showed up on my doorstep."

Ted went to his office door and told one of his assistants to take his calls. He closed the door, returned to his desk and took a seat across from Roy, whom he had always addressed by his middle name, Lee, from their childhood growing up together. There was a quick rap on the door and his assistant cracked the door open to tell Ted that Bill Russell was on the phone. Ted excused himself to Lee and picked up the phone.

"Hi, Bill, how's it going? Yep, he's here now, and it turns out he's an old friend from my hometown. We were close friends in elementary and high school."

Ted listened for about two minutes and hung up.

"Sorry, Lee, that was the owner telling me to listen to you and not to ask questions, at least not until he gets here tomorrow. Lee, in the last two days it seems my life has been turned upside down. I've gone from head golf pro at a top East Coast resort to the CEO of same with two murders of employees on my hands—murders that for some reason brought in the FBI and then the Secret Service—now I'm running the place but I can't ask questions. As my ole pappy used to say, 'It's a hell of way to run a railroad,' know what I mean?"

Roy shifted in his seat, smiled, then got up and walked to the window behind Ted, looking out to the marina.

"Ted, I can tell you this much now, and really it's about all I know. This resort is scheduled to host a high-level meeting of government officials. The people I work for are extremely worried about security, and they think there is a tie-in between the murders and the meeting. My charge as it now stands is to bring you up to speed, and to keep a lid on things to preserve the meeting security and secrecy. I know that the owner here, Mr. Russell, has some association with the people I work for, but I don't know what that association is, or any background."

This comment brought a noticeable look of surprise from Ted, which Roy picked up.

"You didn't know your boss was involved with the Secret Service, Ted?"

"Um, no, but nothing involving Bill Russell surprises me anymore. So let's see, in the last forty-eight hours I've been elevated from golf pro to CEO of a five-star resort, two murders have been committed at the resort, I find the owner is involved with the United States Secret Service, and his resort is going to host a meeting with the President of the United States, that is if we can keep the murders secret."

"Hold it, Ted, nobody said anything about the President; don't get carried away."

"Well, Lee, that's what you do, isn't it, protect the Prez?"

"Yes, we do, but we protect many other officials as well and a lot of other things, so don't jump to conclusions. In fact, I think it's a stretch to think the President will be here. By the way, does anyone here, or anyone for that matter, know that you were a Navy SEAL?"

The expression on Ted's face turned black. "No one, and how did you find out?"

"It's part of my job, Ted. Even though we are old friends I've still got to follow proper protocol. I've read your Navy file and there is nothing to be ashamed of. To the contrary, you have an outstanding record."

"OK, I'm asking you to keep that to yourself and put a muzzle on these other government boy scouts running around here. I have my reasons."

9

Executive Knowledge

POTUS walked back and forth in front of his oval office desk and rubbed the back of his neck as his Director of National Intelligence, Gill Chambers, watched from a side chair.

"God damn it, Gill, no President, no person in the history of man, has been put in the position that I now face. This information that Admiral Bobby Lee Simpson gave you to pass on to me is—I don't have the words. The knowledge we possess will change the course of civilization on this planet forever, people are dying over this, and I'm being asked by my military and security people to cover up the story. And if I do, if I authorize the highest level of security possible and they decide to reveal themselves to the public, there is nothing any of us can do to stop them, nothing."

Gill Chambers got up and walked to the window behind the Presidential desk. "Mr. President, all of our security people feel that it is not likely that they will do anything but continue to work with us in secret as—"

The President raised his hand to silence the DNI.

"All of our security people? How about a handful of our security people, and the Air Force Chief of Staff, and none of them know the full story, hell I don't know the full story, compartmented security, need to know, what a damn mess."

The intercom buzzed and the President almost yelled into the thing.

"Director Cummings is here, sir."

"Send him in."

The door opened and Barry Cummings walked into the oval office.

"Mr. President, good to see you, sir; and Gill, how are you and how is the security of our homeland?" Chambers just smiled and opened his hands in a so-so gesture.

"OK," the President said, "let's keep the small talk for another time. Have you met with Russell and set everything up so this meeting will go off as planned, and what does he know?"

"Russell will be fine and give us any and all the support we need. I had him meet me at our sub base in San Diego to insure secrecy. I ran him up and down the bay a couple of times to instill a little fear but more than anything to instill the need for secrecy. He knows and believes what I told him, which is that this is a secret meeting with selected world leaders to address a new plan to attack terrorists.

POTUS walked behind his desk, put his hands on the back of his desk chair and turned it towards the window and looked out onto the South Lawn. His gaze dropped to the floor and he said just above a whisper, "Damn, I wish that is what it was."

President Horton looked up and turned to Cummings and Chambers. "Those two men killed at the Great River Resort may have been working undercover for Bernie Jarvis and World Dynamic Resources, according to information found on one of their computers."

Gill Chambers was looking at a file.

"The latest we have from the CIA analysts is that the men discussed an offer from Jarvis, but that was as far as it went. CIA says that all indications point to them staying loyal to the agency."

POTUS nodded and said, "Still, something about this stinks. Bernie is mixed up with a lot of high-level government work, secret work. If their execution came from inside this government, the son of bitches responsible will pay, fuck national security."

Cummings and Chambers had never seen POTUS like this, and there was no doubt that he meant every word he said. The President walked over to Barry Cummings.

"Barry, I understand the need for a top-secret facility at this Great River Resort for enhanced national security. In fact, if it's only used for this one operation it will be worth the cost and effort. I think putting two CIA operatives on site there to monitor the coming and goings of the regular guests made sense. It was a good plan—and then some numb nuts brain dead jerk out at Langley gets his wires crossed and sends the two guys to a classified MJ-12 meeting at Dugway Proving Grounds and exposes them— in fucking error!—to the most highly classified matter on the planet. They return home and within a day end up dead, executed, for God's sake. Then we find out that that prick Jarvis had tried to hire them. This stinks like shit and if it's an inside job I'll personally fry every bastard involved. I want answers and I'm going to get them."

POTUS turned to his chair and collapsed into it like the drained man that he was. There was quiet for what seemed like five minutes but really only about fifteen seconds, then Chambers said, "Mr. President, I talked again with Director Rutherford at Langley in depth about the whole matter and he said he was in the dark as to how Smart and Dunn ended up being sent to Dugway. He did say that one investigation seemed to implicate that

Bernie Jarvis was the root cause.

"You see, Jarvis again. God damn it, Gill, look at Jarvis and you'll find he's at the bottom of everything." After a pause the President continued. "Look, Gill, I don't mean to snipe at you, and I think you know that I have the highest respect for you and your intellect and you are a personal friend, but in my entire career I have relied on my gut feelings and they rarely let me down. In this case something just doesn't feel right and in my mind it all centers on Jarvis. I'm also concerned about Director Rutherford. You were here when he went way over the top in arguing against the meeting and maintaining top-secret classification. I tell you, he knows a lot more than he's telling us, you can take that to the bank. My own CIA director withholding intelligence from me, now isn't that a hell of a note. If the decision coming out of the meeting with other heads of state at Great River is to declassify MJ-12 and go public, and he continues to obstruct the release of information, I'll have no choice but to relieve him."

Barry Cummings stood. "Mr. President, I understand how you feel and will do anything that I or the service can do to get to the bottom of this matter. With that said, parts of this are so highly classified and so compartmented that getting the real story is going to be an almost impossible task. The Service will do its absolute best to keep you informed on anything that comes our way. However, I feel it will be very little as the MJ-12 matter is really out of our ballpark. In fact, I don't even know who they are or what they do."

POTUS acknowledged with a slight nod and Cummings continued. "In any case, we must move ahead with the business at hand. Bill Russell has taken on a partner, or at least has offered a partnership in the resort to the head golf pro and his best friend. He wants a managing partner and feels Ted Carter is the right man. We've done a background check on Carter and found that he is a decorated Navy SEAL who has held a top-secret clearance. He was involved in a black operation that is now sealed so I don't know what it was but it left him with scars and now he won't even admit he was in the Navy. Anyway, Carter needs to be brought into the loop on our interest in the resort, and I need to get there and look it over myself. I expect to have final clearance on Carter this evening and will go to the resort tomorrow morning to meet Carter and tour our facility with him."

POTUS got up and shook hands with Cummings.

"OK, Barry, let me know how things are over there when you get back," he said as he led Cummings to the door. POTUS turned back to Chambers.

"Gill, when do you expect to hear from Admiral Simpson again?"

"I really don't know, sir, he said he would contact me when the time was right, whatever that meant."

"OK, Gill, I want you to tell him he's got my attention and I want to meet with him. Tell him I'll give him Secret Service protection and bury him and his boys away so tight that no one will find them. I'll turn him over personally to Barry Cummings and I don't even want to know where Barry hides him. Also, get into the MJ-12 matter with the CIA and the FBI, and see what the NSA may have, and don't take any crap."

10

Plan Adjustment

A white unmarked van sat beside a hangar complex complete with 7500-foot runway on a deserted ranch north of Laredo, Texas in La Salle County near Artesia Wells. In a large room below the hangar floor the two men from the New Braunfels Park were trying to pull themselves back to the conscious world. The room looked like a combination dormitory, medical facility, and dining room. Both men had been shackled to the steel cots they were lying on, and stripped to their underwear.

Just to the left of the cots a door to an elevator car slid open and two men wearing jeans, polo shirts, and Western boots stepped into the room. Both men approached the cots and stood at the foot of each. They smiled at the men on the cots and the one on the right spoke.

"Did you two fools really think that you could take a group of rag tag Mexican thugs and in a month turn them into skilled killers and drug runners? Your people would have been chewed up before you got 100 yards across the border."

The Mexican tried to spit at the man, only to have his effort land on his own chest.

"Now, now, amigo, that's the type of thing that could keep your family from ever seeing you again. Speaking of your family, it's been a while since you have been with them, and, well, I thought you would like to see some pictures of them taken just yesterday. Here are your boys playing in the front yard, and your daughter sitting on the front steps. And of course your wife, here she is dressing after taking her morning shower. You are a lucky man; she has a beautiful body indeed. As you can see we are capable of getting quite close to all of them undetected. I know they mean a great deal to you and you would do anything to insure their safety. Well, you'll have that opportunity, my lucky man."

It was clear that the blood pressure of the Mexican was far above the danger stage from the color of his face, but the pictures got his attention and kept his mouth shut.

"Now, Felix, your friend Omar there is not as lucky as you since he doesn't have a fine family. Omar, you don't fit into our program. There is no way we feel confident that we can control you. We are going to take you out of here—if you behave yourself." The men walked to the cot and unlocked the cuffs on each wrist then re-cuffed each wrist in front of the man. Going to his feet they removed the leg shackles and stood him up. Taking him by each arm they moved him across the room and set him on the edge of a metal examining table in the medical area.

"I'm going to put a blindfold on you before taking you outside. Just behave yourself and all will be fine."

After placing the blindfold, the man doing the talking returned to the side of the bed. Still lying on the bed, the Mexican, looking between his feet, could see the other man reach behind his back, remove a pistol, turn and fire a shot at the head of his Middle Eastern friend. Although the shooter blocked his clear view of the shot he saw blood and other matter spatter the back wall as the body was blown over the table and on to the floor behind. The spokesman looked down at the Mexican.

"I said I was going to take him out of here. I didn't say he would be alive." He walked over and looked behind the table.

"This is a mess, Bobby. Would you get a blanket and cover him up?" If the Mexican had anything on his stomach it would have come up; as it was, he could only wretch. The spokesman got a chair and returned to the side of the bed.

"OK, my friend, do we have your attention?"

The Mexican nodded.

"Good, now there is a change of plans for you and your people. You are going to work for us, and if you are very, very careful and don't try anything stupid you may just live to see your family again. But let me warn you, if I or any of my associates see any hint that you have the faintest idea of doing something stupid we will start killing your family, one by one. There are several hundred of us and we all know about you. Two are within reach of your family as we speak and will remain there until we release you from your task. Oh, one other thing—you'll get the rest of your money, plus another hundred thousand for your trouble, but you are going to have to work a little harder and a few days longer than you expected." The other man walked over and took the left wrist of the man on the cot and snapped on a one-inch-wide silver bracelet.

"This will give us your location at all times and monitor your actions and conversation. If you try to tamper with it we will know and start the killing, so I would treat it with the utmost respect and care. Do you still understand?"

Once again the man nodded in the affirmative.

"Good, now let's discuss our new adventure."

11

CECPC

Barry Cummings arrived at the resort helipad at 8:00 AM sharp and was whisked by electric car through the tunnels to Bill Russell's office in the main building. Bill, Ted Carter, and Roy Lee Steele were at the conference table finishing a light breakfast when Cummings arrived. Bill arose to greet Cummings with a handshake, then introduced him to Ted. Steele shook hands with his boss. Cummings waved off breakfast but accepted coffee from a waiter who had been standing in the corner. After the coffee was poured Bill dismissed the waiter.

"Barry, this is your show. Ted has no knowledge of our little secret and perhaps neither does agent Steele, so what you want them to know is your call."

Cummings nodded. "From now on this conversation and what you will see is top secret and everyone in this room is well aware of what that means and involves."

Ted interrupted, "Hold it; I'm not cleared for secret information."

"Oh yes you are, as of last night," said Cummings. "You held a top-secret clearance in the Navy and it was a simple matter to get you cleared again."

Bill looked at Ted. "The Navy? I didn't know you had been in the Navy!"

Steele flushed and tried to show he didn't have a part in this.

"He was a Navy SEAL to be exact, a decorated Navy SEAL," said Cummings.

"I have asked to have that matter remain confidential, but it appears that no one gives a good God damn about my wishes."

"Mr. Carter, you are involved in a matter concerning a serious national security issue so your wishes take a back seat. Right now I'm not concerned about the petty interest of any one person and that includes every one, you, me, or the President of the United States, so get over it."

Ted stared at Cummings for several seconds then held up his hand in defeat. He had gotten the picture, even if he didn't like it.

"OK," said Cummings, "here it is in a few words. The Service has for some time wanted a secure place close to D.C. that the President and other high-ranking government officials could be quickly taken to in case of a national emergency. Also, we wanted a secure a secret place where the President could meet with whomever, when necessary. Camp David is somewhat secure but not secret and though we do have other places—you may recall our former facility at the Greenbrier, for instance, and perhaps you've heard of the very secret Mt. Weather—but we had nothing this close. Bill and I have been friends for a long time, so when I heard he was planning this resort an idea was born, developed, and carried out. There is a lot more to this place than you know." He raised his hand and spoke into a small device.

"Bring the car, please." Then looking around the table, he said, "Gentlemen, shall we go?"

Outside of Bill's office they were met by another agent, introduced as Agent Jackson, and escorted to a service area. They all got into an electric car, with Agent Jackson driving, and returned to the elevator that accessed the reception area. Jackson ushered them in and inserted a card, which hung from a chain around his neck, into a reader in the elevator control panel. The elevator started, but instead of going up, it went down, obviously startling Ted. After traveling a distance of what seemed to Ted to be about two stories, the elevator stopped and the doors opened into an unfurnished room about twelve by fifteen feet. The elevator doors closed behind them and Jackson placed his hand onto a reader. A green light flashed and he inserted the card into another reader. A slight hissing sound was heard as a wall slid back, opening into a beautiful room. The focal point of the room was a crystal chandelier hanging over a rich, deep blue carpet.

"This is the reception area of the Chesapeake Emergency Command and Planning Center, or CECPC," said Cummings.

A long, walnut reception counter was to their left. Moving straight ahead and through a pair of walnut doors they entered a small but very plush auditorium. He motioned for them to follow him to the front and had them take seats in the front row.

"This facility is about fifty feet below grade and built of reinforced concrete. It was not designed to withstand a nuclear blast but it is very secure. The exact construction details are not part of your need to know. However, in addition to what you have seen, the facility has twelve suites with two bedrooms, a parlor, and a small kitchen area in each. There is a men's dorm and a women's dorm that will accommodate up to fifty persons each, a commercial kitchen, dining room, fully equipped medical suite, communications room, situation room, and conference room. Any questions so far?"

"Not yet from me, but I'm sure there will be a few shortly. I'm still trying to digest all of this stuff," said Ted.

"OK," said Cummings. "Let me bring in two of our fine agents to brief you on the meeting."

The doors at the rear opened and in walked two agents, who looked familiar, as well as the resort's chief engineer who, to the surprise of Ted and Bill, was also an agent with the Secret Service.

"Gentlemen, we will now give you an outline of the conference to be held here in two weeks, and what we will request of each of you," said the senior of the two. Ted was amused, surprised, and puzzled, and all at once had a lot of questions, questions about the murders, questions that would not be answered.

12

The Dirty Dozen

After Felix Lopez was taken from the park in New Braunfels, his car was unlocked using his keys, which had been removed from his pocket, and it was driven south to the La Salle county ranch. After overnight indoctrination, Felix was told to leave and return to the ranch within twenty-fours hours or less with his twelve men for additional training. The two men who had entered the dorm the night before and shot Omar were Jake Barnett and Bobby Lee. They also handled the indoctrination and helped a much-shaken Felix to his car. Before letting him get into the car Jake reminded him again that his every action and spoken word would be monitored by people very close to him.

"Felix, my friend, I hope that you don't get a feeling of security when you get your twelve men together and then try something stupid, because this is what will be the result of acting on such a foolish thought."

About 1,500 feet in front of the auto was an old tandem axle dump truck. Jake pointed at the truck and they all heard a whoosh of sound as an anti-tank missile vaporized the truck in a huge fireball. Jake and Bobby expected the blast and were prepared for it, but Felix was knocked to his knees. As Jake helped him up and opened the door to the car a wet stain appeared across the front of Felix's pants. It was clear he was impressed with what he had just observed.

As Felix drove off, Jake and Bobby Lee returned to the building and strode into the rear portion, which was in fact a large hangar containing a Fokker 100 regional jet that had been converted for their use. They approached a man sitting on the edge of a table under the port wing of the aircraft.

"Watcha' rubbing your chest for, Omar?"

"Listen, you two," replied Omar, "the next time one of you takes the dumb-dumb, that son of a bitch hurts."

Bobby laughed. "Hold on, Omar, you're the rag head in our group, that's your job."

"Pricks," muttered Omar, then he raised his shirt to reveal a melon-sized bruise. Jake went to Omar and put his arm around his shoulder.

"Just kidding, buddy. I know how it feels, I've been there, but at least our friend Felix bought our little ruse. Now we better get ready as he was scared shitless when he left and he may be back a lot sooner than the twenty-four hours we gave him."

A door opened on the side of the hangar and a young woman hurried over to the group and handed Jake a sheet of paper.

Jake read the message. "Well, it looks like they will be here shortly. Our buddy Felix is on his cell now trying to round up his men with instructions to meet him in Laredo in four hours with a van big enough for all of them." Jake paused and thought for a few minutes.

"Bobby, get a couple of the boys to pick them up on I-35 as they head back and escort them in, and make sure they keep them away from the sensitive areas. Omar, why don't you go back to communications with Betty and get a message off to the boss and bring him up to date? Keep the message plain vanilla; we don't want him to get fucking nervous and show up here. OK, let's get to work."

13

Plan from the Grave

The meeting in the CECPC took about three hours, along with a very brief tour of other parts of the facility. However, it was clear that they still hadn't seen more than twenty-five percent of the facility, and that was by design. Their instructions had been made clear, as was what they could tell the senior resort employees. Bill and Ted returned to Bill's office and over lunch set up a quick plan.

Bill had a legal pad and was making notes. "OK, bud, let's review the basic outline. Heads of state from the UK, Germany, France, Russia, India, Japan, Spain, Australia, and perhaps three Middle Eastern nations will arrive at Andrews AFB, Langley AFB, Oceana NAS, Norfolk NAS, and Patuxent NAS. They'll be choppered here on a tight schedule over a four-hour period. They will spend two nights and leave the morning following the second night on the same four hour schedule they used to arrive."

Bill stopped writing and looked up at Ted. "Personally, I don't see how they can expect to do this without someone finding out about the meeting. How the hell can almost a dozen world leaders meet in one spot on this planet without someone smoking it out?"

"I agree," said Ted, "but that's not really our problem. We just need to keep the lid on our people and go on with business as usual. As I see it, that's the only reason we were even brought into this mess. What does bother me is that your buddy Cummings said there would be armed troops at the pad and in the surrounding woods, as well as service guys all over the place. That has got to be noticed and disruptive, not to mention potentially dangerous to our guests."

Bill nodded agreement. "But you brought it up and they said they know how to handle such things, so let them worry about it."

"Yeah, well, if one of our good guests has too much wine for dinner and decides to take a late night walk in the woods and some trigger happy trooper puts a round through his head, well, then it becomes our business—excuse me, your business, since we haven't had the time to get into your partnership offer."

A slight smile crossed Bill's face as he rubbed his chin.

"Ah, yeah. I've been thinking about that and I'm having the papers drawn up as we speak. Don't think for a minute that I intend to go into this alone with my bare ass on the line. Oh no, you will be my partner, like it or not. I'm going to make you a multi-millionaire no matter how much you kick and scream."

Ted knew that Bill was making light of the subject, but he also knew that he was serious about the partnership. Ted wanted the position—who wouldn't—and at that moment it was a done deal. The details were all that remained, and they would be resolved in the next day or so.

They called a meeting of the senior people and told them that they may notice some unusual activity over the next couple of weeks, but to ignore it and not to discuss any unusual activity with anyone except one of them. It was said that this activity was part of the ongoing investigation into the murders and should be ignored, or if they had questions to come to one of them.

Ted took a call from Ruth, who asked if he planned to have dinner at home, and if he wanted to invite Bill. Ted told her about Lee Steele and asked if it was OK to invite him also. Dinner was set for 6:30 and Bill told her he would be there by 5:00.

About 3:30 PM Ruth was getting the kitchen organized for dinner when a runner from the reservations office at the hotel knocked on the back door. He handed her a sealed mailing envelope with "Ted Carter-Personal" written across the front.

"Ms. Bennett, this was found with some of Mr. Smart's things in the front desk safe and it has Mr. Carter's name on it. I was told to take it to him but he wasn't in his office so I thought I should bring it over to his cottage."

Ruth thanked him and put the envelope on the coffee table in the great room without much thought. Ted arrived a little before five.

"Babe, I could sure use a Jack and water and some company."

"Well, place yourself on the patio and I'll get us both one, but the way you look I don't think one will do it."

Ted smiled. "You are so right; every day is crazier than the one before. If this continues I'll be a babbling idiot in a month." She brought the drinks and sat down.

"What went on today?"

"Well, a lot of stuff, most of which I can't tell you about, at least I don't think I can, but—" His voice trailed off and he looked up at her with a little shake of his head.

"Ted, I don't like the way you look. Is it that bad?"

"It's not that it's bad, it's just that Bill is into some heavy stuff with the government and the resort is ground zero. Think about it, we have FBI, CIA, and Secret Service people all over the place. That alone is way beyond the pale even for a double murder."

"I have thought about it, lover, thought about it a lot, but we really haven't had much time to talk so I've kept a lot of stuff, questions, to myself. I know the pressure you must be under and I don't need to add to the pressure. I'm a patient girl and I know you'll tell me what you can when you can."

Ted reached his right hand behind her head, gently pulled her to him and kissed her lips, then placing both hands on her cheeks, looked into her sparkling eyes.

"I'm a fool if I don't marry you tomorrow before somebody snatches you away from me."

"Is that a proposal?" she asked.

"Well, I guess you could say it's more of a warning, but when this mess is straightened out—"

She placed her hand over his mouth.

"One major event at a time, lover. As I said, you don't need any more pressure, and no one is going to steal me away."

She got up, walked behind him, placed her arms around his neck and nuzzled his neck.

"Oh, I forgot, someone from the front desk dropped off a package they found in the safe. I'll get it, sit still."

Ruth returned and handed the envelope to Ted. He opened it and pulled out a second envelope. He opened the second and found a one-sheet typed letter and a brass key. Opening the letter he started to read:

> Dear Mr. Carter:
> Although we have not been close, I have directed this to you because Mr. Russell is rarely here and I know he has complete trust in you and your ability. What I'm telling you here should also be shared with him.
> I have, through error, been given information of a very sensitive nature. This information must be given to the President of the United States as quickly as possible. Mr. Russell has a contact with direct access to the President. I am asking you to be the intermediary to Mr. Russell so he can get this information in the hands of the President. In doing this I'm putting you, Mr. Russell, and others close to you in great danger, and that is something I deeply regret,

but I see no other choice as I have limited time.

I have reason to believe the resort is at the center of what will soon be the most startling revelation in the history of mankind. Powerful people want to conceal this revelation and will stop at nothing to do so. I say again, please heed this warning. You are in danger, Mr. Russell is in danger, and those close to you are in danger. Trust no one! You will receive instructions on how to use the enclosed key shortly and the key will answer many of your questions and explain much more.

To survive this will require great strength, both physical and mental. I know of your military background and I know you have the required strength. Keep your eyes open and always watch your back. You will be hearing from me again.

God Bless,

Billy Smart

Ted dropped his hand with the letter in it to the table and looked up at Ruth and she saw the shock in his eyes.

"May I read it?"

Taking it from his limp hand, she started reading and as she did she pressed the tips of her fingers to her lips and blood drained from her face.

"Ted, what in God's name does it mean?"

He looked into her face. "I don't know, but I do know what I'm going to do right now." He got up and went to the bedroom. Going into his closet he took down a case from the top shelf and set it on the bed.

Opening the case he took out a 9mm Glock and a 380 Colt Pocketlite. He checked the clip in both and racked a round into the chamber of each and put on the safety. He decided to carry the small Colt and put the Glock into the nightstand drawer. He turned around and Ruth was standing behind him. He took both of her hands into his.

"Ruth, I want you to go back to your house until all of this is over; things are getting out of hand and—"

"Stop it, Ted," Ruth interrupted. "What about the resort employees? Are you going to send them home, the housekeepers, food service people, and all the women? If you tell me you need them I will go home because you would be telling me that you don't need me, and I would find that very offensive! No, Ted, I don't cut and run, that is, unless you have a little cutie on the side, and if you do I'll get my pound of flesh or 1.5 million, whichever comes first. Do we understand each other, big boy?" She turned on her heel and headed for the kitchen. "I've got a dinner to get ready."

Bill showed up at 6:15 and apologized for being early. Ted waved him off and told him it was perfect timing as there was a letter he needed to read. After Bill got over the initial shock they decided to wait until at least the morning before disclosing the existence of the letter to anyone else.

"Ted, I'm going out on a limb here and tell you something that is confidential but you now are cleared and I think you have a need to know, although this need-to-know stuff is probably not my call, but to hell with it. I was in San Diego several days ago meeting with Barry Cummings when I told everyone I was in Orlando on business. Barry wanted to brief me on the meeting here in three weeks and in essence give me my orders. The meeting was like a chapter out of a James Bond book. The President is going to be here, as you now know, and they are going to great lengths to keep that and the meeting secret. Anyway, what we were told today the meeting will be about is pure bull shit—Barry told me it had to do with world terrorism and some of my people could be killed if things didn't go right. I don't know what he meant by 'if things don't go right,' but the picture is getting a little clearer."

"I don't know about clearer, but it sure as hell is getting scarier. By the way, Ruth has some beautiful New York strips that I've got to grill outside—you want to cover me while I cook?"

"No, Agent Steele will be here, I understand, and that's his side of the street. Look Ted, all joking aside, there is one other thing I want to pass on before Steele gets here. I had a call this afternoon from Bernie Jarvis, owner of World Dynamic Resources. He said he just wanted to say 'hi' since we hadn't talked in a while, but that is BS—Bernie doesn't call anyone just to shoot the breeze. Anyway, he asked how things were at the resort and finally told me he understood I had been lucky enough to book some high-level secret government meetings this fall. I told him that his information was incorrect as the only large meeting we had booked this fall was for one of his Hollywood buddies who would remain unnamed. However, if he had any high-level contacts in the government that needed a place to hold a secret conference, this would be a piece of cake for us and to put me in contact with them. This seemed to take him back a bit, and he cut the conversation short."

Ted rubbed his forehead with the tips of his fingers. "That doesn't sound good. It seems to me to be information that should be passed on to Steele or Cummings. It sounds like the meeting has been compromised. Aren't Jarvis and WDR companies big into defense contracting?"

"The biggest, and he's a ruthless bastard who will act like your best friend and stab you in the back if you get in his way. He has direct access to the White House, which makes him rich, powerful, and ruthless, a very dangerous combination. You're right; I'll tell Steele when he arrives."

14

The Mole

Bernie Jarvis operated his empire from a suite of offices on the top floor of his Crystal City office building. He had just poured scotch into a couple of glasses and lit a Don Diego.

"He said he didn't have a government meeting planned and it sounded on the up and up."

"Come on, Bernie, we know damn well that a meeting is planned there with a bunch of world leaders."

Bernie looked at his guest with eyes as cold as ice. He was not used to being talked to in that tone of voice.

"We don't know shit, Brad. We fucking suspect based on what your White House source told you, but we don't know shit. I've known Russell a long time and he's a goody two shoes who doesn't lie. He can be a tough businessman, but he doesn't lie."

The guest needed to do some backing and filling as he didn't want to piss off a man who makes Al Capone look like a choirboy.

"Sorry, Bernie, I was just so sure my info was accurate."

"You civil servants can afford to be wrong. I can't. See what you can find out. I'm going to pick Rutherford's brain, which should take ten or fifteen seconds."

Both laughed, and Brad felt the tension lift, which was good. His host didn't suffer fools gladly; he killed them.

"Brad, you don't need to know the why or where, but if this meeting is fact and it is held it would be devastating to my business. I need to hit the resort to disrupt the meeting, and my people in Texas tell me they need about five days before any meeting to pull this off. If the meeting is in fact going to be at Russell's place we need to hit it about three days prior to the meeting. I need proper intelligence. I can't operate on a best guess."

Brad nodded his understanding, but in reality he didn't understand any of this. If he had any choice in the matter he would turn this mad man in, but his option to do that had long since passed. When he was working out of the Pentagon in military procurement and took that first $10,000.00

to pass on confidential contract information, he sold his soul to WDR and Bernie Jarvis. A college buddy who had gone to work for WDR found him in the Pentagon and this little gambit was formed. A nice piece of cash just to give some harmless insider information to a college buddy to help him secure defense contracts seemed so insignificant. How was he to know that it would mushroom and he would end up dealing directly with this psycho? He moved from the Pentagon to the White House as an assistant to a White House senior military aide. He met and was now sleeping with a young lady on the President's staff, who had access to confidential information. Pillow talk was big in Washington, and Bernie Jarvis paid big bucks for good information. The problem was that once you worked for Bernie, you always worked for Bernie. The life expectancy of someone who left Bernie's circle of informers and spies was measured in minutes. He was trapped. Why was this meeting about terrorism or whatever so damn important to Jarvis? So important that he was going to "hit" the place, whatever that really meant.

"Brad, I need more information. You need to press your source a little more, and if it takes more money, that's not a problem." •

"Bernie, you know I'll do my best, but she may not have anymore information to give. This is really above top-secret stuff, or so it seems, with only two or three people in the know."

Bernie wanted to walk to his desk, take out his Sig and blow this simple cocksucker's head off, but he just smiled. Later, he thought, later; he is still necessary to have around for information and I don't need a diversion right now.

"I understand that, Brad, but see what you can do anyway. I'm counting on you."

He got up to indicate the meeting was over. He walked to the door, opened it, took the glass from Brad's hand as Brad approached, shook the other, and closed the door as Brad stepped past the threshold. Jarvis walked to his desk and placed a call.

"He just left, so when and where do we meet?"

Thirty minutes later a limo with dark windows stopped in front of the Jarvis building and picked up Bernie Jarvis. Bernie settled into the rear seat beside retired Air Force General Curtis Hammersmith, former chairman of the Joint Chiefs of Staff. Jarvis and Hammersmith were co-directors of intelligence for MJ-12.

"I assume this limo is secure."

"Yeah," replied the general. "The driver can't hear a thing. My boys all but built it."

"OK, good. I'm afraid that my source has about dried up, or he may be under suspicion as a leak and is being fed false information. I called the owner of the Great River Resort and he convinced me that no government meeting is scheduled there."

The general shook his head. "Bernie, doesn't it stand to reason that the owner would deny knowledge of such a meeting?"

"Look, Curtis, I know this man and lying is not something he's good at doing. If he had to lie he would beat around the bush, and that didn't happen. I can read people and I'm about ninety percent sure that nothing is scheduled at that resort. Since I'm not 100 percent sure, it stays in our sights while we continue to gather information. Is there anything new on our NSA friends?"

The general shook his head. "Nothing that you don't know. Admiral Simpson and two of his deputies have disappeared from the face of the earth. Rutherford at CIA thinks they may have been in touch with the President, but he says the President won't tell him shit. My take is that Rutherford knows more than he wants to tell me and is possibly playing both sides of the street."

"What a hell of a mess," muttered Jarvis. "I wouldn't be surprised if that idiot Horton didn't go on television and tell the world about the entire MJ-12 operation. He's a dangerous son of a bitch that needs to be stopped."

Hammersmith didn't respond to Jarvis's idiocy. He wondered how this maniac could have become such a leader of industry. It once again confirmed his belief that most industrialists were nothing but money-grubbing fools, and that military leaders were the true force behind world progress. He agreed with Jarvis that MJ-12 and its work should remain a black project and something worth fighting to preserve. The difference between him and Jarvis was that he felt it would be truly harmful to mankind if MJ-12 secrets became public knowledge. Jarvis on the other hand could give a whit about his fellow man; he was only concerned about the devastating effect on his own business. With him it was pure greed.

"Curtis, we've got to assume that those three want to expose the existence of MJ-12 and have gone to the President to convince him to do just that. We can discredit most on the inside that decide to go public, but it will be something else to try to discredit the President."

"Bernie, I agree with all of that, but what do we do about it, that's the question?"

Jarvis closed his eyes and rubbed his forehead with his hand, then turned to Hammersmith. "General, we must act before we have to react. Number one, we must find our NSA friends and convince them of the error of their ways, and second we must find out if there is to be a meeting with the President and other world leaders, and if one is planned it must be disrupted so it will at least be postponed. We need time to develop a new plan and damage control."

Hammersmith couldn't believe what he was hearing. This son of a bitch was out of his mind and because of his association with Bernie he could become a part of some insane plot. He couldn't allow that to happen.

15

Instruction/Destruction

Ted walked into his office at 7:45 AM to a ringing phone.

"Mr. Carter, sorry to bother you so early," said the dock master, "but Ms. Russell is arriving today aboard the *Swamp King II* and we are trying to make room for her, all 88 feet of her—"

"Now Bert, is that any way to talk about Ms. Russell?"

"Oh no, Mr. Carter, not Ms. Russell, I meant the *Swamp King*, their new Broward."

"Just a little humor to start the morning, Bert. Go on with what were you saying."

"Well, Mr. Carter since—well, you know, uh, uh—what I'm trying to say, Mr. Carter, is, well, I know you don't like anyone touching your boat—well, I don't mean not touching it, but since you really don't like anyone else to run her—well, would you mind coming down and moving her to help make room for the *Swamp King*. I'm really sorry to ask you to do this...."

"Bert, Bert," Ted interrupted, "have one of your fellows do it. I really don't mind."

Ted had to fight from laughing into the phone; Bert was a nice guy but a second Barney Fife. A year before, Andy Griffith, the actor, was aboard a large motor yacht that had stopped overnight at the marina. Griffith met Bert and swore he had to be a Barney Fife clone.

"Thanks, Mr. Carter, we'll be gentle with her." As soon as Ted hung up the phone it rang again.

"Shit," he muttered, picking it up.

"Mr. Carter, I have a call for you from a Mr. Smart in Ft. Worth. He says he is Billy Smart's brother and he wants to talk to you."

"OK, Katherine, put him through."

"This is Ted Carter, Mr. Smart."

"Mr. Carter, I'm Billy Smart's brother. I have a message for you from Billy."

Ted was so stunned that he couldn't get words out for a couple of seconds, so Smart continued.

"I received a sealed envelope from Billy a few days ago with the instructions not to open it unless he passed away. He told me by phone sometime prior to that that he was sending some legal instructions for his estate just in case something happened to him. When I received the envelope I wasn't concerned, then this happened...." Smart's voice began to break and he tried to regain composure.

"Mr. Smart, we are all deeply saddened by Billy's death. Is there anything we can do for you or the family?"

"Mr. Carter, thank you, but no, except to keep me informed of the investigation. I am his only kin, and the police have not been helpful."

"You can count on it, Mr. Smart, and what was the message?"

"Oh yes, the message. I was simply to call and tell you this: 'Maryland State Bank, Crisfield, Maryland, lockbox number 1101.' That's the entire message; I hope it means something to you."

It wasn't until Ted hung up that he put the lockbox together with the key he received in the note from Billy. He picked up the phone and placed a call to Bill, when the building shook from what he first thought was a tremendous sonic boom. He got Bill's voicemail and left a quick message. When he turned to the windows overlooking the marina he saw black smoke rising from the docks and realized that what he thought was a sonic boom was in fact an explosion in the marina.

Running from his office in the executive suite, he sprinted across the main lobby and out through the bar side entrance to the marina walkway. He stopped on the top landing of steps to the marina where he saw the burning hulk of his Pro Line. Two marina workers were getting a hose to play water on the burning hull, which was still tied to the dock, and Bert Riner was working to unlock a dock box. Ted ran down the steps and when he reached Bert he could see the young man was sobbing while pulling a blue tarp from the dock box. Looking up at Ted, Bert pointed to the end of the dock, and then Ted saw it, the badly mangled and obviously lifeless body that obviously had been blown out of his boat. Bert was getting a cover for the body of one of his young dockworkers.

Ronnie Stone arrived about twenty minutes after the explosion, followed by the state police. The remains of the boat were kept from sinking by three of its four dock lines. The center console had vanished, so it was apparent that that was the location of the explosion. Within an hour it was determined that the explosion was not an accident but a bomb wired to the boat's ignition. It was time to bring Steele up to date about the letter from Billy Smart.

16

Key Instructions

Ruth Bennett was the strongest woman Ted had ever known, but when he called her at his cottage just minutes after the explosion to tell her what had happened, and that he was OK, her strength cracked and she broke down in sobs. However, what shocked Ted the most was not her loss of composure but what she managed to say. Until that instant Ted had only thought about the explosion being an accidental gas explosion, but when she said, "Ted, I think someone tried to kill you," the thought went through him like an electric shock.

After the initial investigation indicated that it was in fact a bomb, Ted returned to his cottage to check on Ruth, discuss the events with her, and to make sure she was safe. If someone wanted to kill him, she could also be a target.

At 11:00 AM he returned to his office for a meeting with Bill, Ronnie Stone, Richard Dill, and Roy Steele. The line of questioning from Stone and Dill, especially Dill's questions, irritated Ted, but he managed to keep his temper in check.

"Look, I understand your questions but I don't have a clue why someone tried to kill me. I haven't been threatened by anyone, and as far as I know everyone around here, especially the club members, love me." Ronnie Stone and Bill laughed, bringing questioning looks from Dill and Steele.

"It's an inside joke, fellows," said Bill. "You see, Mr. Carter here views the club members collectively as a bunch of wealthy pricks, and they know it, and yet still pay his hugely inflated lesson prices."

"I think I understand," Dill added, which brought more laughs.

Stone spoke up. "OK guys, now it's time to hit on a touchy subject. I think it's time to consider that it may be necessary to close the resort, at least until we can get a handle on what is going on. We have had three murders in the last few days, two of which have been taken out of my jurisdiction by the feds and one of which is under my jurisdiction, at least as it stands for now. These events indicate that innocent people may be at risk, and we need a sealed crime scene. Comments, please."

Bill Russell spoke first. "Sheriff, this may surprise you, but that thought has crossed my mind more than once. Now Mr. Steele's boss was adamant that the resort should stay open, but this latest event may change his thinking. Mr. Steele, he's your boss, so why don't you call him and discuss the matter, and then have him call me?"

"He knows how the Bureau feels," Dill added.

As the meeting was breaking up, Ted tapped Roy Steele on the arm to indicate that he wanted him to stay, at the same time Dill's cell phone rang. He answered it, listened a few seconds, said "Yes sir," and hung up.

"Sheriff, that was the director—he wants to talk with you as soon as we are through here. You can contact him from our field office."

Stone and Dill excused themselves and headed for the FBI's temporary field office. Ted closed his office door, went to his desk and took out the letter from Billy Smart and handed it to Steele. Steele scanned over the letter then read it over a second time, and looked up at Ted.

"You told all of us that you didn't know of any threats against you. Don't you think this is a threat and aren't you concealing evidence?"

"Mr. Steele, I have been advised that I have a top-secret security clearance and as such have been made aware of some very sensitive matters. I have also been advised that matters involving my security clearance are governed by federal law. With that in mind, Sheriff Stone was not cleared for information that may potentially tie into security matters around here. Also, since I've told you about it, I have concealed nothing; now you and the Service can do with it as you please."

"Mr. Carter, you get an A+ as you have the correct answers to my question. Now, who knows about this letter?"

"You, Bill, Ruth, and I told our head of beverage services, a good friend of mine."

"How did this fellow in beverage service find out about it?"

"His name is Mango, and Ruth and I went to the hotel bar after you and Bill left last night for a nightcap with Mango after he closed the bar—we do that a lot. Mango is a close friend, so I told him about the letter. Mango is straight as an arrow and keeps his mouth shut."

Steele shook his head. "Ted, you just said you didn't tell Stone because of security matters but yet you tell a bartender friend!"

Ted's face turned red. "Lee, God damn it, that was pre-explosion not post explosion, and at that time I didn't see any possible tie-in between the letter and the security issues I have knowledge of. As a matter of fact, I think the possibility of a tie-in is slim at best."

"OK, bud, let's move on. There is nothing that we can do about it anyway." Steele felt the same about Ruth but knew he would be pushing a hot button with Ted to bring her into this conversation.

"We need to get to Crisfield, Maryland, and I should be able to get a chopper here by mid-afternoon, unless there is a better way."

"Maybe I've got a better way," Ted said, looking at his watch. He picked up the phone and dialed the boatyard.

"May I speak to Lawton? Thanks. Lawton, it's Ted. Are you doing anything?"

"Hell no, Ted, I'm just sitting over here with my thumb up my ass playing with myself, just the same as always."

"Well, glad you're in a good mood."

"Sorry, buddy, but not one thing has gone right today. I'm going to lunch, but it's going to be on my boat in the middle of the bay—to hell with this place."

"In that case, I've got a proposition for you—how about your usual fee of $2,000.00 an hour for your boat and you as captain for a quick trip to Crisfield? If I remember correctly, that's the price you gave the other Secret Service boys and I've got another one here now, and we need to get there in a hurry."

"Sure," said Lawton, "but I quoted the two $1,500.00." Ted ignored Lawton's comment and looked at Steele.

"About two hours each way or $8,000.00 total. What do you say?"

"I say yes, if we can go right away. It will cost that much or more to get a chopper here."

"Lawton, we are ready when you are."

Lawton laughed. "I get it, I get six and you get two. I'll pick you up on your dock in fifteen minutes."

17

The Group

POTUS leafed through the file and looked up at Barry Cummings and Gill Chambers.

"Gill, when did you first hear of this MJ-12 Group?"

"Mr. President, I heard rumors back when I was Secretary of Defense, but nothing concrete until Admiral Simpson contacted me to get through to you, and then of course through your briefing to Barry and me about Simpson's messages to you."

"How about you, Barry, when did you first hear of MJ-12?"

"From your briefing, Mr. President, but I had also heard rumors, the same as Gill." The President nodded.

"Admiral Simpson is passionate in his belief that this all should be public knowledge, but he says he will only discuss the reason behind his passion with me face to face. Curious isn't it?" POTUS tapped his pen on his desktop.

"Barry, I want you to hide the Admiral and his two deputies at a secure location, and I don't even want to know where until I'm taken to meet with them. I gave him your private cell number and told him to call you in the morning to give you time to work out the details. Is this all workable?"

"I could handle it right now if he called. All I need to know is where to pick them up."

"OK, great. Also, I understand none of the three are married. I know the Admiral lost his wife several years ago, but I'm sure they have close family. Do you have the resources to put a detail on their close family?"

"Yes sir, I was going to ask you about doing that."

"Outstanding, Barry. By the way, the Admiral says he knows you well and trusts you."

Cummings smiled. "Yes sir, we have some history together."

POTUS grinned. "Anything you care to share about that history?"

"No sir, not a thing."

"Mr. President," said Chambers, "the CIA boys going over the Smart and Dunn computers say they are now sure that neither worked for Jarvis.

Jarvis made them an offer but they didn't act on it. However, Smart knew his life was at risk so he sent detailed information to Ted Carter at the resort, information he wanted Carter to get to you, using Bill Russell's connections with the government."

"Let me get this straight, Gill—this Ted Carter fellow has MJ-12 data, he's in the loop?"

"No sir, we don't believe so, not yet anyway. Indications are if Smart put these documents and the letter found on his computer together, he probably didn't have time to get them to Carter before he was killed."

"Well, let's hope not," said POTUS. "We don't need any more complications; although in the scheme of things it's not really a big issue, or at least not one we can't control if he does find out. Barry, you are close to the operation at the resort. See what Carter knows, and Gill, get me copies of what was found on those computers."

POTUS picked up the file once again and started flipping through the pages.

"The names of the current MJ-12 Group are beyond belief, at least some of them are. How the hell did so many private citizens get into the group? There are names here I don't know—the president of such-and-such company, the CEO of some instrument company. It just doesn't make sense. I'm the President of the United States, charged with looking after the national security of the country, the commander-in-chief of the military, for God's sake, and some of the most important information in the history of mankind has been kept from me by a government agency run by a group of civilians and a handful of civil servants. My own CIA director is in the group and I don't know about it. He has been keeping this secret from me. It's like this is some shadow government. As soon as this is straightened out I'm going to fire that prick. And what the hell is Bernie Jarvis doing in this group; he's nothing but a God damned thug."

Gill Chambers started smiling. "I guess, Mr. President, for the same reason he's been at two White House state dinners this year."

POTUS saluted the Director of National Intelligence with his middle finger.

18

Jake

Bernie Jarvis was screaming into the phone.

"Wonderful, you blew up the wrong man; you are all nothing but fucking incompetent bastards. One simple fucking job so simple a God damned moron could do it, and you can't get it right." His hands were shaking; the veins in his neck looked like fire hoses. "What else? Just tell me the rest of the story, you God damned incompetent."

He listened for twenty seconds longer and slammed the phone down. He walked to his bar and poured a stiff scotch and threw it down in one gulp. He knew he was wrong. In the old days he kept his cool, but now he blew up; he had lost his control and that was a big problem. Self-control was necessary in his business, but immense success, and possibly age, had robbed him of his self-control. He knew that its loss could result in his downfall; he knew he must fight this weakness to continue to survive.

The scotch helped. He picked up his phone and dialed a number.

"Jake, I need you, Bobby and Omar on the Fokker and here as quickly as you can get here. I need you in a chopper over the bay this afternoon, so go for wheels up in less than thirty, and bring the usual toys." Jake had motioned for Bobby and Omar to come over and he had cut on the speaker.

"Uh, boss, we are in the middle of a major operation and twelve highly trained Mexican gentlemen are headed here as we speak."

"I don't give a fuck if Poncho Villa is on his way. I want you here in three hours or I'll come down there and shoot all three of you sons of bitches myself. I'm fed up with excuses from incompetents. I'll meet you at the Eastern Shore airstrip in three hours. Call me on my cell when you are in the air."

The phone went dead and Jake looked at Bobby and Omar.

"Omar, get in touch with the boys. Tell Hank to get our friends in here, feed them, put them to bed and we'll be back tomorrow or as soon as possible. As I see it we have two choices—we go do what he wants and come back here, or we go there and kill the son of a bitch and come back here."

Jake Barnett had been with Bernie Jarvis for thirty-two years and was now director of "field operations," or, as Bernie liked to say, "director of my black projects." Jake grew up in Louisiana and as a teen had several arrests for petty theft. However, Jake was smart, knew how to handle himself, and could put himself on any level and fit into any situation from honky-tonks to country clubs. His intelligence helped him get through his teen years without serious trouble and he found his way into the rough world of oil field work.

Bernie first met him while Jake was a foreman on a Gulf Coast oil rig, and Bernie was inspecting the installation of equipment that one of his father's companies was installing on the platform. Bernie had been moving up in his father's business empire and had decided that WDR needed the ability to carry out clandestine operations from time to time. This feeling was not shared with his father, as his father was a man of deep-rooted integrity. Bernie, on the other hand, had become involved in industrial espionage behind his father's back, and the need to operate undercover and use strong-arm tactics, in his opinion, had become an absolute necessity. Bernie saw in Jake just the man he needed and hired Jake as his personal assistant.

At six feet two inches and 190 pounds, Jake was solid and a match for most any man, but he was not a killer at heart. After Bernie's father passed away and Bernie took over control of WDR, their black operations increased. When Bernie finally stepped over the line and decided it was necessary to eliminate a problem, the job fell to Jake's end of the operation. Although Jake was not a killer he knew people who were and he hired them. As with so many things in life, once you do something difficult, the next time it becomes easier, and so on. Now, after fifteen years of "eliminating" problems, the method had become Bernie's first choice, not a last resort. Jake had become sick of the job and the man he now considered a nut case. Jake wanted out but he was trapped, just like all the others who carried out Bernie Jarvis's dirty work.

The ranch-and-hangar complex was Jake's home and office. He designed the complex and ran the black operations from there. It had a staff that ranged from twenty to thirty people, all hired by Jake and funded by Bernie. Jake loved the place, he called the shots and it was 1700 miles away from Bernie.

Jake had alerted the ground crew to get the Fokker ready, and he had gone to his quarters in the living area of the building and put a change of clothes in a small carry-on. He stood outside the hangar watching the plane being rolled out. The two pilots were already aboard doing their preflight. As he watched, he thought how simple it would be. He knew Bernie would be in the parking area when the plane landed. He would be alone; it was always that way; Bernie never met him with anyone else around. How simple, he would step off the plane and as always quickly walk over to Bernie and shake hands, then take out his 9mm Glock and shoot him in the head, load his body in the plane, fly back to Texas and bury Bernie deep in the LaSalle County brush country. How simple, but he couldn't do it, not now anyway.

19

Across the Bay

Lawton was there in exactly fifteen minutes and Ted, Bill, Steele, and Ruth were standing at the gas dock when he arrived. Ted had asked Ruth to come along because as he was worried for her safety staying alone in the cottage. Steele had objected but Ted told Steele it was just for the ride and it was no different than having Lawton along. Steele acknowledged the point and dropped the objection.

Lawton gently laid the stern of the big sport fisherman against the dock and the four stepped into the teak cockpit. The custom yachts that Lawton crafted carried his name and this beautiful Lawton had just been launched the month before. He slipped the clutches of the two big 550 HP Cats ahead and the 53' Lawton boat idled out of Ball's Creek, and under the high-rise section of the new Tippers Bridge. Lawton shoved the throttles ahead and the big yacht shot up on plane as Ted led the others up the cockpit ladder to the bridge.

After about three minutes Lawton pulled the throttles back to dead slow. Steele, who had just taken a seat on one of the side bridge seats, jumped up.

"What's wrong, why are we stopping?"

Lawton pointed left. "See that marina and restaurant over there? Well, we pull a pretty big wake and if I didn't slow down I would put a bunch of those boats you see over there in the restaurant bar, and I like to eat there every now and then."

Steele was agitated. "Well slow down, but don't stop!"

Lawton shook his head. "You city people are an impatient bunch. It's like this: if I slow down and get off plane I pull a bigger wake than when on plane. So, you go to dead slow, let the stern rise and the wake drop out, then you can speed up."

Lawton pushed the throttles ahead a little and the big boat picked up several knots. He looked around and winked at Ted and Bill.

"This boat is for sale, Mr. Steele. Why don't you buy her and let me teach you all the tricks of the trade. Then you can quit your high-pressure

Washington job, move to the islands and start a charter business."

Steele sat back down. "From the size of your fee for this trip, I thought the boat purchase was included." Everyone laughed and the mood eased as the boat made its way down the Great Wicomico River towards the Chesapeake Bay. Lawton was busy with some electronics with which Ted and Bill were familiar, but Roy Steele seemed fascinated. He got up and walked over to Lawton in the captain's chair.

"What do all of these electronics do?"

"Well, boats today almost run themselves, at least boats like this one. I'm old fashioned, I like to run her myself, but after a while I turn it over to the electronics. This is the radar, this is a GPS receiver, over here is the autopilot, and I'm programming the chart plotter. All of this stuff is interfaced together; they talk to each other, I'm told, so the GPS tells the chart plotter where we are and the plotter puts our location on this electronic chart. See that little flashing light right there? That's us. And see, it's moving out of the river into the bay. Now I've put our course to Crisfield into the plotter; if I throw this switch on the autopilot, the plotter, using data from the GPS, will tell the autopilot where to steer the boat."

"I'll be damned," said Steele. "If the boat had eyes it could run itself."

Lawton said, "Well, you could say the radar is its eyes. See here, as you know we are the center of the sweep. This target is the Great Wicomico Light you see over there; here's the boat off our port. It's too congested in here but in clear open water I can set an alarm for any given distance and it will sound if any target enters that zone. Really, this is pretty basic stuff. If you've got the money you can set a boat up like a spacecraft. It's too sophisticated for me and it's getting more so every day."

Steele nodded and took a close look at all of the electronic gadgets. Lawton noticed his interest and showed him how he could play around with changing sweep distances on the radar.

The Chesapeake Bay is beautiful any time of year but fall is a special time. Today there was no wind and the bay was calm, or as the locals say, "flat cam." The big sport fisherman was a picture of elegance as she cut through the blue-green silky water at twenty-eight knots being pushed by her big Caterpillar diesels. The sun reflected off the water and sea gulls dived on schooling bait fish pushed to the surface by the feeding rockfish and bluefish below. Across the bay to the east a huge freighter was making her way up the main ship channel to the port of Baltimore.

Ted thought of Lawton's comment earlier about his day and the need to get on the water. He saw Lee was playing with the radar and looking ten years younger in just the last few minutes. He thought how he and Ruth always took the boat out when the pressure started to build. The sea has been a mistress, a lover, to man from the beginning of time, and Ted felt sorry for those who had never come under her spell.

Bill and Lawton were in deep conversation about Bill's plans for his new home here and work he wanted Lawton to do on *Swamp King II*. Ruth had gone below to rest in the forward stateroom. Ted walked over and tapped Steele on the arm.

"Let's go below and I'll show you around."

They went down the bridge ladder and into the main salon. The smell of finished wood and rich leather was heavy in the air-conditioned air. The richly finished woods were so polished that it appeared you could look into them. The plush carpet had a full-size sailfish embroidered in the center while the galley featured stainless steel appliances and granite counters.

Steele said, "I can't get over how quiet it is in here. There are two big diesels pushing us along at almost thirty knots, and it's so quiet in here I can almost hear the hiss of the air conditioning. How much does this rig cost anyway?"

"About two million, give or take a couple of hundred thousand."

"Man, it's really something."

"You think this is plush, wait until you see the master stateroom and master head. But before that I've got a question for you. When I gave you the letter from Billy Smart I thought you would want to bring it to the attention of some of your fed folks, but you are acting on it alone or with Bill and me, but no other officials. Why?"

Steele thought for a moment. "Ted, there are several reasons, but for now I'm only going to give you one. One of my jobs is the security of POTUS. Before I give this information to any other agency, I want to see what's involved and if it is a threat to POTUS."

Ted replied, "Is it possible that you don't trust the other agencies?"

"Ted, I said that was all I was going to tell you at this time."

20

Bernie's World

Bernie Jarvis had never been one to reflect on or question his actions, but as he drove his black Escalade across the Chesapeake Bay Bridge to Maryland's Eastern Shore that is exactly what he was doing. He had the uneasy feeling that things were starting to come apart. It's a feeling that he had never encountered and he was unnerved by the unwelcome experience. He felt like a dying man who was seeing his life pass in front of him. He thought of his father and the empire of companies he had built in aerospace manufacturing, weapon systems, electronics, and even heavy equipment. Bernie had grown up in the business and had been spoiled by the tremendous power at his disposal. He knew people respected, even feared, people with great power. His father, a gentleman and a gentle man of great intellect, had used this power wisely. Bernie, who grew up in the business, saw this power, embraced it, became spoiled by it and in the end was corrupted by it.

Bernie was an only child and the apple of his father's eye. His father's greatest desire was for Bernie to take control of his empire and run it as he had. It was also Bernie's desire to take control of the empire, but his approach to running it would be far different than that of his father. Bernie had his father's intelligence, if not his ethics, and knew he must conceal his real intentions, and in fact his real self, from his father if he was to inherit the business.

In the 1950s the United States came upon some startling technological discoveries. To unravel the discoveries the U.S. employed companies with advanced technological skills to study and experiment with these discoveries in utmost secrecy. WDR companies were major players in this endeavor. All personnel involved went through a most rigorous and involved security check. They were then indoctrinated about maintaining security with their work, and if they breached security they would suffer the most severe of consequences. The indoctrination sessions were carried out at the Army's Dugway Proving Grounds, a remote Utah location that in itself was frightening, and the perfect place to instill the fear necessary to keep people's mouths shut.

When Bernie became executive vice president of WDR he also went through the security process, only Bernie wasn't frightened, he was excited. He had no problem keeping secrets; he loved them, as it made him feel superior; but more than that it meant more power, and what he was finding out gave him unimaginable power. It was about this time that he developed the idea that he needed the means to conduct clandestine operations, and it was also about this time that he met Jake Barnett.

Ten years later Bernie's father passed away and Bernie assumed total control of WDR. He had developed close relationships with the highest-ranking military officers and politicians, and connections with every occupant of the White House. He became a leading industrialist in the U.S. and his wealth and power soared.

Some years later a member of the super-secret MJ-12 Group passed away. This group was the controlling authority handling the technological discoveries of the 1950s in which WDR and Bernie were deeply involved. Because of his background Bernie was asked to fill the position, along with Hammersmith, as directors of intelligence. The position involved maintaining security and secrecy, something that was a natural for Bernie Jarvis.

In this position and behind the back of the other MJ-12 Group members, Bernie used Jake and his people to maintain secrecy. They did this through intimidation and threats, physical attacks and murder.

Jake was never told the true nature of his boss's work, only that people needed to be taken care of because of various threats they presented. Jake hated this work, he had grown to hate Bernie, but what he didn't hate was the one million a year that Bernie paid him, so until now, he had kept his mouth shut and did as he was told.

Most of the MJ-12 Group members were, in varying degrees, patriots. Most felt that the matter they were charged to investigate and research should be done so in total secrecy to protect this country, her people, and civilization in general. The exception to this was Bernie and several other U.S. industrialists, who were all part of the MJ-12 Group.

Bernie was the driving force within this small group of five or six men that were part of the larger MJ-12 Group. They knew that if these very dark secrets that had been worked on now for over forty years were exposed, then much of their power and fortune would vanish.

Acting on his own while these men looked the other way, Bernie over the years authorized and committed acts that would put him on death row if exposed. Now, there was an MJ-12 defector, someone who wanted to go public and was exposing MJ-12 operations to the President, and Bernie thought Horton to be an idiot. Presidents didn't need to know, in fact should not know, about black operations. Presidents were temporary, they talked too much, and except for politics, were not very smart.

As Bernie took Route 50 south toward Easton he thought about the two CIA plants at the Great River Resort and how through a major error they had been exposed to the whole MJ-12 secret. They had been taken care of but not before one had come up with a plan to pass on some of what he knew.

Bernie's mind was racing trying to figure out the details. His informant had alerted him about the boat trip to Crisfield and before that about the letter and key from Smart to Ted Carter. But he didn't know what the key opened; he guessed it was to a safe deposit box, but that was merely a guess. He had to assume the boat trip involved the letter and key. That was a problem that had to be eliminated. Those people had to be eliminated.

Bernie was in damage control and he hated it. He was reacting, and damage control carried great risk. He was heading for the MJ-12 secret compound on the Eastern Shore near the Choptank River. It was a small but heavily guarded fortress where MJ-12 had gathered for meetings since the 1950s. Everything from its double run of chain link fence topped with razor wire to the sealed blockhouse spelled high security. It also had a main operations building along with a seven-thousand-foot runway and hangar.

Funding for MJ-12 operations was mostly at taxpayer expense, but like all black projects the amount, where it came from or where it went was never revealed. He would meet Jake there in thirty minutes, transfer him to the chopper and brief him on his target.

21

Tangier

Lawton pulled back on the throttles as he passed the outer Tangier Island channel marker. Tangier Island, Virginia is a picturesque little island that sits in the middle of the widest part of the bay just south of the Maryland/Virginia state line. The island is so small that there are no automobiles and all travel is by foot, bicycle or motor scooter. The island was settled by early Virginia colonists, and the inhabitants still speak with a distinctive old English accent. The residents of the island make their living primarily from the water.

Ruth had gotten up from her nap and was on the bridge.

"I love the trip through here, it's so quaint and charming. It must be wonderful to live here—except in a nor'easter, I suppose."

Lawton said, "Used to be that if you were born here you stayed here, generation after generation. Now I understand the kids have started to leave to find a life out in the big world. I guess life here has started to change; it's a hell of a shame."

The town was on the south side of the waterway, or the boat's starboard side, and the shoreline was lined with workboats of various sizes, shapes, and condition of repair, tied to the docks. The largest dock was used by an excursion boat from the mainland that made day trips to the island and docked so people could go ashore and have a seafood lunch at the local restaurant.

Lawton made a sharp turn to port and headed the big boat out the back channel and into Tangier Sound. He accelerated to plane after the last marker and set a course to the harbor at Crisfield.

A regional jet caught Roy Steele's eye as it appeared to be making a final approach to what he assumed would be the airport at Salisbury. Something seemed strange about the plane and its approach but he couldn't put a finger on it.

22

The Admiral

Barry Cummings answered his cell phone on the first ring.

"Is this Director Cummings?"

"Yes it is, Admiral. How are you?"

"Well, Barry, I'm fine right now but how long that will last, I really don't know."

"Billy Joe, the President tells me I'm to be at your disposal and to tuck you away somewhere so secure that even the Almighty himself can't find you, so you tell me where to pick you up and I'll have you secure before you can bat your eye."

There was a pause.

"Barry, you are one of the few people on this planet that I trust but I'm still nervous. I don't know how much you know but I'm not playing with fire, I'm playing with molten lava. OK, I'm at the Patuxent River Navel Air Station Navy Lodge—can you handle that, and when?

"Not only can I handle it, buddy, it's perfect. Give me thirty minutes to get clearance and get there; you check out and tell the desk you'll be leaving your car for a few days. When you hear the chopper move out, bring all your gear and hop aboard. I'm going to keep her spooled up. Any questions?"

Twenty-five minutes later the admiral and his two assistants were in the lodge lobby. They had their heads buried in the USA Today when they heard the sound of a chopper approaching low and hot. They grabbed their gear and sprinted through the automatic front entrance as the Sikorsky S-76C was settling onto the almost-vacant parking lot. The men reached the chopper as the door opened, all three jumped in, and the bird was back in the air, all in just over fifteen seconds.

The two friends shook hands as they flew out over the bay and headed south. Simpson introduced his assistants and wanted to know where they were headed. Even in the presence and care of an old friend he was anxious. Cummings put his hand on his friend's shoulder. "Billy Joe, everything is fine. We are heading to a little facility just a few miles down the bay. You remember the facility we had at the Greenbrier? Well, we built another at the Great River Resort, except it's more modern and more secure. We can slip you in there and no one will be the wiser, and we can bring the President in the same way."

The admiral seemed to relax a little as they flew down the bay past the mouth of the Great Wicomico River. They turned west over Indian Creek and then north just beyond Route 200 to approach the concealed helipad from the back of the resort and avoid coming in over the main lodge. As soon as the copter settled on the pad the men were out and into the receiving area elevator and down to the facility. Safely in the lobby area, Cummings introduced six agents who would be protecting the three men and looking after their needs.

"Billy Joe, the President said to give you the same protection that he receives, and you can bet I'll carry out those orders. He also said for you to let me know when you want to meet with him, be it today, tomorrow or next week, it's your call. My people have access to me at any hour of the day, but do you have any questions or comments before I head back to Washington?"

"Barry, thank you, and please thank the President. Let us settle in and gather our thoughts overnight and I'll talk to you in the morning. By the way, can we get anything to eat here?"

Cummings laughed. "This place has a galley set up to feed the President, his staff, and senior officials of the government and is presided over by an executive chef. I think it will be to your liking. Have a good evening and we'll talk tomorrow."

23

Air Assault

Lawton laid the boat against the pilings of the Crisfield city dock at the end of Main Street. The bank was a short walk up Main Street so Ted and Steele headed out as soon as the boat touched the dock. It was just before 2:00 PM when they walked into the bank and asked for the manager. They were taken to the office of Vernon Moore, a young man with a pleasant smile who in his best banker's manner asked how he could help them.

"Mr. Moore, I'm Roy Steele with the United States Secret Service, and this is Ted Carter, president and chief executive officer of The Great River Resort."

Steele handed the surprised banker his credentials.

"I'm going to have to ask you to do something strictly against bank rules and policy. We need to get into a customer's safe deposit box."

The banker was reading Steele's credentials and immediately started shaking his head.

"Mr. Steele, I can't do that, not even for the Secret Service. What's this all about anyway?"

Steele put his hands on Moore's desk and leaned forward in his chair.

"Mr. Moore, this is all I can tell you: the customer in question is deceased and before he died he gave permission to Mr. Carter, permission by letter, to the box and its contents. This letter was received by Mr. Carter after the person's death, along with the key. I will also tell you that this person was an employee of the resort."

"You have the key?"

"Yes, right here," said Ted.

"May I see the letter?" asked Moore.

"No, you may not, it contains confidential information," replied Stone.

Moore rubbed his head for a few seconds and turned to his computer and started typing information from Steele's credentials. After a few minutes he printed out his work and asked Steele to read it and sign the paper, which Steele did.

"It may not help me much if the shit hits the fan but at least I don't feel quite as vulnerable. OK, let's go."

They entered the vault and Ted handed the box key to Moore. The manager inserted the key along with the bank's master key into the proper keyways and opened the slot door. He removed the lock box and handed it to Steele. Once the men were in the vault, Moore used Ted's key and the bank's master key to open the slot door. He handed the lock box to Steele, who set it on a small table, cracked the box and peered inside. He looked up at both men and raised the top a little higher.

"Mr. Moore, there is no cash, bonds, securities, jewels, or anything else of apparent value. In fact, there is nothing in here." Ted reached for the side of the box and looked inside. Steele then opened the box all the way so both Moore and Ted could see inside. The three men stared at each other without saying a word.

Finally Steele said, "I can assure you, Mr. Moore, that you will never hear of this incident again in any way."

He nodded to Ted and they turned and walked out of the bank.

"Let's get back to the boat and the hell away from here."

Lawton saw them coming and saw Ted spin his finger in the air. He got the message and had the engines running and the lines off when they reached the boat.

"Lawton, let's get away from here."

Lawton had to hold his speed down in the no wake zone—the marine police would jump boats pulling too much wake in a flash. When they passed the marker into the harbor he hit the throttles and they were flying back to Tangier Island.

There was little conversation on the way back. What could you discuss about an empty safe deposit box? Bill had gone below and tried to contact Bonnie to see if she had reached the resort, and to take a quick nap. They made the slow crawl through Tangier and headed back across the bay. There is an area just west of Tangier called the "Target Ships." Two old WWII liberty ships were flooded and allowed to rest on the bottom for use as targets for military aircraft training. It was in this area that they noticed a private chopper showing interest in them. The chopper orbited several times, getting closer with each pass. Steele tried to call his boss to see if it was a service chopper but there was no cell service.

Lawton had the boat on autopilot and plotted for the mouth of the Great Wicomico River. He had decided it was five o'clock somewhere and he wanted a drink. Ruth thought that that was a wonderful idea and headed to the salon with Lawton and drink orders. Ted and Steele kept watch on the bridge.

The chopper had moved off but was now returning. It approached them head on and flew past their port side only about fifty feet off the water. They could see three men inside, since the doors were off. Passing the boat the bird pivoted around and came up on their stern. Ted was getting ready to wave when he saw flashes and the bridge was racked with bullets tearing into the fiberglass. Both Ted and Steele jumped behind the bridge control console as bullets tore across the top of the entire boat. The copter dropped its nose and pivoted back around. Both men grabbed the bridge ladder and slid down it into the cockpit. Ted pulled the salon door open and both men rolled inside. At the same time the port side windows started exploding, with glass blowing all over the salon. Lawton had gone below to get a rifle; Ted and Steele were still on the salon floor and Ted yelled for Ruth to get down, but before she could respond she took a hit that spun her around and up against the big side-by-side refrigerator. Ted saw her slide down the front of the refrigerator and crumple onto the galley floor. Bill came up the companionway steps into the salon and immediately took a round in his left shoulder. Steele had his Glock out and he crouched below the windowsill and started to fire through the broken side window at the bird that now tried to match the boat's speed. When he saw he was being fired on, the chopper pilot jerked the bird up and away from the boat.

Ted had gotten to Ruth to see how badly she was wounded. He could see blood oozing from a wound in her side so he grabbed a kitchen towel and pressed it to the wound. Lawton came up from below with a rifle fitted with a scope.

The chopper once again had met the boat head on and raked it with fire as it flew past. It dropped its nose and pivoted for another run at the stern. Ted grabbed the rifle from Lawton, who was trying to help Bill down the companionway stairs, and told him to hold the compress on Ruth's wound. He moved to the cockpit doorjamb, braced himself, and made a quick scope adjustment. Ted watched the copter through the scope as it approached the stern of the boat. He could see a man leaning out the left side with an automatic weapon; there was a man beside him who appeared to be holding him in some manner and the pilot was in front of both. Ted saw the man leaning out the side of the copter raise his weapon; as he did Ted squeezed off three quick rounds from Lawton's beautiful Weatherby.

Jake Barnett was ready to rake the boat once again with gunfire and he wanted to locate the position of the person that had fired on them. Omar was sitting beside him holding on to his belt. As he raised his AK-47 he saw a reflection inside the open door of the salon, only it wasn't a reflection, it was muzzle flashes from the Weatherby. In that instant the front bubble of the copter exploded—followed by Omar's head.

The pilot had several shreds of Plexiglas lodge in his upper body, one of which blinded him in his left eye. By some miracle he was able to keep the damaged copter out of the water and flying. Jake had been temporally blinded by blood and other matter from what had been Omar's head. He was finally able to regain his vision after wiping his eyes on his shirtsleeve. The impact of the bullets hitting the copter had caused Jake to drop his weapon into the water, and he was now trying to tell the pilot to head back to the base, a decision the pilot had already made.

Although the boat had tremendous cosmetic damage, she still continued to run on autopilot as before the attack. Ted and Steele attended Ruth's wounds; she had substantial blood loss and seemed to be in shock. Bill had come back to the salon and he now sat on a sofa holding a compress on his arm. The bullet had passed through a fleshy part of Bill's upper arm without hitting bone. Lawton was on the radio with a mayday call to the Coast Guard, and at the same time trying to keep an eye on where the boat was going.

Ruth was still able to talk and it was decided to try to get a med-flight copter to meet them at a little marina just inside Cockrell's Creek at the mouth of the Great Wicomico River.

It took Lawton precious minutes to get the Coast Guard to understand what had happened, but after some back and forth they got the picture. The Coast Guard started working on the med-flight and sending both air and sea assistance just in case the boat went south. The local private sea rescue group had also picked up the call and was sending a boat out of Reedville on Cockrell's Creek as an escort.

Ruth had seemed to stabilize, although she was still on the galley floor. Both men held a compress to her side to slow the bleeding. Ted had elevated her legs with a pillow and covered her with a blanket. Lawton stayed on the bridge to look after the boat and to see if the controls all worked. Blasting into the marina only to find he couldn't stop the boat would not be a good thing; also he needed to stay in constant voice contact with the Coast Guard.

Ruth was squeezing Bill's hand as he rubbed her forehead.

"You were pretty cool, big boy," she whispered, "and where did you learn to shoot like that? Been hiding something from me?"

Bill kissed her forehead.

"Let's just get you fixed up and then have a long talk about my secrets."

She smiled and closed her eyes.

24

Complications

Flying the copter now was like holding a dangerous snake just below his head. The wind felt as if it was turning his eyelids under themselves, and the blood and gore had made him wretch. Self-preservation had taken over and the horror behind him was fading, especially since Jake had released Omar's seatbelt and shoved him out of the chopper into Tangier Sound.

Bobby Lee had stayed behind on the Fokker to brief Bernie on what had been going on in Texas. It wasn't his idea—the thought of being alone with Jarvis sent chills down his spine—but Bernie asked him to do it, and Bernie asking was the same as an order. They were at a desk in the front corner of an open hangar when Bobby heard the sound.

"I hear a chopper." They both stood and walked just outside the hangar doors. The chopper was coming in hot, just above the trees and heading for the hangar. Reaching the hangar pad, the pilot tried to flair the bird but finally lost control. It hit hard on its right, rolled more to the right, with its rotor hitting the concrete pad and spinning it around. In the process the rotor also hit a small cart sitting on the pad, shearing off its tubular pull handle and slinging it into the open front of the chopper and impaling the pilot, through his chest, to his seat. Jake, on the other hand, was uninjured and quickly jumped from the thing almost before it came to rest. Bobby ran to Jake and helped him into the hangar while Bernie stood transfixed watching the events unfold, seemingly unable to move or speak. Bobby helped Jake to a chair at the desk.

"Jake, what the hell happened?"

"They had guns, something big, I never counted on that," he said, almost gasping. Bernie had become unfrozen and moved to the desk. He didn't speak but his mouth gaped open.

"We raked the boat pretty good a couple of times and were making another pass from behind when they shot out the windshield."

Bernie finally spoke. "That's impossible; bullets won't go through that stuff."

"Look, Bernie, go over and take a look for yourself. Not only did the bullets go through it, they blew off Omar's head."

"Oh shit," said Bobby, "I forgot about Omar. Where is he?"

"In the bay somewhere. I pushed him out."

"You did what, you stupid son of a bitch?" screamed Bernie.

Jake started giving serious thought to pulling out his Glock and then remembered in was also in the bay.

"His head was blown off and shit was shooting out of his body—would you sit next to that? I did it without thinking."

Bernie spun on his heels and walked into the hangar. He had to think and he had to think quickly. He could get his security people in here to clean up the chopper and get rid of the pilot's body, but he couldn't do much about the body the damn fool pushed into the bay. Things were coming apart faster than he could act. He was reacting and that caused problems and errors.

25

Fitting Pieces

Emergency personnel from the local rescue squad were on the dock to meet the boat. Ruth was stabilized, placed on a stretcher and into a med-flight chopper along with Ted and emergency personnel. The chopper lifted off for the seventy-mile flight to Richmond and the Medical College of Virginia hospital.

Bonnie was also waiting for the boat and rode with Bill, whose wound was less serious, in the rescue squad ambulance to Rappahannock General Hospital in Kilmarnock. Lawton and Steele took the boat and returned to the boatyard where June, along with their sons and daughter, and Barry Cummings and two of his people, met the boat, which now had become a floating crime scene.

Roy Steele knew it would be a long night of debriefing for him as well as Lawton. He was used to it but he was not sure how Lawton would take to it. Once the boat was secure Roy took his boss aside.

"Director, I know you and the guys want to debrief Lawton and me ASAP, but you've got to understand that Lawton is one tough, independent cookie. If you try to get pushy he's going to tell you to stuff it. My suggestion is to ask him if we can all get together in his office and go over the day's events while still fresh in our minds. From what I can tell he's a good guy, but not one to respond meekly if he thinks he's being pushed around."

"OK, Roy, I get the picture, but keep in mind the other boys are going to want to get a piece of this as soon as they get the word, and my guess is they have gotten the word and are on the way here now."

"You mean the FBI boys, I assume."

"I mean FBI, CIA, NSA, NRO, all of them."

"Boss, what the hell is going on here?" asked Steele.

"It's big, Roy. It's so big I don't really know much of the story. Hell, POTUS doesn't know much of the story, not yet anyway. OK, let's talk with Mr. Crockett."

26

Proposal

Ted was with Ruth in an emergency room cubical waiting on an orthopedic surgeon. The ER staff had been alerted to their arrival and had already done an evaluation of Ruth's wounds.

Although serious, they were found not to be life threatening. The wound in her side was just a flesh wound without damage to any internal organs, but she had also been hit in her left shoulder, which was a somewhat complicated wound. Ted was on his cell phone talking with Bill, who was being attended to at the hospital in Kilmarnock.

"Ted, I've put my copter at your disposal and have permission to use the hospital helipad. The pilot will be in touch to work out timing and details. How's Ruth?"

"She's sedated and the doc's say she is very lucky as the wound is not life threatening. A few more inches over and, well, you know."

Ruth was holding Ted's hand and squeezed it gently.

"How are you?" asked Ted.

"Oh, I'm fine, just a little sore. The good folks here in the emergency room at Rappahannock General did a great job; the doc said the bullet went through flesh without much damage. He just cleaned it and dressed it, so Bonnie and I will be leaving for the boat. She was so impressed with the hospital that she invited the whole hospital staff for dinner at the resort.

"The resort is under military security and is being shut down. I will need you back here for a couple of hours or so as soon as you are comfortable leaving Ruth. You can go back and forth between here and the hospital in the chopper as much as you want, but we'll have our hands full until the guests are cleared out."

"OK, Bill, let me see what the orthopedic surgeon has to say and when he wants to operate and I'll be on back. I can't believe all of this is happening, and today. My God, who would have thought when I got up this morning that someone would try to kill me by blowing up my boat, then try to kill me again in the afternoon, and then almost kill my soon-to-be wife."

The last statement started the tears flowing from Ruth, who was now really squeezing Ted's hand.

"Well, Ted, congratulations, old boy. I didn't know you had popped the question."

"I hadn't until just then."

"All I can say, Ted, is that's the strangest proposal I've ever heard."

"You know me, Bill. Well, let me go. I've got a lady here that wants to talk to me."

A nurse had seen Ruth sobbing and rushed in, and through sobs learned the story. She was now hugging Ruth as Ted closed his cell, and the surgeon walked in. It took a few minutes for him to get the picture that this was in fact a very happy scene.

"Ms. Bennett, I've looked over the charts and x-rays and I'll tell you that you are very lucky. I think you will only need some minor surgery, which I will schedule for 10:00 in the morning. I want you to get a good night's rest. We'll do the surgery in the morning, keep you tomorrow night, and if everything looks good, let you go home the following morning. Now let's have a look at the wound."

While the doctor was with Ruth, Ted got a call from the copter pilot and he told the pilot to pick him up in an hour. He wanted thirty minutes alone with Ruth before he returned. He knew he also had pressing business at the resort and he would need to be back at the hospital in the early morning. It was going to prove to be a busy night.

27

Commencement

Lawton and Steele had been debriefed in Lawton's office at the boatyard and Steele was now at the resort. He was meeting with his boss, Barry Cummings, in Bill Russell's office and going over the note from Billy Smart to Ted while they waited for Bill to arrive. It was 8:00 PM when Bill returned, dropped Bonnie off at the boat, and went to his office to meet Steele and Cummings. He opened the door to his office and found Cummings and Stone sitting on his sofa.

"Well, buddy," said Bill, "when we met in San Diego you said some people may be killed but I didn't think you meant me. What kind of terrorist would want to kill me?" Bill shook his head as he walked over to shake hands with both men. "I don't know whether to be pissed off, scared, amazed, bewildered, or all of the above. I hate to say this, Barry, but I'm starting to get the feeling you have been less than forthcoming with me. What's the real story?"

Cummings rubbed his forehead with the tips of his fingers and thought for a few seconds.

"Bill, you're correct, I have not been completely honest with you. There is a meeting scheduled here with world leaders, a very secret meeting, but it's not about world terrorism and it's not being threatened to be attacked by terrorists, at least not the kind of terrorists we are most familiar with."

Cummings got up and walked to the window behind Bill's desk and looked out onto the now-deserted, landscaped garden paths.

Bill said, "Please continue, Barry."

Cummings continued to stare out the window and then turned to Bill.

"I can't, Bill, that's as far as I can go. You don't have the need to know."

"Hell, Barry, what do you mean I don't have the need to know? Two of my key people have been murdered, you feds are taking over my resort, someone tried to execute my partner, then later they tried to kill him and me, now my resort is going to be shut down, which, I may add, will cost me about $400,000.00 a day in lost revenue. I don't know how you have the balls to tell me that I don't have a need to know. I say bullshit."

Cummings straightened up and gave Bill a cold stare.

"Go over to the couch and sit down."

Bill was worked up and had felt in command, but he noticed the coldness in the stare that Cummings now fixed on him. It was chilling and deflating, and he did as Cummings requested. Barry Cummings went to the front of Bill's desk and sat on the front edge, facing both men.

"Roy, you have been kept out of the loop on this, as have all department agents, but in light of the events of today and what I expect in the future I guess it's time for some in-depth background. Bill, I still don't know if you need this information but I'm going to override my better judgment and say that you do." Cummings rubbed his chin as he thought and continued.

"Just after the end of the second World War, the United States came into the possession of some very sensitive, or to put it another way, some earth-shattering technical information, something that made the A-bomb pale in comparison. To properly handle this new information and insure security, then-President Harry Truman signed a document authorizing a special group of twelve military personnel and scientists to oversee dissemination of these secrets and to maintain security."

Cummings hesitated, then said, "Now, what I've just told you is fact. From now on what I'm going to tell you are assumptions and bits and pieces of the puzzle I've picked up from various sources. Since the inception of the group, it has grown in size and now includes military personnel, scientists, and movers and shakers of major industry, primarily military contractors. The group has become so powerful that it is almost a shadow government. I believe the group now numbers thirty plus members that direct several thousand employees operating in total secrecy with a budget in the billions, and being funded by taxpayers as a black project."

He stopped for a moment and walked to small wet bar and poured a half glass of water. Returning to his perch on the front of the desk he continued.

"It appears that recently one or more of the group has become dissatisfied with the group or its actions and wants to go public through the President. The director of a government agency who is part of the group has dropped out of view and has contacted the President through an intermediary. This individual, Admiral Billy Joe Simpson, director of the National Security Agency, has given the President some very basic background on the group. He wants to meet with the President and give him the full story, if the President will agree to go public with the information."

Cummings took a sip of water, allowing Bill to jump in.

"Barry, are you saying that the President of the United States didn't know about this group until this group member contacted him? How the hell can that be when the group was set up by presidential order?"

Cummings shook his head. "I knew I was opening Pandora's box when I got into this, but yes, that's what I'm saying. After Eisenhower, it was decided that presidential knowledge should be limited for security reasons. Kennedy knew a fair amount about the group and what they were doing. It is believed that he wanted the secrecy of the program lifted, and this really upset the group. They couldn't allow that to happen."

Cummings stopped for a moment and looked hard at the two men and took another sip of water. A light bulb came on in the heads of the two men at the same time. Bill raised his hand.

"Hold on, Barry, you are not suggesting that Kennedy...uh...was uh—"

Cummings interrupted. "I'm not suggesting anything. I don't know, but one of my jobs is to protect POTUS, so I look at everything. I guess you are starting to get the picture of why the Secret Service is so involved in all of this."

Bill got up and went to the bar.

"I want a drink. I need a drink. Who'll join me?" Roy Steele looked at his boss and Cummings nodded his approval.

"It's well after working hours, and it's been a hell of a day. Why not, I'll have a scotch on the rocks."

"Just a beer is fine," said Steele.

Bill poured a stiff Jack Daniels for himself. "I don't really believe all that I'm hearing. Some nut group within my own government is trying to kill me over something that I don't even know about!"

"Bill, take it easy. I don't think anyone is trying to kill you, but they did try to kill Ted Carter because for some reason Billy Smart gave him classified information. Right now I can't make those pieces of the puzzle fit."

"What is this group involved in that's such a big secret?"

Cummings walked back to the window and looked outside for a few seconds. Then he turned to Bill and smiled.

"If I told you I'd have to kill you."

28

Lesson Learned

The MJ-12 compound had a well-trained security force. It had an equally well-trained accident recovery team that was used to recover and examine far more exotic remains than this simple copter mishap. The copter and the pilot's body were gone in thirty minutes, leaving no sign of the accident. Bernie did give some thought as to whether the pilot had a family, but didn't dwell on it.

The compound didn't exist to the outside world. Local authorities knew that there was a government facility in their jurisdiction, but they didn't know what it was except to speculate that it was some sort of CIA facility. Every employee that worked there had been through a lengthy security check, and before starting work signed a statement that if they divulged where they worked or anything that went on there, they would be prosecuted under espionage laws of the U.S. and imprisoned. Employees were shuttled in and out of Andrews AFB in an unmarked MD80. Entrance by car was only allowed to MJ-12 Group members, and most of them preferred to use aircraft, as they had private use of the plane during non-shuttle hours.

In Bernie's mind, the chopper pilot would just disappear. He would have his car removed tonight from the Andrews parking lot and dropped off at a mall parking lot in Waldorf, Maryland. Bernie was back in his environment. He was acting not reacting, and he was in control.

He still didn't have good intelligence; he didn't know the background on the meeting, or if there was to be a meeting, or what Carter may have found in the safe deposit box. He needed to put the squeeze on Brad, and he needed more info from his contact at the resort. He would call both as soon as he got Jake on his way back to Texas. Now Bernie was in the hangar putting on his war face, as he called it. He was going to dress down Jake just for good measure, make him feel like a piss ant, and smack him back in line.

Bernie stepped out of the hanger and saw Jake standing beneath the Fokker's wing. Jake had gotten a new Glock from the weapons locker on the plane and was loading the magazine. Bernie called to Jake, who slipped the magazine into the pistol and strode over to Bernie.

"Listen to me, Jake. You did a shitty job here today, and I don't expect that type of work from you in the future. Apparently I overestimated your intelligence, because the way you performed today indicates you're nothing but a God damned ignorant hill ape. Now, get your big dumb ass on that plane, go back to Texas and bring all of those Mexicans here. I'm going to bring cots in and house them here in the hangar. I want them at my disposal so I can act quickly if and when I have to. Do you understand all of this or is it too deep for you?"

Jake was looking into Bernie's eyes. A smile crossed his face and he said very quietly, "Bernie, let's go into the hangar. I've got a couple of questions and I don't like standing here in plain view under these apron lights."

Bernie turned and walked into the hangar just behind a sliding door panel. He said, "Is this alright, numb nuts?" as he turned to face Jake.

At that instant, Jake's left hand grabbed Bernie in by the throat and threw him against the hangar door, his head hitting the door so hard he almost blacked out. When his vision returned, the barrel of a Glock was shoved against his teeth.

"You little insignificant motherfucker, if you ever talk to me that way again I'll blow your God damned head off. I'll go get the Mexicans and bring them back here, but from now on you better watch your back, our time together is limited, so it's going to be you or me before this gig is over, I promise you that. Now do you understand me, you God damned ignorant hill ape?"

With that Jake threw Bernie sideways, and he skidded across the hangar floor on his left shoulder and crashed into the desk. To put a final emphasis on what he said, Jake fired one round into the side of the desk about two inches from Bernie's head.

Bobby had asked the pilots to start the plane while Bernie and Jake were talking so he didn't hear the shot. Jake bounded up the stairway and told Bobby to get in the air. Jake went straight to the bar and poured a drink as the wheels started moving. By the time the Fokker rotated off the runway Bobby knew the full story, and why Jake's hands were shaking.

29

Sleight of Hand

Ted arrived at the resort helipad just before 10:00 PM. He desperately wanted to get to his office in the hotel or to his cottage before anyone saw that he was there. He needed access to one of his computers before he talked to anyone.

When Roy Steele opened the safe deposit box at the bank in Crisfield, Ted had seen something that Steele and the bank manager had missed. The light in the vault cast a shadow inside the box, concealing a tiny object from the view of the other two. Ted had seen this object and casually laid his hand on the side of the box while expressing surprise at its being empty. He had looked Steele in the eye and palmed the small object using his little finger, a trick he learned some years ago from a Navy SEAL buddy. Actually he was only trying to conceal it from the bank manager and had planned to tell Steele about it on the way back across the bay. He was getting ready to show it to Steele when the gunfire started. Now, after reflecting on the day's events, he decided that he wanted to see what he had before he told anyone about it. The object he palmed was a flash card from a digital camera and he wanted to get to his computer and see what was on it.

He sneaked around corners and down corridors in an effort to get to his office. He passed Bill's office. The door was shut and he heard a muffled conversation going on inside. As he was easing past the office, the door opened and Bill stepped out and was surprised to see Ted.

"Uh, I was just about to knock. I just got here."

"Well, come on in. I was going to get some more ice. We're having a drink; would you like one? Ted stepped into Bill's office and shook hands with Steele and Cummings.

"What's the latest on Ruth?" asked Bill.

"Surgery on her shoulder tomorrow at 10:00 AM, and the doc says she should be able to leave the following day. I'll leave about 7:00 AM, stay with her until it's over and she's alert, and come back here."

Bill said, "That's great. Now look, our folks are doing a remarkable job of getting the social guests out of the resort. We are promising to bring each guest back and throw a big seafood bash for them, all at our expense, of course. From what we can tell, if they are not happy they at least understand. All is fine on that front so why don't you go on to your cottage and get some rest. It's been a hell of a day for all of us."

Ted sensed that Bill was trying to get rid of him, but he was too pumped about finding out what was on the flash card and too tired to care that he was being brushed off.

"Ted, I think that's a good idea," said Cummings. "You've had a hell of a day. Now I do need to talk with you, but get some rest and get these personal issues behind you and we can talk when you get back here tomorrow."

Ted nodded. "Thanks, I appreciate that and I think I'll pass on the drink. I would really like a nice hot shower, a sandwich, and some sleep. See you folks tomorrow."

He turned and left Bill's office for his cottage.

30

Rally the Troops

Bernie was bruised, his rib cage hurt, and he couldn't raise his left arm above his shoulder. No one had ever talked to him or touched him in that manner, and he was badly shaken. In his mind, he told himself that Jake was a dead man, but in reality he was frightened of the man. He realized he hadn't paid attention; he let his ego get out of control and pushed the wrong man too far. He didn't need this now; he needed Jake and he needed him on his side. How could he have made such a major fuck up?

Bernie decided that he would call Jake when he got to Texas and apologize. Tell him that he was under terrific pressure, and that he just lost his head. He would tell Jake that he didn't blame him for the way he reacted, and let him know that all was well and good and what happened was in the past and forgotten. Then, when all of this mess was resolved, he would kill Jake, before he did the same to him.

The administration building in the compound looked like a cross between an upscale farmhouse and a Southern antebellum mansion. It had three stories above grade with a large parlor, library, dining room, kitchen, and two bathrooms on the first floor. The second and third floors had living suites periodically used by group members. Beneath the first floor was 24,000 square feet of computer rooms, communications rooms, laboratory, staff offices, a medical suite, and a fifty-seat auditorium/classroom. Depending on the time of day and current situation, there was a minimum of thirty and up to a maximum of 100 staff on duty 24/7. The most sophisticated and secure communication equipment in the world tied the compound to the Defense Intelligence Agency, the National Security Agency, the National Reconnaissance Office and several military bases, the most prominent of which was Wright-Patterson AFB.

Bernie got into the electric cart he used to drive around the facility and returned to the administration building. The assistant director of security, an Army lieutenant colonel, saw his civilian boss arrive, noticed the cuts and abrasions, and asked if he was OK.

"Yeah, I'm fine, Colonel. I slipped coming down the stairs from the plane and took a good lick on the tarmac. I just need to get to my suite and clean up. I'll be fine.

"Sir, let me get one of the medics to look you over, you look pretty beat up."

"What the fuck do you mean, beat up, Colonel, I said I'm fine, I just need to get cleaned up, now drop it," he said as he walked away from the somewhat taken-aback officer.

After a shower and fresh clothes, Bernie contacted General Hammersmith, CIA Director Derrick Rutherford, the Defense intelligence director, and the National Reconnaissance director, and asked them to meet him here at 9:00 AM in the morning. Although he didn't trust any of the MJ-12 Group to share his point of view and operating philosophy totally, he felt he needed some guidance. The DIA and NRO directors had to do some shuffling of schedules, but they all agreed to the meeting.

After he set up the meeting, Bernie called Brad, his inside man at the White House, and his inside contact to the resort, and got into some heavy arm twisting. He needed solid intelligence and he needed it at once, and if it took threats to push these people, so be it.

He had one more urgent matter to attend to and that was a call to Jake in Texas. Once that was out of the way he would finally have the luxury of time, time to think and plan. He needed to identify and prioritize the intelligence requirements.

He realized some data would be impossible to get, such as the location of NSA Director Simpson and his two associates. Other information, such as what Simpson had told the President, if in fact the President was going to have a meeting with world leaders to discuss Simpson's information, where the meeting would be, and the timing of the meeting, he hoped would be easier to obtain. Finally and perhaps easiest to get would be what Smart had passed on to this Ted Carter person. He hoped his inside men at the resort would be able to get all of this information, but if not he would go there himself and choke it out of this dumb local yokel.

31

The Beginning

Ted had gone to his cottage, fixed a drink and started up his computer. He inserted the flash card and downloaded the pictures. The first picture was actually a photo of a memo addressed to Ted from Billy Smart.

Dear Mr. Carter:

First let me apologize for getting you mixed up in this situation. However, in my opinion this is the most important matter to ever face mankind. I have information that needs to be brought to the attention of the President with all due haste and then be made public knowledge. Having had precious little time to develop a plan I chose you to get this information into the proper hands because of your military background, your relationship with Mr. Russell and his access to the President through Director Cummings, and your proximity to me.

Now for some background:

I have worked for the CIA for eighteen years. I won't go into details because it's not necessary, but I was trained in hotel management for a CIA operation some years ago. When the Great River Resort was selected to also be a secret government installation, the CIA felt it was wise to place a couple of agents inside on a permanent basis. Mike Dunn and I were the logical choices. We applied for employment while the resort was still under construction and started working when the resort opened.

Several months ago my boss, Mr. Rutherford, hosted a meeting at the resort with some other intelligence agency heads as well as some industry leaders. The meeting was more recreation than an official meeting, as most brought their families. The meetings and activities were held in the regular resort, not the secret area, and although my boss knows about the secret facility I don't think the others did. During that time Mr. Bernie Jarvis was here for less than a day. While here he approached me and asked for my business card and one from Mike Dunn. He then told me that Mr. Rutherford had told him that Mike and I were undercover agents for the CIA. I of course denied this but he just smiled and ignored what I said. He then said if Mike and I wanted to go to work for his company at a substantial increase in salary to call him. He gave me a card with his private number and walked off.

Six weeks ago we (Mike and I) received orders to attend a meeting at Dugway Proving Grounds, Utah. The instructions indicated that it would cover extremely sensitive data but beyond that we were in the dark. In fact we now know that we were the wrong people—two other CIA agents from Langley were due to be transferred to an operation known as MJ-12 Group, a group of people, including Mr. Jarvis, directing an operation to disseminate the super-secret data you will find on the accompanying photographs.

From what we can determine, Mr. Jarvis put our names into a database of names at MJ-12 headquarters. Somehow our names got crossed up with the proper people and we were sent to Utah by mistake.

Something didn't seem right but we kept our mouths shut and went through the indoctrination. Keep in mind, we still thought the agency wanted us there, and everyone out there thought we should be there. The dam burst when Mr. Jarvis came out with Gen. Hammersmith to give a talk on maintaining security and spotted us. Without going into detail, I'll just say we were pulled out of there in a hurry.

An Army major actually got us off base and to Salt Lake City to catch a flight back east. During the drive to Salt Lake City he told us that that Bernie Jarvis was a very dangerous man. He was certain that Jarvis would attempt to eliminate both of us as soon as possible. The major said that there are a lot of good people in this MJ-12 operation that are fed up with the secrecy and want the story told, as the benefit to mankind would be enormous. He gave me the documents you see in the accompanying photographs and pleaded with me to do everything in my power to find some way to get them to the President. He cautioned me about trusting my own agency but he didn't elaborate. I thought of Mr. Russell's friendship with the Secret Service director as the perfect tool to get this information to the White House. Since Mr. Russell is in Florida and you are close to me, I'm working all of this through you.

You see, I believe the major, so I'm writing this memo to you on the plane because when I return to my cottage I'll get a few things together and try to get out of sight for a while. The same for Mike.

I have written a brief note to you that I'll put in the office safe along with a key to a safe deposit box. On my drive in from BWI Airport, I'm going to put the flash card in a bank safe deposit box somewhere and figure how to get that information to you. I'm afraid to put it in with the note as it may get into the wrong hands. Please find some way to get this data into the hands of the President. I'm sure Mr. Russell has the connections to make that happen.

I apologize for this rambling note, but I wanted to give you as much background as possible since I'm putting you in a less than desirable position.

God Bless You,

Billy Smart

Ted read through the note twice then went to the next picture. The picture was of a government document stamped "TOP SECRET/MAJ-12 - A REPORT FOR PRESIDENT ELECT EISENHOWER."

At that point there was a knock on the back door, so he clicked out of the file. He had laid his Glock on the desk beside his computer, but he picked it up and put it in a side drawer. He also had his little Colt Pocketlite in his hip pocket. He took it out, racked a round into the chamber and put it on safety, and went to the door. The back door was half glass and the porch light was on. Ted had closed the blinds over the door glass, but around the edge he could see Mango standing there with a blender pitcher in his hand.

"Damn," he thought, "what timing."

He opened the door to a grinning Mango.

"Man, you've had some day! Thought you might like to relax a little."

"Come on in, Mango. You are right, it has been a rough day and I was just getting ready to go to bed." Mango stepped into the kitchen and Ted closed the door behind him making sure it was locked.

"Well, how about a nightcap?"

"Thanks, but I have a drink. I was just checking my e-mails when you came."

Mango nodded. "Anything new on the letter from Billy or what the key was for?" he asked in his thick Cuban accent. Something didn't seem right to Ted. Mango didn't ask about Ruth.

"Nothing new, Mango. I just gave it to the authorities to let them do their job. I've got my hands full with this place and an injured close friend in the hospital."

Mango nodded again.

"There is talk of the President holding a meeting here but nobody has told me to do anything special. You know about it?"

Ted saw a red flag. This was all very wrong, as his old friend didn't seem like his old friend anymore.

Ted said, "The President of what?"

"The President of the U.S., man, that's what I heard."

"Mango, look, I'm really tired. Let's talk about this stuff tomorrow. I don't have a clue about any of that. Look, the place has closed down; we've had murders and attempted murders here—don't you think this would be the last place on earth the President would want to visit? Now I've got to go to bed."

"OK, man, I just wanted to make sure you OK."

As Mango was heading to the door there was another knock and a voice. "Ted, it's Roy."

With a sigh Ted let Mango out and Steele in.

"I'm trying to get some rest, if my good friends would leave me alone."

Roy held up his hands in a surrender signal.

"I just wanted to tell you that we feel you need some added protection. We have guards around the resort but I'm also putting three MPs outside your cottage."

"Roy, you'll have no objection from me. To be honest, I have gotten just more than a little stressed. By the way, I didn't like the flavor of the conversation I just had with Mango. He never asked about Ruth, only about Smart's note to me and if I knew anything about the President holding a meeting here."

Roy stared at Ted for a few seconds.

"Have you got his cottage phone number, and his cell number?"

"Yeah."

"Write 'em down," said Steele as he flipped open his phone.

After Steele left, Ted locked up, turned off the lights, and returned to his computer. It took about three pages to really start to comprehend what he was reading, but once he did it was as if the wind had been knocked out of him. Each page was a new revelation and his emotions went from wonder and amazement to anger at the deception imposed by so few on so many. It would take days for the impact of what he was reading to sink in, but even now he knew why it was so important for what he possessed to become public knowledge. There would be little sleep tonight.

32

Reflections and Regrets

Jake Barnett was back in Texas and in the process of getting plans together to get Felix and his twelve men back East when he was called to the phone. He listened for almost a minute before speaking.

"Bernie, you can talk all you want to, but I know and you know that you won't forget what happened. It's history and you can't change history. You stepped over the line with me, Bernie, you know that now, maybe you even regret it. I don't know, I don't care. I'll bring these people back and I'll do my job, but I'll be watching my back, you can count on that. You can expect our arrival around 10:00 AM in the morning."

Jake didn't want a reply nor did he wait for one. He simply hung up the phone and returned to setting up the flight back East. Jake was loading arms into the plane when Bobby walked up.

"Felix and his boys have bedded down in the dorm. Our cook made two large pans of enchiladas and those Mexicans devoured both pans. The only problem was they couldn't get the stuff hot enough. They put all the Texas Pete hot sauce we had on them and that still wasn't enough. Felix wanted some habañeros and the cook had a jar. They would eat a bite of enchilada and then take a bite of a habañero, then scream in pain and laugh. It was a damn show; I've never seen anything like it."

Jake just smiled as he kept on working.

"Are they secured, Bobby?"

"Yep, locked in tight and they are monitored by video."

"OK, I want wheels up at 6:00 AM in the morning; we'll have burritos for them on the plane."

"I already told Felix that they will be up by 4:30 AM and seated on the plane by 5:45 AM."

"That's good, Bobby. Tomorrow should be a very interesting day."

"Jake, do you have any idea what Bernie's plan is? What does he want these men to do? To kill, is that it? These guys have been trained to kill people but you still need a plan that fits the situation."

Jake stopped loading the plane.

"Bobby, I don't know what is on his mind, I really never do, but let me tell you this, if you haven't figured it out already—these people have been trained to think they have been trained, but the fact is a small group of rent-a-cops could take them out. Bernie brought in Omar from somewhere, I guess the Middle East, to round up some Mexicans and train them to be drug runners. Now Bernie wasn't going into the drug business, he wanted cheap, expendable killers; we all knew that—everybody, that is, except Felix. Omar told Felix that he worked for al-Qaeda and the plan was to damage the U.S. by flooding it with drugs using many trained cells of men, just like the ones Felix brought in. They put the fools into one of Bernie's planes, flew them around for a few hours, landed out here at the ranch, put them up in tents and told them they were in Afghanistan. Omar oversaw the training and was out here for two weeks with Felix and his mob. When our boys picked them up at the park, Omar had just given Felix a fifty percent payment for the men. He was to turn them over to Omar in Laredo the next morning and Felix was out of the picture.

I got all of this directly from Omar, not Bernie. He didn't elaborate; he was trying to pick my brain to see if I knew what Bernie was up to. You and I were not supposed to know any of that stuff; our only knowledge was pulling the scam on Felix. Of course, that is how Bernie has always operated: never tell any of us the full story."

"Jake, I sensed something like this, and I'll tell you what I think: I think Bernie wanted an expendable disruption for something. We both know he's mixed up in some high-level secret government crap and maybe it involves that work. Damn, do you think the government does that kind of stuff, the same stuff we do?"

"Bobby, I'll give you my take, and in general I think you are dead on. We know he owns and runs World Dynamic Resources out of Crystal City, but the compound in Maryland is strictly government and very secret. Now he has the run of the compound, as do a few other high-level government people that I've seen there from time to time. I think he is part of something similar to a board of directors for this secret government agency. My guess, it has to do with the development of military weapons, but that's just a guess. As you know, we are paid by WDR, and our job is supposed to be in the area of undercover operations, industrial spying and so forth, but in the past several years we seem to be more and more involved in Bernie's government interests.

"I believe it's like this: Bernie is operating behind the backs of the others involved in this government or military project. I can't put my finger on any one thing, but over the past few years I've seen a lot of little things that indicate that's the case. Bernie is a ruthless bastard and I wish I had never hooked up with him. I'm not saying I'm a saint, and I certainly let greed take over my better judgment, but I wish I could take back a lot that I've done. I'm going to pay for it in the end, so are you, my friend, but I just hope I have the chance to properly repay Bernie before my time comes."

"Jake, it's not a pretty picture, but we both went in with our eyes open. I just wish I knew what he had on his mind. It would certainly make life a little less stressful."

Jake laughed. "Are you sure about that? Look, Bobby, for what it's worth, I don't think he has a plan as yet. He just wants those men close at hand in case he needs them. Something big is going on that involves the compound. I don't think that was a WDR competitor he got us to shoot up. If it makes you feel any better, if things get too crazy we'll just shoot the bastard, fly back here and disappear. Now let's finish and try to get a few hours sleep."

33

Revelations

Barry Cummings had spent the night at the resort. He had a lot to look into concerning the security of POTUS since Horton was not going to cancel or put off the meeting. The world leaders scheduled to attend had heard about the problems at the resort and were sending advance teams to look into security also, as well as work out logistics and schedules.

The resort actually bustled with activity, just as if it hadn't been closed to the public. The advance teams for the various world leaders, crime investigators from the FBI, CIA agents, Secret Service agents, and other unnamed government operatives, all trying to upstage each other, had filled the resort.

Cummings and Steele met in the resort office conference room at 6:00 AM to put a report together on the events of the last two days that would be presented to POTUS later in the day. Ted had gotten about four hours of fitful sleep when he called Bill around 5:30 AM on his cell and asked if he would meet him in a half hour. Bill grumbled a little but told Ted to meet him on the *Swamp King II* at six. Ted arrived promptly at six carrying his laptop, and found Bill sipping coffee in the cockpit of his boat.

"You're on time. How about some coffee?"

"Bill, let me start my computer, then I'll get some. I want you to see this."

Ted went to the salon dining table and set up his computer. When it was booted up he brought up the pictures from the flash card.

"Bill, when we opened the safe deposit box, I saw a small object that the others didn't see—a camera flash card. I quickly palmed it before the bank manager saw it, and if you remember we got out of there fast, so I didn't tell Roy Lee what I'd done. I was about to tell him when the gunfire started so he still doesn't know. I want you to take a look and then we'll decide what to do. It's set up as a slide show so just click from page to page."

Bill sat down in front of the computer with his coffee, and Ted went to the galley to get a cup. When Ted returned with his coffee, Bill's hands

·

were trembling and he was visibly shaken. He looked up at Ted, then back at the computer screen, and continued to click through the pages without speaking. Ted walked to the large side window in the salon that overlooked the river and Tippers Bridge. The Secret Service folks were doing their job well and had the Coast Guard in inflatable boats patrolling the waters around the resort, and in particular the *Swamp King II*. Things had become so much clearer with these new revelations, but at the same time there were so many new questions. Ted's cell phone rang, and he heard a sleepy voice on the other end.

"Hi, big boy, did I wake you?"

"Hi, babe. No, I'm on Bill's boat going over some issues before I leave for the hospital. How do you feel?"

"Oh, fine. I just want this over with and to get back there. The doc was in again after you left last night and said he didn't think he would even need to put me under, just use a local. When will you be here?"

"I'll leave in about an hour; I should be there about eight or so."

"OK, hurry, I miss you—oops, here comes the nurse, got to run, see you shortly."

Ted hung up and returned to Bill, who now was in deep concentration with his chin resting on interlocked fingers. He looked up at Ted.

"The world just changed forever, bud, be that good, bad or whatever. Once this gets out, nothing will ever be the same."

"You know, Bill, that's exactly how I felt last night after going through all of that stuff, but after sleeping on it, I'm not so sure. We've grown up as a people; we've lived through wars, the threat of nuclear war and the H-bomb, and worldwide terrorism. We've put people on the moon and we fly in space. My guess, people will be surprised, but when all is said and done, things will go on as always. Now I think we should take this stuff to our Secret Service friends and let them deal with it."

Cummings and Steele were bent over a couple of legal pads on the end of the conference table when Bill and Ted walked into the conference room. Ted plugged in his computer power supply and booted it up while he explained the background on the flash card. The two SS agents pulled up chairs and looked at the first documents. As Cummings clicked through each page he appeared unmoved, but Steele on the other hand appeared shocked by what he was seeing, although he said nothing. After about ten minutes of reviewing the data, Cummings placed a call on his cell phone.

"This is Cummings, please put me through."

It was just a short wait until POTUS got on the line.

"Mr. President, I'm at the resort with Agent Steele, Bill Russell and Ted Carter. Mr. Carter has received the package we discussed from Billy Smart.

Both Mr. Russell and Mr. Carter have seen the contents, which appears to be somewhat more detailed than the data you received from Admiral Simpson."

He listened for a few minutes. "Yes sir, I can do that." Cummings placed his phone on the table. "Mr. President, it's on speaker phone now, sir."

"Gentlemen, this is President Horton. Can all of you hear me?"

Cummings answered for the group. "Yes sir, we can all hear you fine."

"Mr. Carter, I'm deeply sorry you have become involved in this mess, but you and Mr. Russell have seen some of the most classified information in existence anywhere on this planet. I'm not going to remind you of your security classification or anything of that sort, but I will ask you as patriots to please refrain from any discussion about what you have seen in those documents until such time as I have been able to sit down with both of you and brief you on the matter. It is my wish to meet with you within the next twenty-four hours, there in our facility at your resort. As you can understand, anytime the President moves, especially in secret, it takes some doing, so twenty-four hours is just a target. Director Cummings will keep you up to date on the schedule. Barry, can you meet me here at 3:00 this afternoon?"

"Yes sir," replied Cummings.

"Fine. Now Mr. Carter, Director Cummings tells me you have a lady friend, actually your bride-to-be, who was injured when you were attacked yesterday and is being operated on this morning. I know you want to be with her, so why don't you go on to Richmond and see her through the operation? When you get back, hopefully we'll have the meeting set up. One more thing: if there is anything I can do or my administration can do for either of you, you only have to ask. Both of you are making a big sacrifice for your country and I will personally see that you are taken care of. Thank you, gentlemen, and Barry, I'll see you at 3:00 PM."

There was quiet for a couple of minutes after the President got off the line, and then Ted spoke up.

"Bill, there is an issue with Lawton. His boat was really ripped up and it will require some substantial repairs. I wonder if there is any way the government can help with the repairs."

Cummings put his hand on Ted's shoulder.

"Gentlemen, consider it done."

34

Damage Control

It was 8:00 AM when the shuttle from Andrews touched down at the compound. Included with the staff workers on the flight were General Hammersmith, CIA Director Rutherford, DIA Director Roger Dowell, and NRO Director David Lamb. The men were driven to the administration building where they, joined by Bernie Jarvis, had breakfast.

After breakfast they moved to the library and Jarvis started the meeting with a recap.

"Gentlemen, as co-directors of security for MJ-12, General Hammersmith and I have done substantial research into problems concerning Admiral Simpson. This is where we stand on the matter as of this moment.

"One: It appears that the Admiral has broken ranks with us and decided the work of MJ-12 needs to be made public knowledge. Two: The admiral and two of his top assistants have gone underground. As of this moment we have not been able to determine where they are located, but believe they are probably in protective custody requested by President Horton. Three: It is our belief from sources within the White House that Simpson contacted Horton through Gill Chambers, and passed on some basic MJ-12 documents. He will meet with the President and divulge all he knows about MJ-12 operations, if the President will agree to go public with the information. Four: Although I have not been able to get any hard evidence, there is speculation that Horton has scheduled a secret meeting with a number of world leaders, and MJ-12 matters may be the subject of the meeting.

"That's what I think, but our source said the subject was world terrorism. Now, if such a meeting were to be held, one likely place would be the secret facility at the Great River Resort, just because of its close proximity to D.C. Again, that's speculation and I've been unable to get any solid data one way or another, so all of this is just for your consideration.

"Five: Two of Derrick's boys that worked undercover at the Great River Resort were accidentally sent to one of our indoctrination seminars at Dugway. They were there for almost the entire seminar before the mistake was discovered. Now how the hell the CIA could fuck up that badly is beyond me, but it's an academic point as both of the men have apparently been eliminated by Derrick's people."

Rutherford jumped to his feet.

"Goddamn you, Jarvis, you know we didn't have anything to do with killing those two men. From what my people at the resort are telling me, it looks like an internal matter that involved sex. As far as CIA sending the wrong people, our own investigation shows the fuck-up came from here and is pointing right at you, old boy."

Bernie was doing a slow burn, but he knew he had to retain composure, at least for now. Rutherford was an idiot who could be dealt with later, but for now he needed his help and the help of everyone else in the room, or at least their support.

"Derrick, I apologize for those statements. I was out of line. This problem has us all on edge and I've lost a lot of sleep since it came up."

Roger Dowell spoke up. "Bernie, I'm not going to mince words. I've got some concern with you. I believe most every member of the MJ-12 Group has the best interest of our country in mind—indeed, the best interest of all the citizens of this planet in mind. We feel that if we divulge what we know to the general population it could have an adverse effect on the psyche of the population. We also believe that the technology we now possess could, if placed in the wrong hands, create a worldwide threat. That's the way most of us feel, but I don't believe that you, or possibly several other members that you are close to, share those feelings. My take is that you are only concerned about your empire, about lost revenue from your energy operations and holdings. To put it bluntly, Bernie, I don't think you give a shit about mankind, and your interest is totally self-centered. You may not know this, Bernie, but as a young man I worked for your dad, and he was a good man, a great man. Bernie, I don't think you are cut from the same cloth and to be honest, my friend, I think your appointment to this group was a mistake. Would you care to address what I have just said?"

Bernie Jarvis sat back in his chair with a smirk on his lips.

"Director Dowell, I'm sorry you feel that way. I guess my methods and the manner in which I conduct my business gives the impression that my interests are purely self-centered, but I'll assure you that is not the case. However, I am not going to spend a lot of time trying to convince you or anyone else otherwise; you can believe whatever you want. I have a job to do and I'm asking for input, so let us move on to that and away from these personal attacks."

Bernie looked at each of the others and continued. "The sixth and final point in this recap of events: My inside source at the resort tells me that one of the men sent in error to Dugway sent a letter to a top executive at the resort indicating that he was going to pass on some important information to this executive. Whatever that information is, it was not stated in the letter, but you would assume that it had to do with his unfortunate visit to Dugway. I do not know if this information was passed on before the man was killed, but I am proceeding as if it was."

David Lamb spoke up. "Bernie, the news is reporting that a pleasure craft from the Great River Resort was shot up yesterday out in the bay. What do you know about that incident?"

"I have no idea what you are talking about, Dave. I've been consumed with the matter at hand for several days and have not looked at the news on TV, or looked at a newspaper, for that matter. I don't know why you are asking me about this incident. I don't see the relevance."

"Bernie, the relevance is that the resort owner and the resort CEO were both on that boat. You are telling us that a top executive at the resort probably has MJ-12 information, then two top resort executives get shot up and you don't see the relevance?"

"I told you I haven't seen or read the news, but I'll look into it and see if there is a connection."

This meeting was not going at all the way Bernie had anticipated. He was back in damage control and losing control. The meeting was a mistake and he needed to find a quick way to end it. To hell with these people. He would handle matters and keep them on the outside.

Then it hit him—how could he have been so stupid? His plane from Texas was due to arrive here in less than thirty minutes, and if these people saw the Mexicans when they arrived, it would not be good. They had all seen his plane here from time to time, some had even flown in on it, but they had never seen it unload a dozen Mexicans who would take up residence in the hangar.

Roger Dowell stood. "Bernie, when I get back to my office, I'm going to call President Horton and ask him to meet with General Hammersmith and myself. We'll lay out our reasons for secrecy and hope he sees it our way. I don't know what else we can do; the cat is out of the bag. It's inevitable that the situation will become public knowledge at some point in the future; perhaps the time is right. Maybe we should consider this an opportunity to still control the information, just admit the basics, and keep a lid on the hard core stuff."

Bernie's mind was racing now.

"OK, Roger, if you think it will do some good, fine. I just remembered I've got to make an important call that I almost overlooked. Please excuse me for a couple of minutes." Bernie left the library, went into the parlor, and placed a cell call to Jake.

"Jake, there is a change of plans. Divert to Richmond International Airport, rent a couple of vans, and put the men up in a motel close to the airport. Call me when you get settled and I'll tell you what to do."

When Bernie returned to the library, the others were getting ready to leave.

Dowell spoke up. "Bernie, the general and I will try to see the President as quickly as possible, and will of course keep you informed. For now I think it's best for you to return to your business matters and put MJ-12 activities on the back burner."

With that the group left the building for a return flight to Andrews AFB.

35

Wedding Plans

Ted had spent a little over an hour with Ruth before she was taken to the O.R. He went outside and called Bill for any updates, then went to the gift shop and bought a magazine. He hadn't been in the waiting room but fifteen minutes when the surgeon came in to tell him the surgery was complete and everything went as planned. He said that he expected Ruth would be able to leave in the morning. After a brief discussion of the surgery, he told Ted that he could wait in her room, as she should be out of recovery in about a half hour.

He was in the room reading his magazine when Ruth was rolled in from the recovery room, groggy but alert.

"Hi there, big boy, been waiting long?"

"Nope, not too long. The doc says you are a good patient."

"Really? Well it's hard to be a bad patient when you're in la-la land. What are you reading?"

"A travel magazine. Would you like to see it?"

"Not now. Are you planning a trip?"

"Actually, babe, I'm planning a honeymoon."

"Oh, that's right, you did propose didn't you? Well, did I accept?"

"As a matter of fact, you didn't."

"Hmm..., well, why are you planning a honeymoon if I didn't accept?"

"You know me, once I make up my mind to do something I'm going to do it, and I hope this doesn't come as a shock, but you are not the only fish in the sea!"

Ruth looked at the nurse who had been helping her into the bed.

"Nurse Miller, what do you think about all of this?"

"Ms. Bennett, I think you better accept his proposal with all due haste."

"You do, even after he called me Charlie the Tuna? I don't know—tell me this, big boy, where are you thinking about going on this honeymoon?"

"Well, I'm torn between Paris and Rome, so I think I'll do both."

"Well now, I do sort of like the sound of that. What do you think, Nurse

Miller?"

"What I think, Ms. Bennett, is if you don't accept real quick I'm going to throw my hat into the ring. Now I better get out of here before I get into trouble. Just ring, hon, if you need anything."

When the nurse left, Ted walked to the bedside and kissed Ruth on the forehead. She took his hand and squeezed it and they just looked at each other for a few minutes. Ruth finally spoke.

"What's going on back at the ranch?"

Ted had been waiting for this question but still didn't have a good answer.

"Well...uh, I talked to the President this morning."

"The president of what?" asked Ruth.

"I talked to the President of the United States."

Ruth let go of Ted's hand and reached for the bed control box and raised the head of her bed into a more upright position.

"So you talked to the President of the United States this morning; and what was this little chat all about? My health, I assume?"

Ted smiled. "Why, yes, as a matter of fact, that did come up."

Ruth glared at Ted for several seconds. "Are you going to tell me what's going on before I get angry?"

"Ruth, here is what I can tell you now. There was—uh—something in the safe deposit box, a photo flash card, and no one saw it but me and I was able to get it out of the box unnoticed. Later, on the boat, just as I was about to tell Roy Lee about it, the shooting started. When I finally got home last night I put it in my computer and opened it up. What I saw was shocking, not bad, but shocking. Early this morning I showed it to Bill, Roy Lee, and Director Cummings. Cummings immediately called the President, and the President asked all of us not to discuss the contents until he could arrange a meeting with us, and that meeting should be within twenty-four hours. That's all I can say, babe. I'll tell you all about it as soon as I can."

Ruth looked out the hospital room window and Ted could tell she was in deep thought, troubled thought.

"Ted, you say it's not bad but we seem to be in great danger. I don't understand."

"The danger, babe, is that some people don't want this information to get out. I'm not sure why, but that's the danger."

"I guess you'll have to get back to the resort soon. Ted, please be careful, I love you, and I want to go to Paris and Rome, damn it."

36

Wasted Plans

Bernie Jarvis was on his way back to his Northern Virginia office and was still angry that he had made the mistake of calling the morning's meeting at the compound. He had control of twenty-one of the nation's most advanced defense contractors and energy producers. In addition, he had assets in place in sensitive areas around the world. He had inside sources at the White House and the resort, and he had moles all around D.C. and in all of the intelligence agencies. He didn't need these people, except he still didn't have enough intelligence to develop a plan.

He was on the Bay Bridge when his cell rang. He answered and a voice said, "Secure callback."

He hung up and enabled the secure feature. When the call came back it took about forty seconds for the secure feature to go into effect.

"Simpson and the other two are here at the resort."

"Are you sure?" asked Jarvis.

"Bernie, this place is crawling with feds. We put some bugs in the public johns and picked a couple of agents talking about 'the admiral' that they had stashed away."

"Damn. Can you get to them?"

"Hell no. I don't think a company of Marines could get to them."

"OK, just keep this to yourself; I'll get back to you."

In the National Security Agency at Ft. Meade, Maryland, a transcript of the brief cell call to Bernie Jarvis to set up the secure call was made and recorded. The information would eventually end up in the hands of the acting director.

As he rode back to his Crystal City headquarters, it had become clear to Bernie that he really only had one course of action. Horton and Simpson had to be eliminated, and this had to occur before the meeting with the world leaders took place. If not, if this new technology that up until now had been so highly classified became public knowledge, it would make the petroleum and to some extent even the petrochemical industries obsolete. Jarvis's investments in these industries were worth several billion dollars;

he could not allow that information to become public knowledge. A plan was forming, a plan so simple that he actually smiled as the pieces started to fit together. Everything was a perfect fit, if President Horton met Director Simpson at CECPC, and that seemed the only logical thing Horton could do.

Jarvis placed another secure call to Jake Barnett. Jake answered on the second ring.

"Plans have changed. Get those men on the plane and back to the ranch. I'll call you tonight."

He was in a hurry now to get back to his office and his secure landline phone. He needed to get in touch with his controls company in Pensacola. They designed and installed the HVAC system in the Great River Resort and he wanted the plans. He also had to find out for sure if and when Horton was going to the resort to meet Simpson. That information was critical and he would make an all-out press to get it. Finally, he had to fly to Honolulu to see a director of one of his little known projects.

37

Travel Plans

POTUS was sitting behind his desk tapping the end of a ballpoint pen on a leather binder.

"OK, Barry, what's the plan?"

"Mr. President, we'll slip you out of here tonight at 8:00 in an unmarked service Suburban. Two others will join up for added security and we'll get you to Andrews. Marine One will take you to the resort for your meeting and fly you back."

"Just that simple? You sure no one will pick up on it?"

"Mr. President, trust me, we're really good at this stuff."

POTUS smiled and looked over at Gill Chambers, who was also smiling.

"What say you, Gill, think it's a plan?"

"Yes sir, Mr. President, I think it's a plan, but are you sure you want Carter and Russell included?"

"I absolutely want them included. They are in the middle of all of this and in some danger, wouldn't you say, being shot at and all. They have been brought into the loop by circumstances beyond our or their control. They've seen some of the classified data and I think they deserve to know the real story. To put it another way, they are cleared and they have a need to know."

Things started to happen faster and faster. Director Chambers was getting intelligence data on this matter from all of the agencies, really only bits and pieces, but a picture had started to develop—still a bit cloudy, but a picture nonetheless, that got clearer with each new revelation. POTUS was going to see Admiral Simpson tonight and Director Dowell at the DIA, and General Hammersmith had called his office and requested a meeting with the President.

Unfortunately, everyone on the list of MJ-12 Group members was looked on in an adversarial light. This group had lied to this and other Presidents over important national defense issues. President Horton was not happy and was inclined to fire or relieve all the members and possibly sign an executive order eliminating MJ-12. He would wait until all the facts were in, if that was possible, but they had a lot to explain.

"Gill, when I arrive I don't want anyone but your necessary people, the Admiral and his people, and Russell and Carter in the CECPC. No service and support personnel, no CIA people, no one except those mentioned."

POTUS turned in his chair and looked out onto the South Lawn. He was quiet for a couple of minutes and Chambers and Cummings looked at each other as if trying to think of something to say next. The President turned back around.

"As my old pappy used to say, we have some people who are wearing two hats, if you get my drift. People who work for us but who don't necessarily play on our team. To be honest, I don't trust anyone with the exception of you two. I certainly don't trust this MJ-12 bunch, and when I see that most of our intelligence directors are part of MJ-12, and operating behind my back and the backs of other Presidents, well, I don't like it one damn bit. Then when I hear talk of a shadow government I get real upset."

POTUS thought for a moment. "I want you both to understand that we are going to get to the bottom of all these matters. We are going to start tonight, and tomorrow I am going to meet with our friends Dowell and Hammersmith—and when they leave this office they'll know they met with me."

38

CECPC Disclosure

Ted spent the afternoon with Ruth discussing wedding plans and the situation at Great River. They were both concerned about the long-term effect that the two brutal murders, and the attempted murders, would have on the resort. Since the events at the resort were in the news, Ruth and Ted were sort of mini-celebrities. When the news of their engagement spread, nurses and doctors started stopping in to offer congratulations.

Bill had called Ted in the early afternoon about the 8:30 PM meeting and asked Ted to meet him at the resort for dinner before meeting with the President. Ted stayed with Ruth through her dinner at the hospital, and left for the resort at 6:30.

Marine One sat down on the resort helipad at 8:30. The President was whisked into the reception area, to the elevator, and down to the CECPC reception area. Ted and Bill, along with Barry Cummings and Roy Steele, met the President and Gill Chambers in the reception area. Introductions were handled by Cummings, and the President thanked everyone for being there on such short notice. He also asked Ted about Ruth's present condition. It was a small gesture that left a very positive impression with Ted.

"OK," said the President, "let's move on to meet Admiral Simpson. Barry, please lead the way."

The group followed Cummings through a pair of guarded and locked doors, down a well-lit hall and to a door that opened into a conference room. Seated at the far end of the conference table were Admiral Simpson and his two assistants. Behind them stood Secret Service agents Jackson "Jack" Hardin and Angela Hughes.

Both the Admiral and his assistants seemed nervous and somewhat put-out at the sight of both Ted and Bill. The President handled the introductions and gave a brief summary of Ted and Bill's background and why they were there. This seemed to relax the Admiral and his people. The President asked the two agents to step outside of the conference room and the meeting began.

"Gentlemen," said the President, "everyone here has a top secret clearance. Everyone here by my order has a need to know all that will be discussed in this room tonight. Please be advised that all matters discussed in this room will stay in this room until I authorize the declassification and release of part or all of the matters to be discussed. Any questions? Good, then let's begin."

The President opened a folder and took out some documents, and handed them to the Admiral.

"Admiral, these are the documents given to Mr. Carter by the CIA agent who worked undercover in the front office here at the resort. This is the same agent sent to Dugway by mistake. Would you look these over and tell us if they are authentic?"

The admiral, along with his two assistants, read the cover letter, and then started reading the documents and looking at the pictures. Smiles crossed their faces as they flipped from page to page.

"Yes sir, no question they are authentic; the three of us have seen all of them before. It must have been one hell of a screw-up for this stuff to get out."

"Yes, Admiral, it was. Now you want my assurance that I'll make this stuff public before you tell me more—well here is what I'll do. I'll go public with the basic information you sent to me through Director Chambers. I can't go beyond that as I see some potential national security issues involved."

"Mr. President, that is all we want. I agree that the public shouldn't have, perhaps couldn't handle, the full story. The full story will come out as it should over months and years through the press. I think all the public can really handle now is the basics."

"OK, then, Admiral, how about giving us the full story?"

"Mr. President, the full story is an ocean cruise and would take far more time than I'm sure you have tonight. How about a paddle around the lake and we'll work out the cruise later?"

The President got up from his seat at the end of the table and went to a wet bar and poured a glass of water. He then offered to serve the others, creating a ripple of surprise.

"I was not anointed, gentlemen. I'm just a normal fellow temporarily holding the office of President. Admiral, you have the floor."

Admiral Simpson stood and clasped his hands in front of him.

"I'm sure you have all heard the rumors of a flying disc that was supposed to have crashed near Roswell, New Mexico in 1947. Well, it happened—actually, two crafts crashed in a twenty-four-hour period.

The Army recovered the craft and extraterrestrial beings, both living and dead. The craft and beings were shipped to Wright Patterson Field, and held there for study. Because of this and other previous events involving what was believed to be extraterrestrial craft, President Truman, after he conferred with General George Marshall, authorized a highly secret group called Majestic 12 to investigate these incidents."

The President held up his hand.

"Admiral, I'm sorry to interrupt—yes, I've heard these rumors many times, but I've always discounted them for one very simple reason. It's hard to believe that some very advanced civilization is so advanced that they have ability to fly across the vastness of space and visit us, but yet, when they get here they start wrecking their craft like some sci-fi demolition derby. Not to mention that these very advanced folks just leave their wounded and dead lying around for us to pick up and examine. That's a picture that's never made any sense to me, Admiral."

"Mr. President, this is the most complex issue in the history of mankind. Most questions will be answered in time, but let me address your question, as I was about to get to it anyway. The craft were probes, like an advanced version of the probes we sent to Mars, and came from motherships several thousand miles in space. The beings were androids, manufactured beings, which actually were part of the craft. It took us about two years to figure that out. They were from a civilization that just wanted a look around, just curious, just like we are with our probes. However, in the overall scheme of things, they were not really important, except they got us involved in the study and research into extraterrestrial visitors. Our real interest was in the second civilization of visitors we discovered, visitors who had been around since life began on this planet, and we found to our amazement, these visitors were our ancestors."

This statement hit every person in the room like a blow in the gut, and Admiral Billy Joe Simpson was having a hard time keeping a smile from his lips. He let that message rest for a few seconds.

"Uh...ancestors, Admiral?"

"Yes sir, our ancestors. Life was placed on this planet by a civilization not too many light years away. They placed their own people here and since that time have watched over us and protected us. They are wonderful spiritual beings, who care deeply for us. Although they have not interfered with our development, they have watched us closely."

Again, the Admiral stopped for a few seconds to let this all sink in. He well knew how difficult the information was to comprehend, and what a mental shock it could be to the uninformed. The President spoke again.

"Uh...Admiral...uh.... By the way, if I sound speechless, I am. Admiral, you said, "Protect us." Protect us from what? Are there others out there who perhaps wish us harm?"

"Mr. President, let's say there are other civilizations out there, especially the newer ones, like ours, for instance, that may be more aggressive towards us if allowed to be so."

"How many are out there, Admiral?"

"We don't have any idea. There are many; we only know of fifty-seven to date."

Again, total silence as each person tried to digest each new revelation. Admiral Simpson had been in this position before, explaining the discovery to the newly informed and seeing the look of total bewilderment on the face of each person. There were so many questions but no one knew what to ask.

"Gentlemen, let me address one important issue before we move on: that is the fear factor—there is nothing here to fear. What I'm telling you has existed from the beginning of mankind on this planet. Please understand that if these beings wished us harm that would have happened long ago."

Gill Chambers raised his hand to ask a question.

"Do we communicate with these beings?"

"Yes. Our primary involvement at the NSA is communication with our friends—that's how we refer to them—and that's really the job of James and Michael here. We started communication in the late '60s after an initial meeting not unlike the one portrayed in *Close Encounters of the Third Kind.*"

"I'm almost afraid to ask what they look like," said the President.

"They look like us, slightly oriental, but human, because in essence they are human."

The questions started to flow and went on for over an hour. It became apparent that each question only raised ten more and to cover the subject in detail would take months. Admiral Simpson had to halt the Q and A session to bring the issue of MJ-12 and disclosure to the table. This was the issue at hand and it had to be discussed tonight. The Admiral stood and moved around the conference table as he spoke.

"Gentlemen, we must now put our questions aside for a later time and discuss MJ-12 and the public disclosure of this information. The MJ-12 Group is nothing like the original panel authorized by President Truman. It has grown to thirty-two members and is made up primarily of leaders of the military industrial complex. This resulted from early attempts by the U.S. government to have industry and scientific institutions study and back-engineer biological and mechanical components of the vehicles and biological entities in our possession. The people who were allowed into this secret loop of knowledge became very powerful. They were able to operate in total secrecy with almost unlimited funding. Secrecy has become so obsessive that I fear some on the inside believe that nothing should be ruled out to maintain security."

The Admiral paused to let this thought sink in before continuing. "The scientific information gathered from our study of the recovered craft has been enormous. Fiber optics, computer chips and so many other things were a direct result of back-engineering alien technology. However, what worries MJ-12 as a whole is not what is now in use, but what has been developed that is not in use. The extraterrestrial vehicles used a power source that requires no fuel, no energy whatsoever. It is my understanding that we now understand and in fact have this technology. It is feared by some that this technology would, if it becomes public knowledge, cause the collapse of the world economy. Also, the technology has been applied to develop new advanced weapon systems; this brings up legitimate national security issues.

"Now, many also fear that disclosure would cause the collapse of our religious institutions. Let me say here that these beings, our friends, are very spiritual in nature and worship a divine being. This unfortunately is not an area where I have great knowledge or strength, but it is my understanding from some of the other MJ-12 members that modern religion had its origins in the spirituality of our ancient extraterrestrial ancestors. Think about the arguments over creationism, the story of Adam and Eve."

Opening his hands for effect, the Admiral paused and waited for questions. There were none so he continued.

"There are at least 100 billion stars in our galaxy alone. We assume that most have a solar system with planets revolving around a sun just like our own. Our galaxy teems with life in all stages of development—this we have been told by our friends. When a civilization reaches a point in its development where it has the ability to leave its own terrestrial world and explore space, it has reached a point where it must lose its innocence, accept the knowledge that life exists throughout the universe, and become a member of civilizations of the universe. That is a very simplified version of what our friends have told us. The majority of MJ-12 Group members want to continue operating in a cloak of secrecy, as many in the group fear a strong adverse reaction by the population; a few others have a darker, more selfish agenda."

The Admiral stopped, took a drink of water and continued.

"As I mentioned earlier, this is a powerful group of powerful people who have the resources to stamp out any threat to the secrecy of their operation. It is only a very limited few that give me cause for great concern, but I'm convinced that those limited few will stop at nothing to preserve the continued secrecy of MJ-12. The three of us have had far greater contact with our extraterrestrial friends than any of the others, past or present. They have made the case to us that now is the time, in fact it's past time, for the people of this planet to lose their innocence and become members of the intergalactic community. Gentlemen, I know this may appear to be pure science fiction, but it is fact. The three of us feel strongly that the facts need to at least start to be made known. To do this, we decided that we needed to go straight to you, Mr. President, and because of the situation I've just outlined, we felt it necessary for our own well-being to take the steps we have taken, that is, to go underground. In the past there have been others who voiced the intention of going public with their knowledge, and some of those folks died. I have no proof that their deaths were related to their MJ-12 work but I strongly suspect that is the case."

The Admiral stopped and looked around the room.

"Now, that is an very abbreviated version of the situation as it now stands. The matter is complex, and we really have not even scratched the surface, but at least you have a flavor of this intriguing story."

The Admiral once again looked around the room and took a seat. For whatever reason, Ted stood, looked at the Admiral and his associates, and applauded. The president stood, too, adding his applause to Ted's. The others followed suit, one by one, demonstrating their appreciation for the words of the Admiral and the noble work he and his associates had been involved in. When the applause stopped, everyone sat down, except the President.

"Admiral, you've made a compelling case. Now I've agreed to go public with some basic information. Do you have any suggestions on how to do that?"

"Mr. President, you have asked world leaders here to discuss the information you now have. I would continue with those plans, but I would make it clear that you are advising them of what you are going to do, and asking them for their input on how to do it, not whether to do it. Before that happens I would call in religious leaders from around the world and explain the basics, and that this is in no way a threat to the spiritual health of the world. I offer you my assistance in this task."

There was a slight pause before the Admiral continued. "Finally, when you go public, I suggest you invite the world leaders to join you, as well as the religious leaders. Of course you will have had, at some point, to brief your cabinet members and members of Congress and they should be a part of the address. However, I would put the support—and hopefully you will have the support—of the religious leaders in the forefront, backed up by the other world leaders. As you can see, I've given this some thought and that is the way I believe the matter should be handled. Of course, in the end, sir, it's your call."

Again, the Admiral paused and looked around the room. "As far as what is actually said in the address, I think just the basics. Acknowledge that there was a crash at Roswell, but that the vehicle was a type of probe and the occupants were manufactured humanoid robots, or something of that nature. Tell the public that we are visited from time to time by extraterrestrials that are benevolent and mean us no harm. I would not go much farther with solid data, and of course what I just said can be dressed up to make it sound like you are saying a lot more than you really are. Good speechwriters seem to be able to do that quite easily."

This brought a smile and a nod from POTUS.

"Mr. President, I know this revelation to the public will cause quite a commotion for some time. The news people will be hounding you and your press secretary for more and more information. How you handle that will be up to you and your people to address and resolve. It may even be necessary to create a new office, like a modified MJ-12, to handle the matter and the periodic release of information. Of course, we must keep in mind that this is not a U.S. issue—it is a worldwide issue. We suspect that other governments may have had their own "Roswell" and after the U.S. takes the lead with disclosure, other governments will handle the release of information as they wish. However, here's what I'm trying to get to: there will be a commotion for sure, and for some time, but the fear held by many MJ-12 members that the population will panic is in my opinion ill founded. Surveys of the population have found that well over eighty percent believe that there is life, abundant life, in our galaxy. Also, better than fifty percent believe that we are being visited by extraterrestrial beings. In addition, we have lived for some time with the fear of nuclear attacks, we have been to the moon, and space travel has become a common occurrence. We have grown up as a people. I think this will be accepted and life will move on as always."

Ted smiled at Bill when he heard this last statement. Bill leaned over and whispered into Ted's ear. "It looks like you and the Admiral are on the same page, buddy." Ted nodded.

Admiral Simpson took a seat and POTUS looked around the table at each man, then he stood.

"Thank you, Admiral Simpson, for your well-articulated comments and for being a patriot. In the course of the history of our great country, patriots have stepped forward in times of need, thus earning them a permanent place of honor in our glorious history. I think that history will soon add the three of you to that list of honored patriots. Now, it's almost midnight and each of us has a lot to digest. I want everyone in this room, including the agents, and Mr. Russell and Mr. Carter, to consider themselves to be appointed to my uh—until we come up with a better name—my alien advisory board. This of course will be temporary until I can establish a committee, perhaps a cabinet position, to handle MJ-12 matters. We will be meeting again in the near future. In the meantime, I am requesting a report from each of you on your thoughts from what you have heard tonight, and I would like the reports within forty-eight hours. I have a number of quick decisions to make and I need all the input I can get. I remind you again that everything discussed here carries the highest possible security rating until I tell you otherwise. You all will hear from me shortly. Good night."

39

Waikiki Distraction

Earlier that afternoon Bernie Jarvis had returned to his Crystal City office and was deep into the development of a plan to put an end, once and for all, to the idiocy of MJ-12 disclosure. Bernie had a number of aircraft at his disposal, but his favorite was a Boeing 757 owned by his Santee Scientific Electronics Co. Bernie favored Richmond International Airport because it had a good executive terminal and lack of prying eyes. He had just made arrangements for the plane to be flown to Richmond to pick him up for a flight to Honolulu in the morning. The head of security at his Pensacola controls operation, a made-up position for his first cousin and one of the few family members he liked, had gotten a copy of the Great River HVAC drawings and would fly them to Richmond tonight so Bernie could take them to Honolulu in the morning. His phone rang and he saw it was Brad.

"Yeah, what have you got?"

"The spook is at the Great River Resort."

"I already know that. What else?"

"The meeting is going to be next Sunday night at 8:00 PM.

"Damn, that's good news, but I wonder why they are putting it off so long?"

"It has to do with a fire hazard in the air conditioning." Bernie couldn't believe his good luck. The letter about a potential problem with the HVAC system controls had just been sent out. They bought the story and it bought him precious time.

"Brad, keep me informed, and thanks for this good information." He hung up. There was much to do before leaving in the morning. The thought crossed his mind that Brad should have a secure phone, but he knew he would not be of much use to him in the future.

Bernie Jarvis had his own operation to support his black projects. It was located in a modern stone and glass three-story building on property he owned on Oahu just off H-1 near Barbers Point. Known as Oahu Experiment Ltd., it was heavily involved in back-engineering alien technology for the government, but it was also the center for equipment development used in Jarvis's illegal clandestine activities. The person in charge of the operation was Leonard Douglas, a research scientist with a PhD in chemical engineering. When he was a young man he had worked for a competitor of one of Jarvis's companies. It was about the time that Jarvis started to develop the reputation as a shady operator. Taking a chance, Douglas approached Jarvis with an offer to sell him industrial secrets being used by his employer. A friendship of like minds was formed and within two years he was working for Bernie.

Working in this beautiful facility located in the heart of paradise were some of the most brilliant, and at the same time, some of the most corrupt scientific minds from around the world. Bernie Jarvis was a very dangerous man indeed, and these were the people that fueled that danger.

Bernie looked at his watch. It was now 8:00 PM EDT and 2:00 PM HST. He figured that Douglas had returned from lunch so he placed a call to his office.

"Bernie, how the hell are you?"

"Fine, Len. Listen, I'm flying in tomorrow and I would like for you to have dinner with me in my suite at the Hilton Hawaiian Village. Can you work it out?"

"Of course I can work it out. Just give me the time and where at the Hilton."

"The Alii Tower at 6:30. They have their own check-in lobby so bypass the main check-in area. I'll advise the front desk to expect you."

"Fine. Anything in particular I need to prepare for or that you need?"

"I just need one of your special favors. See you tomorrow."

40

Security Matters

It was 6:30 AM and Ted was a few minutes out from the helipad at the Medical College of Virginia hospital. The chopper pilot made a comment about a white and silver corporate Boeing 757 that had just taken off from Richmond International Airport and was climbing out in a southwesterly direction. The plane was of no interest to Ted. He was foggy from too little sleep—he and Bill had stayed up until 2:00 AM discussing the events of the evening, but then sleep had been hard to come by. So many things had happened so fast, his life now felt like a surreal blur. The strange thing was that it really wasn't the extraterrestrial alien matter—he was trained as a Navy Seal to expect the strange and unusual, and to him this was just fascinating science. No, it was the murders, then his attempted murder, the attack on the boat, and now he was an advisor to the President of the United States. Things like this just don't happen to golf pros.

At this same time, Bill and Bonnie were having coffee in the cockpit of the *Swamp King II* and watching a beautiful early autumn Chesapeake Bay sunrise. Bill had tried to explain to Bonnie the sequence of events that created the present situation. They had been together very little since she arrived and she was totally confused by the bizarre events of the last few days. There was so much he couldn't tell her, and that was complicating an already-complicated story.

He and Ted had agreed in their early morning talk that the four of them would have dinner that evening aboard the *Swamp Kink II*, if Ruth was up to it, and perhaps that would make the discussion of the recent events somewhat easier. Ruth knew everything but the classified data, so she could help bring Bonnie up to speed from a woman's viewpoint.

Bonnie had just returned to the cockpit with coffee refills and a plate of sweet rolls.

"Bill, I've listened and tried to understand or at least make some sense of what has been going on here, but it's very confusing when every time you get to something important you tell me it's classified and you can't talk anymore. It reminds me of the movie *True Lies*. Have I been living with a government spy all these years?"

"Bonnie, I'm not a spy."

"Whew, what a relief, my husband is not Arnold Schwarzenegger and I'm not Jamie Lee Curtis. On the other hand, maybe being married to Arnold wouldn't be so bad."

Bill just looked at her and shook his head.

"Look, Bonnie, you know my background with Barry Cummings going back to UVA. Well, when he became director of the Secret Service and found out I was building the resort he asked a favor, a favor I couldn't tell you or anyone about. We had an opportunity to make a contribution to the welfare of our country so I agreed to do this favor for our government. I knew there was some potential risk involved, but nothing like this. Now we have a problem, a big problem, but we'll get through it."

"OK, Bill, fine, but let me ask you this one question that troubles me. We have had two murders here at the resort, horrible homicides. Someone has attempted to murder Ted. You, Ted, Ruth, Lawton, and a Secret Service agent friend of Ted's are shot up on a boat in the bay. Now all I hear about is some secret stuff you can't talk about. Is there an investigation into the murders and the attempted murders? Aren't they important anymore?"

Bill looked at Bonnie. She was right, he thought—has the extraterrestrial issue pushed aside the murder investigation? He picked up his cell and placed a call. A few minutes later he knocked on the door to Cummings's room.

"I'm surprised you are still here, Barry."

"It was so late I decided to spend the night and get back to D.C. early this morning and work on my report. What's on your mind?"

"I'll make it quick and simple: we've been so wrapped up in this MJ-12 stuff that the investigation into the murders and attempted murders seems to have taken a back seat. Is that the case?"

"Not at all, Bill. The Bureau—that is, the FBI—is here and has an active and ongoing investigation into the crimes. I've talked with them several times in the last twenty-four hours; in fact, the deputy director is here now."

"So they know all about the information Billy Smart sent to Ted?"

"No, not all; they know about the letters, and they know that Smart was to send some classified data to Carter, but they don't know what that classified data was. They know the data was classified well above top secret at the MJ-12 level, but they don't know what MJ-12 means or covers. They don't have a need to know to investigate the case. Security matters are compartmentalized on a need-to-know basis, and individuals almost never know the complete picture. With that said, the FBI director Jim Hughes has background on MJ-12 but not the guys working the murders. Let me give you another example. Admiral Simpson gave a good overall view of what has gone on within MJ-12, but he only knows a small part of the complete picture; that is what he needs to know to do his job. The same is true with the other group members and the employees who work within the operation. Hell, until Simpson broke ranks with the group and decided to go to the President, the President, and Presidents before him, didn't know about the operation."

"How could two people on the outside like Ted and myself get drawn into something like this? It's unbelievable."

"Bill, are you OK with what you've heard, and now know? I'm not worried about Carter; he has one hell of a military background and has been involved in secret missions that I can't even see, but I do have concern that these revelations are perhaps too unsettling for you to handle."

"Oh hell, Barry, if you are talking about finding out that there are some real space people out there, I don't really give a shit, to be blunt. To tell you the truth, I always thought that was probably the case. No, it's the murders and attempted murders that have me unnerved, and the fact that I think there is still some danger here. Also, this stuff about Ted's military background shocks me more than a little. What can you tell me about that?"

"As far as Carter's military history, you'll have to discuss that with him. As far as the danger, let me tell you there is still great danger here, and there is a level of security here far above anything you can imagine. My people and military people are here, undercover and in force. Now I believe you and your employees are safe and are well protected, but anyone who knows about MJ-12 and the people around them are in grave danger and need twenty-four-hour protection. This will be the case until the President takes the guts out of the MJ-12 operation, and I hope that will be soon. Until then, this conversation is classified."

41

Presidential Decisions

I t was 7:00 AM when POTUS walked into the oval office with special
agent Joe Martin, the head of his security detail.

"Well, Joe, this is going to be a busy day. I hope you got some sleep
last night."

"Not much sir. I don't guess you did either."

"Nope, not much, about four hours I guess." He hit his intercom. "Ellen,
where is my deadbeat chief of staff?"

"You rang, sir?" A door from the secretary's office opened and Bob Hite
walked in with Gill Chambers. POTUS looked over at his head of security.

"Look at that, Joe—Mutt and Jeff, right on time; I think it's going to
be a good day. Gentlemen, let's start earning our pay. Bob, what time are
Rutherford and Hammersmith due here?"

"Two o'clock, Mr. President."

"OK, Bob, I want every other government employee that's a member
of MJ-12 contacted and at that meeting also, as well as the joint chiefs. I
don't have control over the civilian people but I sure as hell do over my
intelligence directors and the joint chiefs."

The Chief of Staff looked at the Director of National Intelligence with a
knowing smile.

"Mr. President, uh…, what's on your mind?"

"Ball busting, Bob, ball busting. I want 'em all here unless they are out
of the country, no excuses. We'll meet in the Situation Room. And contact
Barry Cummings, I want him here also. I'll give these MJ-12 pricks a
shadow government; I'll shadow them right into a federal prison if they've
broken the law, and I'll bet all I've got that laws have been broken.

"Bob, you weren't there, but we heard Admiral Simpson discuss
the feelings of many in the know that acknowledging the existence of
extraterrestrial life, especially if they are coming here, would have a
negative impact on the psyche of the population. They fear an adverse
effect on the institutions of the world—religious, financial, industrial, and
so on. Personally, I think these attitudes stem from '50s and '60s thinking,

but I want input from others. My cabinet is a start, but I also want to talk with people of science. Get me a list of some of the best scientific minds in the country—astronomers, astrophysicists and any people of science who would have good input into and understand the subject. This needs to move quickly. I'm not talking about weeks or even days. The meeting with heads of state is eleven days from now, and I want a clear course of action in place before then.

"Bob, start working on getting the MJ-12 people in here this afternoon, set up a cabinet meeting for tomorrow morning, and get me a list of people in the scientific community that I should see. I'm going to call Jim Hughes at the Bureau to see how the investigation at Great River is coming, and if they have anything new on our friend Bernie Jarvis."

41

Come Fly with Me

Ruth was released from the hospital at 9:00 AM and flew back to the resort with Ted. She showered, napped for an hour and a half, and was now sitting on the patio of the cottage with Bill, Bonnie, and Ted. Bill had ordered a buffet lunch of oyster bisque, lobster salad, and sautéed soft crabs. Also, Dieter had sent along a dozen of his famous Great River popovers. As the waiters were placing the food on the table, Ted pointed out the popovers to Ruth.

"Babe, look at that, remember what I told you about Dieter and his popovers?"

Ruth grinned and shook her finger in Ted's face.

"You are nothing but a dirty-minded, broken-down golf pro, but I love you anyway."

A waiter opened a bottle of Piper Heidsieck to celebrate Ruth's return and poured a glass for each. The waiters were dismissed, and Bill stood and raised his glass in a toast.

"To my new partner and his beautiful, soon-to-be bride—may you both enjoy a lifetime of happiness together."

Setting down his glass Bill continued. "Bonnie and I want to host, as a wedding present, the wedding and reception here at the resort, and include the use of our plane for two weeks to go anywhere and as many places as you wish."

Ruth reached for Ted's hand and squeezed it. "I'm so stunned I don't know what to say except that I'm about to cry."

"Hell, I know what to say! We accept!"

After hugs and kisses all around it was decided that this show of emotion was allowing a very nice lunch to get cold. It was also declared that there would be no talk of recent events: that discussion could wait until tonight over cocktails. Bonnie and Bill wanted to hear about the wedding and honeymoon plans. Bill had friends and contacts in high places around the world, and Bonnie knew that if she didn't rein her husband in he would take over planning the honeymoon.

The luncheon went on for two hours, along with another bottle of champagne. The conversation went from the wedding to Bonnie and Bill's plans for building and retiring to the resort, and what Bill Jr. and James were doing and their future plans. It was a relaxing afternoon that they all needed. It would also prove to be the last of such for some days.

42

Justification

As lunch at the Great River Resort was breaking up, POTUS was walking into the Situation Room in the basement of the West Wing of the White House. In attendance were Gill Chambers, Director of National Intelligence; Jordan Penny, Director of Homeland Security; Roger Dowell, Director, Defense Intelligence Agency; CIA Director Derrick Rutherford; Director of the National Reconnaissance Office, Dr. David Lamb; Barry Cummings, Director of the United States Secret Service; former Air Force Chief of Staff General Curtis Hammersmith (Ret.); Robert Hite, Chief of Staff to President Horton; the current Joint Chiefs of Staff, and the Presidential security detail.

The meeting was being held in the teleconferencing room of the Situation Room complex. The documents on the flash card that Ted had taken from the safe deposit box had been set for display on the many large flat panel screens located around the periphery of the room.

When the President entered the room, everyone stood, as is the custom. He walked to his chair, stood behind it for a moment, looked around the table at each person, and then took his seat. On the conference table in front of the President was a leather-bound binder. POTUS pulled his chair in to the table, placed his right elbow on the arm of the chair and his thumb and index finger against his lips as he looked down at the cover of the binder. He then looked up, and around the room once again.

"Please be seated." The President had made it clear that he was a disturbed and unhappy man. There was no doubt in the minds of all present that some heads were going to roll.

"I ask that everyone please give the screens located around the room your undivided attention." POTUS nodded to Bob Hite and the first page of the documents came up. The text documents were displayed at a speed that allowed for complete reading; the photographs followed in more rapid procession. Of particular interest to those who had never seen these materials were the photos of the damaged alien spacecraft being inspected by President Eisenhower and General Walter Bedell Smith, director of the

CIA. Some present were also visibly moved by the photographs of the small alien beings, actually engineered androids, but this fact was not known to the uninformed. The next-to-last slide was a list of names of the current MJ-12 Group members. The final slide was a copy of a top secret memo from Gill Chambers to POTUS outlining MJ-12 background information and ending with these two sentences: "It appears that the MJ-12 operation is a well-organized and very powerful black op that has grown to a point that it could be considered a shadow government. It is extremely well funded with both appropriated and non-appropriated funds."

There was absolute quiet in the room as everyone read the screen. Then the President slammed his open hand down on the binder in front of him, causing everyone in the room, everyone except Marine Corps Chief of Staff General Nathan Burley, to jump in their seats.

"A shadow government, a goddamned shadow government, how dare you people! How dare you arrogant bastards keep this from the president—me and my predecessors?"

POTUS sat back in his chair, and put his fingers to his lips again as he looked around the room. He lowered his voice to a normal tone as he spoke again.

"You've been busted, people. Your operation will be broken up, I can tell you that. It may not be dissolved but you can bet your ass it's going to be restructured and the Commander in Chief is going to be calling the shots. The public is going to be told, maybe not much at first, but it's time for them to know."

POTUS knew that the real villains were probably not in this room, although he really didn't trust Hammersmith or Rutherford, but this was a ball-busting operation and he wanted to put the fear of God into these people, his people.

"Now, I'm a reasonable man, I'm not cutting off heads—yet. I'll listen to explanations of how all of this came down and the involvement of each of you. But I warn you, you better come clean, and if you've broken the law you will be punished, that I promise. However, if you've broken the law and come clean, I'll do what I can to minimize the punishment or at least make it fit the crime. If you lie and try to conceal what you've done, I'll find out and nail your balls to the wall; that I promise also.

"I understand that what I know about the issue of extraterrestrial life is hardly a scratch on the surface. The fact is, I don't need to know the complete story. It's far too complex and time consuming, and there is probably no man or woman who does know the whole story. The complex nature of the issue along with the high level of compartmented security should make that very difficult. However, as President and Commander in

Chief, I do need to have a broad understanding of the situation and updated summaries of new events. You must understand that as President I need to be aware of anything that could possibly affect the national security of the United States. I need—all Presidents need—the best intelligence possible on any possible threat to the U.S. It's not up to you to make the judgment call on what is a possible threat and what isn't—that's my responsibility, and that's why I'm so upset. It's hard for me to fathom how dedicated public servants could rationalize a reason to keep this away from the President. Does anyone in this room have a reasonable explanation for that?"

Roger Dowell, Director of the Defense Intelligence Agency, spoke. "Mr. President, I cannot, and will not attempt to speak for the entire MJ-12 Group. However, I will speak for the members present here, in this room. I know these people well, and as public servants we have, shall I say, our own little group inside the MJ-12 Group. We are the members of the group on the public payroll and as such we have banded together to function as one in an attempt to better guide the direction of MJ-12. As I'm sure you understand, each of us holds a particular position within the group. Our positions had several predecessors going back to 1947 when President Truman authorized the formation of MJ-12. There were major organizational changes implemented by our predecessors in the late '60s and early '70s. When each of us was asked, and we accepted a position to serve on MJ-12, we were not aware of the inner workings of the group, and it took time for us to learn. As we got into the inner workings of the organization, we saw a lot that we didn't like. I can tell you now that each of us present in this room feels that the changes implemented back then were both improper and unwise. I can also tell you that you, as President, have the loyalty of every MJ-12 member in this room. You may not believe that, but it's a fact."

"Director Dowell, that's a damn good speech but actions speak louder than words, and your actions don't demonstrate loyalty."

"Mr. President, I realize that's the way it looks, but things were starting to change. We are with Admiral Simpson, but he just jumped the gun. Billy Joe is a good man but he thought we were not moving fast enough, and he may have had doubts that the rest of us were on the same page. We may as well face the facts as they are: the Admiral feared for his life, it's that simple. There are some very sinister elements within MJ-12. If you remember, President Eisenhower in a farewell speech warned of too much power being given to the military/industrial complex. He was aware then of the secrets being discovered from back-engineering the alien craft and the potential danger if these tremendous discoveries were misused. That statement was aimed directly at this issue."

"Roger, who was the last President in the loop on this matter?"

"Mr. President, it was President Kennedy. President Johnson was briefed on it but not in great detail, I understand. He was actually the first President to have knowledge knowingly and willfully withheld."

"Why was that, why was he the first?"

Roger Dowell looked at the other MJ-12 members in the room, then picked up a glass of water and took a swallow.

"This is only speculation, sir, but it was common knowledge on the inside that President Kennedy was going public with the complete story. A timetable had not been set but people in the White House were working on a major address he was planning to make on the subject when he returned from his Texas trip. After that, people in MJ-12 felt they could no longer trust any President to keep the secret."

All eyes in the room were no longer on Roger Dowell, but had shifted to President Horton.

"Roger, are you telling us that President Kennedy was assassinated because he was going to reveal this uh...alien matter to the public. Are you suggesting that he may have been assassinated by people working within this government?"

"Mr. President, I'm not saying, implying, or suggesting anything. I am stating some facts but I am not connecting dots. I will say there are some very powerful people involved in MJ-12 operations, both past and present, who would not benefit, who would be hurt, by these revelations. Also, there are people in other organizations similar to MJ-12 in other countries that are in the same position. A small but very powerful group of people will suffer if this matter becomes public knowledge."

43

Fatal Mistake

It was 4:00 PM EST and 10:00 AM HST when the Boeing 757 carrying Bernie Jarvis touched down on the Reef Runway at Honolulu International Airport. The plane taxied to the general aviation complex near Keehi Lagoon where there was a rental car waiting for Bernie. He loved Honolulu and preferred to drive himself when here. There was something about this big city in paradise that made him feel better than any other place on earth. The climate was part of it: the soft Hawaiian air, and the trade winds with so much less humidity than on the East Coast. But it was also this big bustling city sitting right in the center of paradise that he loved. He lived here sixteen years ago in his big house at the base of Diamond Head. How he missed it.

He put his bag in the trunk of the new Cadillac and pulled out of the general aviation parking lot and headed for H-1. Once on H-1, he stayed right and took the exit to Nimitz Highway, which took him past Kapalama Basin, where the seagoing freighters and huge cranes unloaded the supplies and goods to support this island paradise. When it reaches the beautiful and modern downtown, Nimitz Highway turns into Ala Moana Boulevard. Passing the famous Aloha Tower and marketplace, Bernie remembered the first time he came here as a child with his parents on a ship, and the Aloha Tower was the first thing he saw as the ship approached the island. He was not one for sentimental thoughts, but that is what this place did to him and that's where his mind was as he rode on past the Ala Moana Beach Park and the huge Ala Moana Shopping Center. Finally, Ala Moana winds its way to Waikiki. Bernie turned on Kalia Road and then quickly into the entrance of the Hilton Hawaiian Village Hotel complex. Driving in past the many upscale shops, he swung the car around the courtyard in the reception area. The doorman took his bags, and since he was booked in the exclusive Alii Tower they bypassed the hotel's large open-air registration area and went directly to the tower, where he was shown his twelfth floor suite.

Bernie showered, put on fresh clothes and called to have his car ready.

He left the tower, took a leisurely stroll through the gardens and shops of the village to the main reception area and his waiting car. He left the hotel property, driving down Kalakaua Avenue through Waikiki towards Diamond Head. Taking Diamond Head Road, he went around the base of the crater toward Black Point. He turned on to the brick drive of a beautiful two-story stone and glass modern mansion overlooking the Pacific. The drive turned right into a circle that fronted the entrance to the house. He stopped at the front entrance, got out of the car and took a few seconds to look over the property. The trees and shrubs had grown larger but other than that the property looked about the same as he left it sixteen years ago. There was a large pool and cabana area on the right side of the house and he saw a young girl of about sixteen in the pool while a nurse sat in a chair near the pool and watched the girl. The young girl saw Bernie and waved in sort of a strange, disjointed way. Bernie waved back, and looked up to a second-story balcony off of what he knew was the master bedroom. There was a nine-foot sliding glass wall that opened onto the large balcony, where an attractive woman in her mid 30s reclined on a lounge chair. He waved at her; she didn't wave back. He walked to the front entrance, where he was met by a butler.

"Good afternoon, Mr. Jarvis, it's good to see you, sir."

"Good afternoon, Rick. I would like to see my daughter."

"Mr. Jarvis, I'm sorry, she just sent word down that she did not wish to see you, and for you to please stay away from Jill. Mr. Jarvis, please understand, sir, I'm just relaying her message." Bernie could see the man's hands shaking. God, how he hated weakness in men, but he held his tongue.

"Rick, please inform Pam that I'm going to wait here until hell freezes over or until she sees me. Now you go tell her that and I'll wait in the library."

About five minutes later the young woman walked into the library.

"Pam, it's good to see you."

"It's not good to see you, Bernie. Please tell me what you want, then leave."

"I'm here on business and I just wanted to see my daughter and granddaughter. Why can't you be civil to me? Don't you understand how much I love you? I give you everything you want and need, including this house and servants. Can't we just get along?"

Pam stared at him for a few seconds before she turned, strode briskly to the library doors and closed them. She turned back to him. Her fists were clenched and her knuckles had turned white. Once again, she stared before speaking.

"You fucking, sick bastard, you just want to get along; you want me to be civil to you? You give me everything I want and need. Well, I need a life, give me that back. I want my mother; give her back to me, you God damned bastard. You want to see your granddaughter—you mean your daughters, don't you? You came to see me, your daughter Pam, and your other daughter out there—Jill, my daughter. You son of a bitch, you raped me and you killed my mother and now you ask me to be civil to you. Bernie, I want to see you rot in hell, and if it were not for Jill I would do everything in my power to kill you myself. I keep my mouth shut and take your money because of Jill. That's the only reason I don't expose you. Now get the fuck away from me. Leave, before the temptation becomes too great to resist."

He stared at his daughter for only a brief moment. Her towering rage and hatred seemed to radiate from the very core of her body, and he knew this meeting was over. He turned, walked to the library doors, opened them and walked across the marble entrance foyer and out the front entrance to his car. The young girl in the pool waved again but he didn't notice as he started the car and drove away.

44

Exorcism

The dinner on *Swamp King II* had been enjoyable, but not as enjoyable as lunch. They reconstructed the resort events from the finding of Billy Smart's body to the present. MJ-12 became the "security issue" in the discussion and both Ruth and Bonnie reluctantly accepted that for now they could not be privy to the nature of the "security issue." Bonnie was now up-to-date on the events and understood the timeline as well as the others.

Public relation issues involved in closing the resort to the public were of great concern to Bill and Ted. With the help of the feds, they fabricated a cover story to address the issue. The murders were public knowledge, but at this point they really didn't have a negative tie-in to the resort in the public's eye. Security was required for Admiral Simpson and his people who were still being kept in the CECPC and would remain there at least until the President went public with the MJ-12 matter. Also, the government wanted to keep the resort secure until the meeting with the heads of state was completed. Closing the resort to the public simplified lodging accommodations for the many federal investigators, security personnel and the advance parties for the various foreign heads of state.

The resort actually had about ninety percent occupancy and was running on full staff. The golf course was getting fair play from off-duty government personnel and some of the foreign advance people, especially those from Japan. The only part of the resort to scale back operations was the country club.

Ted and Ruth had returned to the cottage and were having a nightcap on the patio. There were Marines guarding the perimeter of the resort but they were so discreet they were almost impossible to detect. You could just hear the motors on the inflatable boats as they patrolled the water around the marina and resort property, but other than that, the evening seemed like any other quiet night at the resort.

Ruth was sitting close to Ted with her arm around his shoulders and stroking his face with the back of her hand.

"Don't you think it's time to tell me about your secrets? If I remember correctly, you made a promise to do that a couple of days ago."

Ted had expected the question but still didn't know how to handle it. She would soon be his wife so she should know the truth, but it was still so difficult to think about that time, and so much harder yet to discuss it. In fact, he had never discussed it; this would be the first time, and hopefully the last.

Being very careful since her left arm was in a sling, he turned to her and took her right hand and arm that was on his shoulders and raised it over his head and rested it in his lap. He then took her hand and held it in both of his. Ruth could see he was trying to gather himself to do something he didn't want to do. She felt a cold shiver as she sensed this was starting to cause great pain to the person she loved deeply.

"When I graduated from Wake Forest, everyone expected me to turn pro, so I disappointed a lot of people when I enlisted in the Navy. I had become fascinated with Navy SEALs and their history and read everything I could find on them. I guess it was a young man's romantic vision, but I thought they were the greatest fighting force in the world—I still do. Anyway, I requested SEAL training and was sent to Great Lakes for basic training. I had gotten myself in great shape and it paid off, as I did very well. I graduated and moved on to San Diego for advanced training."

Ruth took her hand away and clasped the back of his neck.

"Ted, you don't really want to get into this, do you?"

"No I don't, Ruth, but it's probably necessary. I've never told anyone this story before and perhaps I need to get it out, and babe, you are the elected recipient."

She kissed his cheek. "Go ahead."

"Anyway, SEAL training is tough, really tough, and I loved it—BUD/S training, jump school, SQT, all of it, and it takes almost a year. I was in heaven. It fit me like a glove; but most couldn't take it. I think we lost about eighty percent of my class in dropouts. I can't explain it; I wasn't a tough guy at all. I just loved what I was being taught. It made me feel special. I knew I was part of an elite group that only a very few could join.

"After my training was complete, I was assigned to a team based in Virginia Beach and I moved up in rank. In the mid-1980s we received orders to conduct a top-secret operation in South America, and that's as close as I can go to pinpoint where the operation occurred. I understand that the files and reports on the operation are sealed and no one has access to them. My guess is that the whole operation was illegal, but I really don't know, and don't want to know.

"The mission involved underwater insertion into an area where some bad guys, terrorists, had an operation ongoing with the result being an intended attack on the U.S. These people also had some prisoners that we were to extract. Our mission was to destroy the operation, kill as many of the bad guys as possible, and get the prisoners out. Well, something went wrong. All of the intelligence we had on their equipment, locations, everything was wrong. We came in at the planned location but it wasn't the right location. Everything seemed wrong. We were on a large dock used by oceangoing vessels when we were flooded by lights. The bad guys opened fire with automatic weapons and we immediately lost four men. We took cover around some shipping containers, but then all hell broke loose—grenades, rockets, you name it. Fire was everywhere, explosions, it was pure hell. I was finally able to take out a couple of the lights, which helped some, but our guys were scattered, or so I thought. In fact, by this time most were dead."

Ted got up and walked to the edge of the patio and looked towards the bridge and downriver. His back was to Ruth as he continued.

"I stayed in the shadows of the shipping containers and moved to the back of the dock. There was a ladder fixed to the side of the dock so I eased down it into the water. The shooting had stopped and several minutes later I saw five figures with automatic weapons coming onto the dock. I eased back up topside, hiding behind the shipping containers. They started checking our guys to see if any were still alive. They found one and started to slit his throat. At that point I didn't think, I just stepped out into the open and shot the son of a bitch in the head before he finished the cut. Somehow I was able to get the other four before they could focus on me. My weapon was silenced so there was little sound. I moved around to check my guys and found three injured but alive and able to move. I got them to the ladder and into the water where they were concealed under the dock. I went back up to the dock to check on the rest, but I didn't find anyone else alive.

"On land near the dock there was a two-story frame structure. As it turned out, we had come right to their front door instead of sneaking in their back door as planned. It was an intelligence breakdown, or we were set up by someone on the inside, and I think it was the latter.

"There was a boat tied to the other end of the dock, about a twenty-foot open outboard. I untied it, pushed it under the dock and got my three guys into it; actually, two of the three had less serious injuries and helped with the third. By that time another group of four had left the house and headed towards the dock. I told my guys to stay quiet and went back to the top and waited behind one of the shipping containers. Once the men from the house were out on the dock in the clear I took the four of them out. At that point, why I didn't get back to the boat and leave is a mystery. I had sent a distress message to our support people and they were waiting at a pre-selected location to get us out. Instead of leaving, I got another automatic weapon and went to the house. I was able to get to a window and look inside. Somehow they had gotten Buck Meadows, a close friend in the platoon, and had him tied to a chair. Three men were going at him pretty good, but old Buck was just staring at them and not saying a word, just staring as they kept hitting him."

Ted stopped, and Ruth could tell he was starting to choke up, but then he continued.

"Then one of those bastards pulled out a knife and cut off his ear, just that quick, then held it in his fingers and waved it in Buck's face." Ted had to stop and clear his throat. He shook and his voice quivered, but he continued. "You know what, old Buck never flinched, he just kept looking at the guy square in the eye. I still see that in my dreams at least two or three times a week. I shot that bastard through the window right in the back of the head, blew his brains all over poor Buck. Then I shot the other two, went inside, got Buck free and started to get him out of there, when I saw an assembled RPG-18—that's a Russian-made shoulder-fired anti-tank weapon—which I picked up as we left. Buck was in pain but not seriously hurt and didn't need assistance. We ran back to the dock and I told him where the boat was and to get it fired up. The RPG was no problem for me to use as I was familiar with it. I even knew the optimum range. I didn't know what else or who else was in the house and at that point didn't care, so I took it out with the RPG.

"Buck had the motor running and we took off down the river—. Uh, babe, forget I said 'river,' OK? Anyway, I guess we were about a mile away when there was a huge explosion, so big I though it was going to take us out. I don't know to this day what it was, but it was awful; the shockwave and heat almost killed us. We continued on to the location to link up with our support people and then moved to a secluded location to await being picked up by members of our team. We lost the most seriously wounded man during the wait, but Buck and the other two survived, although one lost a leg."

He turned and looked at Ruth, and she saw tears running down his cheeks.

"Well, babe, that's the whole story."

"Why did you get out? It sounds like you were a hero who risked your own life to save your platoon members."

"That's what our team members and our CO said, but babe I left our guys there—you don't leave your fallen brothers, you get them out and I didn't know how to do it. I still don't know how I would have done it, but it haunts me. And when I destroyed the house, I'm sure the people we were supposed to get out were in there, but no one would ever confirm that to me. My superiors never told me what blew, but they said that it was what was to be used to attack the U.S. and that I prevented a disaster. They said the operation was considered a success even with the horrible loss we suffered. All I have ever been able to think about are the fallen guys I left behind that deserved a decent burial, and the innocent people I probably killed."

"Ted, I can't begin to understand how you feel but I know this: there are times in life when events are no longer in your hands. This was one of those times. You did your best, and in fact you did some superhuman things in my opinion. I'm so proud of you; I loved you before but now even more so."

Ruth didn't sleep much that night as she lay close to Ted. He had a fitful night, crying out often as the demons he had bottled up inside for twenty years were being released.

45

Cattle Business

Bernie Jarvis was sitting in his suite sipping eighteen-year-old Macallan scotch and looking at the people below around the hotel pools and on Waikiki Beach. He had known it was a risk to go to the house and he didn't expect a warm reception, but Pam's hatred had stung him badly. It was costing him millions a year to support the two girls and he thought that she would have mellowed some over the last few years. No, he thought, she hadn't mellowed at all. She was a greedy bitch, just like her mother, and she would be dealt with in good time, but now he had other more pressing matters.

The suite phone rang and the front desk advised that Leonard Douglas was there to see him. A few minutes later Bernie answered a knock on the suite entrance door.

"Len, come on in. Good to see you. How about a scotch?"

"Scotch sounds good, Bernie, make it on the rocks. How is the world of Washington?"

"Just dealing with the usual troublemakers, Len. It seems the world is full of people trying to complicate my life. By the way, look on the coffee table. There are some menus from the restaurants on the property. Look them over and I'll order room service for dinner."

The two men discussed the status of several research projects going on at Oahu Experiment and Douglas brought Bernie up to date on the development of some small laser weapons. Dinner was ordered, and after dinner Bernie got to the point of his trip.

"Len, let's say that I have a hundred or so cattle that I would like to destroy quickly because of disease. You were telling me some time ago about a new or improved device the company developed to dispense cyanide gas in gas chambers. Could something like that be used for my purposes?"

"Under the proper conditions, I guess so, but I'm sure there are better ways to destroy cattle."

"Well, let's just say that the particular circumstances in this case dictate the need to destroy them all together as a herd and instantly."

"I see," said Douglas, except he didn't. "Well, you would need a large amount of potassium cyanide, and the delivery device we have could handle that. The two big problems are that you need an area that is sealed or at least very tight; also, the clean up with anhydrous ammonia is a bitch, and dangerous. Again, I would think there would be an easier way to kill cattle, but if for some reason this meets your purpose I can go over it with you tomorrow at the lab." Douglas knew Bernie well, too well, and he knew cattle were not in his plans. They had played this little game before, and he would give Bernie what he wanted and ask no more questions. "The device is very simple; it dispenses cyanide pellets from an upper vessel into a lower vessel of sulfuric acid. A radio transmitter activates a servo that opens a gate, allowing the pellets in the upper vessel to drop into the lower vessel. It's just that simple. For an area that large, you'll need some way to move the gas, but fans should do that without a problem. The safe range of the transmitter is three miles."

Bernie was nodding as Douglas explained the details.

"Is this something that I could take back with me tomorrow, the device and the chemicals?"

"Sure, we've got everything at the lab. There is really nothing revolutionary to any of it. I'll have everything ready by the time you get out to the office tomorrow, and I'll give you a formula for the number of pellets to use based on room size and effective speed."

"That's great, Len, I'll be there by 9:00 AM. Now it's time for me to turn in, it's been a long day. It's almost 3:00 AM at home so I've been up twenty-four hours."

Riding the elevator to the lobby, Len Douglas wondered what exactly Bernie had on his mind. One thing for sure, once again he was an accessory to a planned murder.

46

Coming Together

It was 8:00 AM and President Horton had been in the Oval Office for an hour looking over his morning intelligence briefing. Now he was sitting on a sofa across from FBI Director James Hughes sipping coffee from a china cup in his right hand and leafing through a file with his left hand.

"It's not a pretty picture, Jim. Our friend Mr. Jarvis is in deep shit trouble. I assume all the wiretaps and listening by our people is legal."

"Yes sir, proper court order on everything necessary, Justice sees to that."

"Good, but I'm surprised he doesn't use secure phones."

"He does, with his people and some of the MJ-12 people, but some of his informants don't have secure equipment and the phones have to be secure on both ends. He doesn't suspect that he is under suspicion so he gets a little loose and that's where we get the bulk of our information."

"Well, Jim, Bernie's not stupid by a long shot and it won't take much to tip him off. I think your time of keeping him in the dark is limited."

"Mr. President, we could take him down right now and put him away for a long time with the laws we know he's broken that we can prove he's broken. What we can't prove as yet is murder, and that's what we want. We know he's been behind at least five and probably many more, but we can't prove it—yet. We've been letting him run and looking for a break, and maybe we just got one."

Horton looked up from the file. "You think you've got a break?"

"Yes sir, but what I've got is new and sketchy. I received a call this morning while driving in to the office from the head of our Honolulu office. Jarvis has a daughter and granddaughter living in Honolulu; we knew that. She called our Honolulu office mid-afternoon yesterday, identified herself and said she wanted to talk with an agent about an important matter. They picked up on who she was, so the head of the office and another agent went over to her home. It seems that sixteen years ago Jarvis killed her mother while she watched, then he turned on the daughter and raped her, now she wants to come forward and testify against him. Those are all the details I have now, but I'll talk with him again around noon here or 6:00 AM there. Right now Jarvis is sleeping in a hotel suite in Honolulu, so we suspect the fact that he's over there had something to do with her call."

The President tossed the file folder on the table. "My God, Jim, what a sick son of a bitch. Damn, how many times has he been invited to state dinners at the White House...." His voice trailed off and he got up, his chin now almost resting on his chest, and walked to the windows behind his desk.

"Jim, do you think he killed those two CIA boys at the resort?"

"We're sure of it, Mr. President, or he had someone do it, but we can't prove it yet and that's the reason we haven't taken him down. We're giving him a lot of rope to hang himself."

The President was still looking out onto the South Lawn.

"What's your plan?"

"Find out if his daughter's story holds water; if it does, get her back here so we can properly protect her. Jarvis is no amateur and he has his own intelligence resources and spies. If he finds out what she is trying to do, he'll kill her. Also, we want to keep playing him to see who else is involved in his adventures, and get all the pieces to fit at Great River."

"Jim, is there any chance that he could get wind of your investigation and run?"

"Sir, yes, we do run the chance that he will smell us out, but take my word for it, if he does he won't get away from us. The worst that could happen is that we would have to take him down with what we've got now."

"OK, Jim, I'll take your word on it, but keep me informed and don't let that bastard get away. Now to change the subject, what do you know about this MJ-12 Group?"

"Not much, Mr. President. We knew there was a group at the center of UFO investigations. We have had our own internal UFO investigation group for years. We were never into it in a big way because every time we tried to find out some background on a particular event a door was slammed in our face. I didn't like it, and to tell you the truth I always thought you and your predecessors were calling the shots. If I had known that there was a government agency not answering to anyone I would have been alarmed, to say the least."

POTUS left the window and returned to the sofa.

"Another thing, Mr. President, but I can't verify it. I've heard that Hoover, during the Eisenhower administration, started raising hell about being kept out of the loop on everything involving UFOs. He called the President about it and Eisenhower told him in a nice way to shut up and butt out, and it's been that way ever since."

POTUS was rubbing his chin. "You ever hear anything about the possibility that Kennedy was assassinated because he was going to go public with the extraterrestrial alien matter?"

The FBI director shifted in his seat and looked up at the ceiling. "Yes sir, I have. We have files on the matter but the investigation didn't go anywhere. It was only one lead and that was looked into and discarded."

POTUS studied Hughes for a few seconds. "Discarded because it was proven there was nothing to it?"

Hughes hesitated, and took a sip of cold coffee. "No sir, our investigation was stopped by someone, but I don't know who."

POTUS thought about this for a few seconds, then nodded.

"Jim, I had a very rough meeting with everyone in the government who is a member of MJ-12. I was damn angry and ready to fire all of them, but I listened to their stories and I'm convinced they were trying to do the right thing and redirect the course this group has been on for so long. They were fighting some very powerful people, Bernie Jarvis for one, but they were trying to initiate change. I think they will be loyal to me and I need them, so for now all of them stay in office. I'm going to tear the guts out of this operation and some of my people think I'm really going to be in harm's way. What do you think?"

"Mr. President, I agree with that assessment, but the Secret Service and the FBI will be looking after your best interest. So you go ahead and tear it up, we'll take care of you."

"Jim, you just made my day."

Joe Martin was in his usual place against the wall, and he was not at all sure it made his.

47

Camp David

Ted's office was far too plush for his taste, but Bill had insisted on the best, arguing that there would be numbers of important people in and out of the office and it needed to reflect his status as chief executive officer of the resort. His desk sat in front of a twelve-foot expanse of casement windows that overlooked the marina, creek and river beyond. The left wall was another bank of windows that faced the golf course and pro shop with built-in bookcases on either side. The room was paneled in walnut and teak and looked like the interior of a fine yacht; in fact, Lawton's people had done the interior.

Ted had insisted on bringing his glass gun case that held no guns but instead housed his prized fishing rods. There was also a framed photo of Ted with Arnold Palmer, Jack Nicklaus, and Gary Player taken at Pinehurst when Ted was a senior at Wake Forest and the runner-up in the U.S. Amateur.

Ted was in a meeting with his executive staff explaining the background on why it had been necessary to close the resort to the registered and booked guests. Although news of the murders was in the media, the extent of the crimes and the involvement of the fed was not public knowledge. The boat explosion was publicly explained as an accident, and the guests had been told that the closing of the resort was due to a mold problem that needed to be eliminated. All boats had been allowed to remain in the marina, and the dockmaster's office, ship's store, and the small marina restaurant continued to serve people staying on the boats. Access to the rest of the resort was blocked off to the marina guests, as was the marina to the government people occupying the hotel.

Katherine Goodly, Ted's secretary, buzzed him to advise him that Roy Steele and Richard Dill were there to see him. Ted dismissed the others and had Steele and Dill sent in, and asked Katherine to have foodservice send up coffee.

When they stepped into the office, Ted started laughing.

"You guys beat everything, suits and ties, one dark brown and one dark blue. You might as well put a sign around your neck 'Government Agents.'"

Dill grinned. "Yeah, and you beat everything, a prick for life."

Ted held up open hands in surrender. "OK, OK, fair enough, one prick and two feds. You know, some may say that equals three pricks. Anyway, I got coffee on the way. What's up?"

Dill walked to the window behind Ted's desk and looked out to the marina.

"Nice view, Ted." He looked out over the marina for several seconds before he turned back. "Ted, our guys have gone over what's left of your boat and say it was simple C-4 plastic explosive rigged to the ignition through a detonator cord and blasting cap. On one hand pretty simple, but on the other it shows a level of some sophistication, not your average thug."

Ted was standing in front of his desk drumming his fingers on the polished top. "What's your take?"

"Well, of course, everything is tied together—two murders, your boat, and the shooting in the bay. We need to put all the pieces together, and find the players."

"Do you think someone on the inside, one of our employees, could be involved?"

"We don't think so."

"Have you looked at the head of beverage service, Mango?"

"Forget Mango, Ted, he's clean."

"Are you sure, Richard? Mango has been acting very strange recently. Roy Lee, you looked into him didn't you?"

"Ted, Richard is right. Mango is clean."

Ted looked at both men. Something didn't seem right: either these two men hadn't done a proper job looking into Mango, or...or what?

There was a knock on the door and a coffee service was rolled in. Ted's phone rang and he motioned for Steele and Dill to help themselves as he picked up the receiver.

"Mr. Carter," said a somewhat-excited Katherine, "the President is on line one."

It took a couple of seconds to register and Ted said, "Thank you, Katy."

Ted punched a button.

"This is Ted Carter."

"Please hold for the President."

A few seconds and the President came on the line.

"Hello, Ted, I hope I'm not getting you at a bad time but I just wanted to see how Ms. Bennett was doing."

"She's doing fine, Mr. President. I brought her home yesterday; she rested and then we had an enjoyable dinner with Bill and Bonnie Russell on their boat. When I left this morning I checked in on her and she was sleeping soundly."

"That's wonderful, Ted, please give her my best, and when all of this mess is resolved, Ms. Horton and I want you and Ms. Bennett and the Russells to be our guests for a weekend at Camp David."

"Mr. President, that is something we will look forward to with great pleasure, and thank you so much for asking about Ruth. I'll let her know you called."

"Good talking with you, Ted. I'll be in touch. Goodbye."

Ted stood holding the receiver in his hand and looked at his two speechless guests. Then a smiling Ted pointed the receiver in Dill's direction.

"You know, Agent Dill, you really should be careful how you talk to me. Prick for life—indeed."

48

Tommy

The 757 with Bernie Jarvis lifted off from Honolulu International at 4:00 PM HST with expected arrival back in Richmond at approximately 8:00 AM the following morning, and perhaps sooner if they had good winds aloft. Bernie would work a couple of hours, have dinner, and sleep for six hours or so before starting the new day back East. Timing was critical; when he landed in Richmond he would only have four days to implement his plans before Horton's meeting with Simpson at Great River—at least that's what he thought.

He would be ready to hit the ground running when the plane arrived in Richmond. A 757 is not a wide body but a large plane nonetheless. The seating area of the plane could be configured in any number of ways, but forward of the galley and just behind the flight deck it had a private stateroom with bath, shower and pullout double bed. Bernie had no problem sleeping on planes; in fact, he loved it and he would be rested and ready to go in the morning.

The stateroom was more like a small executive office, richly paneled with two leather fixed aircraft style seats in front of a desk with a seat on a sliding track. On the outside wall were eight windows, beneath which was a sofa that made into a double bed. The private bath was at the rear of the suite.

Bernie was alone in the suite at the desk making notes on a legal pad. He had a habit of putting the details of any particular situation he was involved in on paper in order to develop an action plan and reduce the possibility of overlooked details. Once the plan was fully developed he would run the pages through an onboard paper shredder.

The task was clear: Horton, Simpson and Simpson's two people would be eliminated as well as this Ted Carter person. Once that happened and Vice President George Stevens took office, all the others with background information could be controlled, because he had control of Stevens.

George "Kingfish" Stevens, senator from Louisiana, had been pushed down Horton's throat as his running mate by some big hitters in the party, including Bernie. Bernie knew "The Kingfish" well and over the years had padded his pockets with several millions of dollars and supplied him with enough women to fill the Superdome. Bernie had Stevens in his pocket and he could shut down this MJ-12 disclosure idiocy in a heartbeat. He would give Kingfish a little background on MJ-12 and then get the new President to issue an executive order making the disclosure of any MJ-12 data a federal crime, case closed. His problem now was that he still didn't have a final plan on how to eliminate Horton, Simpson and his two people, and keep himself in the clear. Carter was no problem; plans were now being implemented, and he would soon be out of the picture. Horton was another problem. Security for POTUS had always been tight but with the increased terrorist threat, Presidential security had been ratcheted up to a new level. Cyanide in the duct system would work, but now he was worried about it being traced back to him; hell, his own company was doing the repair work. He was not as sharp as he needed to be and he knew he needed another sharp mind in the mix.

Hammersmith had been a central part of his original plan, but now the way events had unfolded he no longer felt he and the general were on the same page, and certainly he would not go along with his plans for Horton and the others. No, Bernie only had one person he could trust as an associate in this plot: his cousin from Pensacola, Tommy Jarvis.

Tommy was older than Bernie, an electrical engineer with a brilliant mind, but also a mind that had been warped during the Vietnam War. From stories he told Bernie when they were younger, he knew Tommy probably killed as many American officers as the Viet Cong. The war ruined him and he hated authority. As a youngster, Bernie had always looked up to him and when Bernie started with WDR he tried to get his father to hire Tommy, but his father wanted nothing to do with his older brother's son. After Bernie's father's passing, Bernie wasted no time hiring Tommy and sent him to work under Jake Barnett. However, the two men clashed from the start and it soon became apparent that he had to get them apart or one would eventually kill the other.

Bernie sent Tommy to Pensacola in a made-up position that was nothing more than a holding pattern that allowed Bernie to grab Tommy for whatever special job may arise. Bernie was a powerful man of immense wealth, but he still looked up to his older cousin. In Bernie's eyes, Tommy stood on a pedestal.

Bernie had called Tommy and told him to meet him in Richmond. He would lay the problem out for Tommy in detail during the limo ride back to Crystal City and there was no doubt that when they put their two heads together they would come up with an airtight plan. Also, Tommy would love the new toy he was bringing back from Hawaii, even if they didn't use it in this plan.

49

Three Strikes You're Out

It was 6:30 AM Wednesday morning just a little before sunrise. Ted was making his early morning rounds of the resort. He started at the country club office, where he would make a quick check with the staff on duty, then headed to the golf course pro shop and on to the dockmaster's office, take a quick walk on the docks and end up in the hotel office.

It was a little after 7:00 AM when he strolled down the first dock after talking with Bert in the office. As Ted approached the *High Roller* tied on the end of the dock Tee, the salon door opened and one of the men stepped out and into the cockpit.

"Mr. Carter, may I speak with you for a moment? We have been having a problem with the service here for the last few days."

Ted stopped. "What seems to be the problem?"

"Well, it's not a big deal, but come aboard and let me buy you a cup of coffee and I'll explain."

The two men still aroused his suspicion, and he hesitated for a second before stepping in the cockpit and up into the salon.

"My name is Dave King," said the man, "and my partner pouring the coffee is Ralph Emerson."

"Gentlemen, what seem to be the prob—"

Ted was cut off by King pressing the barrel of a pistol to his temple. The other man also had a pistol aimed at Ted.

"Make no mistake, Mr. Carter, I'll blow your fucking head wide open if you so much as flinch. Put your hands behind your back." Ted obeyed and the partner Emerson put a large plastic tie around his wrists and pulled it tight enough to cut into the flesh. They both shoved him over to a sofa and bound his ankles. Emerson went to the salon control station, fired up both diesels, then went outside and started taking off the dock lines.

"Mr. Carter, my employer wants to know what you got from Billy Smart. He knows he sent you a letter and a key. He wants to know what the key was for and what you found."

The boat had started to move away from the dock and head out of the creek towards the river. Emerson had been running the boat from the bridge to leave the dock. Now he came into the salon and started running it from the lower station.

"I just wanted to give you some back up, Dave, but when I speed her up I'll need to be back on the bridge. When the bow comes up I can't see shit from down here."

"I'm fine, Ralph, just do what you need to do, this asshole isn't going anywhere. Now, how about answering my question—what did you find?"

Ted just looked at the man and a slight smile crossed his face.

"You know what, Ralph? We've got a tough guy here."

He smashed the gun into the side of Ted's cheek, taking out a chunk of flesh.

"What do you think about that, tough guy?"

Ted's gaze was locked onto the man and the slight smile never changed. In his mind he saw Buck again, being hit and hit and then having his ear cut off. This was nothing compared to that, but he knew he was in trouble. He remembered seeing two concrete weights about the size of five-gallon buckets in the cockpit with chains coming out of the tops. They looked like buoy anchors but now he thought they may be intended for another purpose.

The man hit him in the face again and again but Ted's expression never changed—ole Buck was giving him strength.

Emerson had gone back to the bridge and now the boat was moving on plane at about eighteen knots. King had moved to an armchair across from Ted. He had thrown a wet towel across Ted's hands and Ted was wiping the blood dripping from his chin as best he could. King had poured a cup of coffee and was just sitting in the chair looking at Ted. The boat had left the river and was now in the Chesapeake Bay heading east.

King finally said, "Why don't you make it easier on yourself and tell us what we want to know."

Ted had decided that he needed to buy time to try to improve the odds.

"Make it easier on myself, tell you what you want to know and then you'll kill me. How is that making it easier on me?"

"Look, Carter, I don't have to kill you. Give me what I want, we leave you tied up on that deserted little island at the mouth of the river, and by the time someone finds you we are out of the country with two million of our employer's hard-earned cash."

The boat was stopping now and Ted could see they were in the main ship channel. Emerson had come down from the bridge and was shutting down the engines.

"Well," said King, "do you want to cooperate?"

"OK, here it is: the key was for a lockbox in a bank in Crisfield, Maryland. We went over there and the manager wouldn't let us get to the box at first." Ted was dragging the story out, hoping that something, anything, would happen to improve his odds. He could see that both men were getting impatient but he also knew that as soon as he got the story out they would kill him.

"OK, smart guy, get to the bottom line."

Ted knew the chances were slim that he could take both men out with his hands and feet bound, but it was possible and that appeared to be his only option.

"Yeah, we finally got in the vault and opened the box, and it was empty."

When King heard that, he threw his Styrofoam cup of coffee at Ted. "You son of a bitch, do you expect us to believe that?"

"Look, you've got a cell phone. Call the bank now and ask for the manager. He'll verify what I've told you. It's not a complicated matter, my friend, just make the call."

The logic seemed to confuse them, and King motioned for Emerson to go with him into the cockpit. They stepped into the cockpit and closed the salon door. Ted quickly pushed himself up from the sofa and was able to hop over to the galley. He saw a steak knife in the sink and maneuvered his hands into the bowl and picked it up in his fingers. From there it was fairly simple to use his fingers to twist the blade around and cut through the wrist tie. While doing this he noticed through the port window a boat approaching rapidly from the west. He could see through the aft window into the cockpit and saw that King and Emerson had seen the boat also.

It never crossed the mind of the two men that Ted might be armed, so when they bound his hands and feet they didn't check for weapons. Ted quickly cut through the ankle ties, reached into his back pocket, took out his 380 Pocketlite, racked a round into the chamber and took off the safety.

He was watching both men and the approaching boat, which he saw was coming on like a bat out of hell. Then he recognized the boat as *Reprise*, a 38-foot Lawton open sport fisherman. The boat had a pair of huge diesels that would push her forty-five knots; he could see Lawton at the helm.

As the oncoming boat began to slow, King turned for the cockpit door. He jerked the door open and was surprised to face Ted, who had the little Colt in both hands aimed at his forehead.

With a calm voice Ted said, "Freeze and drop the gun."

King had several options and he selected poorly. He started to raise the pistol he held in his right hand. His hand came up about four inches before Ted squeezed off a round. The hollow point bullet impacted King's forehead about an inch above the bridge of his nose. Emerson, obviously not the brains of the bunch, actually made a better decision; he jumped over the transom into the water.

By now Lawton had pulled alongside and both he and Bill were holding rifles.

Ted had stripped off his clothes. "Good to see you guys, but put the guns away and follow me in the boat."

Ted was down to his underwear and socks as he dove off the back of the boat. Emerson was flailing at the water and Ted got to him in about six good strokes. He was no match for the former SEAL, who was in his environment. Ted grabbed him in the collar, wrapped his massive left forearm around his neck and grabbed his shoulder.

"Emerson, I'm going to haul your sorry ass back to that boat dead or alive."

Ted exerted some upward force under the Emerson's chin making him scream and spit water.

"Make no mistake, my friend, I can snap your neck as easy as opening a box of saltines."

Emerson went limp and Ted started to sidestroke over to Lawton, who had backed in close to the pair. Ted asked for a line and Bill threw him a stern line. Ted ran the line around Emerson's chest and under each armpit, tying it in back with a bowline, and flipped the man on his back.

"Keep his head out of the water and tow us back to the boat."

When they reached the *High Roller*, Ted got up on the swim platform and into the cockpit. He got both guns and jumped over into Lawton's boat. Ted and Bill pulled Emerson into the cockpit while Lawton attended to the boat and called the Coast Guard.

Ted handed his Colt to Bill.

"Bill, stand over there and keep the gun on Mr. Emerson—if he moves at all, don't hesitate, shoot him."

This was said more for Emerson's benefit than Bill's, and it worked, as the man didn't move a muscle. Ted's hands were a blur as he bound the man's arms and legs.

"Ted, that's a work of art. Where did you learn to do that?"

"Hooyah," muttered Ted, taking the gun from Bill.

The chant was lost on Bill, but Lawton was ex-Navy and a smile crossed his face as he worked the boat while trying to raise the Coast Guard on the VHF.

Both Bill and Lawton were shaken by the events of the last few minutes, but Ted's mind was clear and focused. He went to Lawton, who had gotten a man named Chief Sherman at the Milford Haven Coast Guard station.

"Lawton, may I talk with the chief?" Lawton handed the handset to Ted.

"Chief Sherman, my name is Ted Carter; I'm the CEO of The Great River Resort. There has been an event in the bay approximately fifteen miles due east of The Great Wicomico River, do you read me, over."

"Yes sir, I read you fine, what sort of event, over."

"Chief, the event is a national security matter and discussion in the clear should be extremely limited. Please call Roy Steele at the following number."

Ted had taken Steele's card from his wallet, and he read the number off slowly, and then repeated it.

"Chief, did you get the number, over?"

"Yes sir, I got it. Who is this person and what should I tell them, over?"

Ted knew, as all boaters know, that VHF radio transmissions in the clear can be picked up by any boat in the area with a VHF radio, which most all have. Also, shore base stations or anyone with a scanner can listen in if they are monitoring that particular frequency, and many do monitor the marine emergency channel 16. There are recreational boaters all over the bay, and those that fish know that if they pick up their microphone and call a buddy to tell him that they are catching fish and where they are, then within five minutes boats will be heading towards them from all directions. This was on Ted's mind as he was trying to get the urgency of the matter through to the chief without drawing in the curious, or even worse, alerting whoever was behind this plot.

"Chief, Mr. Steele will tell you who he is. Tell him he needs to get here as quickly as possible. He can work that out. Please call him now and get back to me, Reprise standing by on 16, over."

"Roger Reprise, Milford Haven out."

Lawton motioned to the *High Roller*. "Ted, we need to get a bow line on her, the tide's running pretty good."

They got a line on the *High Roller* and Lawton idled into the tide, making little or no headway. Bill had gotten a first aid kit and was attending to the cuts on Ted's face.

Lawton was shaking his head. "You know, I used to build boats for a living; never made a lot of money but I had a lot of fun. Then I met you two and what happens, I turn into fucking 007. Next thing you know the President will be down here snooping around."

Ted looked at Bill and smiled.

"Would you two mind telling me how you happened to be out here at just the right time?"

Lawton said, "Yeah, I'd like to hear that myself."

"Bonnie and I were having coffee in the cockpit watching the sunrise, something we've started doing. I went in to pour another cup and saw you walking down the other dock. I didn't think anything of it; in fact, I expected you over on our dock shortly. A few minutes later I saw that boat leave but still didn't think anything of it—that is, until you didn't show up. Then I got a call from Bert, just stammering and stuttering. He was worried about you because you hadn't come back up the dock. One of his boys had seen you get on the *High Roller* and they saw it leave.

"Needless to say, that sent up all kinds of red flags so I called Lawton. I gave him a quick picture of the situation and told him we needed a boat, something fast. The guns I keep on *Swamp King*. The rest you know."

Ted laughed. "'Have Gun, Will Travel – Wire Russell – Glebe Point.'"

"Hell, Ted, that was my favorite TV show, but you're too young—" Lawton was cut off by the radio.

"Coast Guard Milford Haven calling the vessel Reprise, over."

Ted picked up the handset.

"Milford Haven, this is Reprise, over."

"Reprise, please hold position. SAR from Pax River will be bringing Mr. Steele to you with encrypted communication gear. ETA is fifteen minutes. We have dispatched a vessel from Milford Haven. Are you in immediate danger, over?"

"Milford Haven this is Reprise. Thank you, no immediate danger. Will be standing by on 16, Reprise out."

"Milford Haven out."

Lawton pointed northwest. "Looks like a chopper coming out of Pax River."

The chopper was a UH-3H Sea King used by the outstanding search and rescue team out of the Patuxent River Naval Air Station, some of the very best in SAR.

The bird made one close orbit and then, hovering over the cockpit, started to lower a man. The prop wash from the big Sikorsky was tremendous as CPO Carter settled into the cockpit of *Reprise* and hit the release on his harness. Shaking hands all around, he said that Agent Steele was on his way in another UH-3H and he would assist Steele from down here and then go back up.

"Sir, I don't know what is going on here, but you've got some friends in high places. Our radio has been crackling since we got the call to assist. As soon as Mr. Steele arrives we'll back off, orbit, and keep boats out of the area until the Coast Guard arrives."

As Chief Carter spoke, the UH-3H with Steele came into view.

Within an hour, Steele had the story and had reported it in detail to Director Cummings. The Coast Guard had put a crew on the *High Roller* and was taking her, and the body of King, to the Milford Haven Coast Guard station. Roy Steele had taken custody of Ralph Emerson and was in the process of interrogating him on the cutter that was returning to Milford Haven.

Ted, Bill, and Lawton were returning to the resort on *Reprise*. Only now did Ted notice that his hands were shaking, and for some reason, for the second time in forty-eight hours, he told a story he had held secret for twenty years.

Evening cocktails on the Carter patio for two couples would be exceptionally animated.

50

Protection

Richard Dill and his immediate superior met *Reprise* when it arrived back at the resort marina. All five went to Ted's office to detail the story for the FBI. After going over the story, Lawton left to return to the boatyard but the agents had more questions for Ted and Bill.

Dill got up from his chair and walked behind Ted's desk.

"Ted, I want you to think about this. You receive a letter from Smart late in the afternoon. Only your wife—excuse me, your wife-to-be—and this fellow Mango know about the contents. The next morning you receive a call about a lock box in a Maryland Bank. Shortly after you receive the call your boat blows up. Then you take off in a boat to Maryland, without telling us, by the way, check the lockbox and get shot up on the way back. Today two thugs try to get information from you about what was in the lockbox and then kill you. The island stuff was a bunch of shit; you were going to be sleeping with the fish, but of course you know that. Now, you're a smart guy with a hell of a fine military record, I'm told. Hell, you've had better training than I've had, a lot better—the way you handled yourself out there this morning was impressive. Anyway, we would like your take on all of this. Are we missing something?"

Ted studied Dill for a few seconds. "Richard, I was trained for a lot of things but being a cop wasn't one of them. With that said, it's clear that the bad guys are getting information from here by some type of direct pipeline. Someone found out that I was going to receive some classified data, they didn't want me to get it, and within hours they had my boat booby-trapped. The same with the shooting in the bay: somebody put two and two together and figured I was on the way to get the data, which of course I was. Whatever the pipeline is, it moves information real quick, scary quick. Now Ruth, Bill, and Mango are the only ones who knew about the letter and phone call. Ruth and Bill were both shot in the bay incident so I don't suppose you suspect them, or do you?"

"Ted, calm down, you are starting to get yourself worked up. We don't, I repeat, don't suspect Ms. Bennett or Mr. Russell."

"Well I'm damn glad to hear that. That leaves Mango, and you or Steele said he was clean, so where does that leave us?"

"Mango is clean, Ted. We've done a thorough background check and he is as clean as a hound's tooth. Look, Ted, I just wanted you to think through these entire events one more time, just in case you remember some little detail you may have overlooked before. Any little thing you may have mentioned to someone else, just in quick conversation. Anyway, that doesn't seem to be the case."

"Richard, no, no one else was told anything by me. I understand what you are doing, but there is nothing else. So just where are we now with this case? What do you know?"

Dill looked over at his boss, who stood up and walked over beside him.

"Mr. Carter, we know who ordered Smart and Dunn killed. We know who ordered your boat booby-trapped; we know who sent people to shoot up Mr. Crockett's boat, and we know who ordered your attempted murder this morning. It was one man who was giving orders to the two men that you pretty much eliminated today. Those two men were the perpetrators acting on orders from one man on everything but the shooting that injured Ms. Bennett and Mr. Russell. This person was also responsible for that shooting, but he used different people that we have yet to identify."

"Is this person under arrest?" asked Ted.

"No sir, he is not. He is under surveillance but he has not been picked up. Mr. Carter, this case is proving to be far more involved than just this one man. If we pick him up now we run the risk of losing others who appear to be major players. That's about all I can say at this time, except that in less than a week this case will be closed."

Bill Russell got up and walked over to the men. "Gentlemen, that's all well and good, but in the meantime Mr. Carter's life is at risk. There have been three attempts on his life in as many days; sooner or later his luck is going to run out."

"We are aware of that, so starting now, you, Ms. Russell, Ms. Bennett, and Mr. Carter will have twenty-four-hour Secret Service protection. This, by the way, was ordered and approved by the President.

51

Seeing the Obvious

Tommy Jarvis was standing outside of the stretch limo on the tarmac in front of the Executive Terminal when the big 757 taxied to a stop at Richmond International Airport. As soon as the stairs were in place, Bernie bounded down the steps, followed by a flight steward with his luggage. He went to Tommy and embraced his older cousin. He made sure that his belongings were placed in the limo trunk—all except one case, which he personally put in the passenger compartment. Bernie had a few words with the flight crew and then the two men were away in the limo for the two-hour drive up I-95 to Crystal City.

Bernie had been talking continuously since they left the airport. Now passing Fredericksburg, the halfway point between Richmond and D.C., he was wrapping up the situation summary. Tommy had been listening while toying with the device in the case that Bernie had placed in the limo.

"Tommy, would you put that damn thing down and give me some input on this situation?"

"Boss, this contraption is a lot more interesting than the shit you've been babbling on about for the last hour." Of course it wasn't, but that was the way Tommy handled Bernie. He was the one person on earth who could talk down to Bernie, and he did so often and with relish. He also had a habit of calling Bernie "boss," which of course Bernie was, but when Tommy said it to Bernie it came across as mocking ridicule rather than respect.

Tommy put the device back into the case and sat back on the leather seat.

"You want my input, well here it is: I think you've gone fucking brain dead. You have people running around executing people left and right when you only need to get rid of one person, the President. I guess you are worried about the killings getting back to you. You should be—every time one is committed your chance of being caught increases. I can't believe you've been this stupid; you should have come to me earlier."

This was strong stuff, even for Tommy. If anyone else had talked that way to Bernie they would be dead now. Bernie was stung and hurt to have Tommy talk to him that way, but he wasn't angry. Tommy could do no wrong; it had always been that way.

"Tommy, don't you understand that these people knew the story and would go public? They had to be eliminated."

Tommy shook his head. "God damn it, Bernie, plenty of people have known the story and gone public. Pilots, astronauts, military people and civilians who've actually worked on the craft or seen the aliens have gone public from time to time. You've always handled it before with disinformation, made them look like kooks, put out false stories about them. The news people just yawn and go about their business of writing fodder. Most wouldn't know how to uncover a real story if it bit them on the ass. Nothing has changed, except now the President wants to go public, and the position he holds gives him big balls. He can make the story or he can shut it down. The bottom line then is the current President needs to be eliminated, the Kingfish moves into the office and you have him shut the story down. It's just that simple, boss."

"What about Simpson?"

"What about him, Bernie? You do the same thing to him you did to the astronaut that went public about the ship they saw on the moon. You put out a story about his drinking and womanizing and then strong arm a couple of fellow astronauts to say he's gone off the deep end. Simpson's no different. Get Stevens in office and let the President's office leak some disinformation on him. From the beginning you should have been thinking about one thing: get rid of Horton, everything else will take care of itself."

Bernie was nodding in agreement. Tommy was right. How could he have been so stupid? What was happening to him? Bernie Jarvis didn't make these errors of judgment, not in the past anyway.

Tommy could read Bernie like a book; he knew exactly what was going on in his head.

"It's history, Bernie, get over it. We have a little less than five days to come up with a plan to get rid of Horton and to execute the plan. Even with your resources that's a tall order. Tell me again, what assets do you have in the area?"

"I've got Dave King and Ralph Emerson on a motor yacht in the area. They are the two who took care of Smart and Dunn. They are my go-to people for jobs like this."

"Yeah, the two who did a nice job framing some chef when they killed Smart and then, with the chef in custody, they kill Dunn using the same MO and blow the frame up. Brilliant operators, Bernie, perfect people to handle killing the most guarded person on the planet. Who else do you have?"

"Jake Barnett and Bobby Lee have twelve Mexicans at the ranch that the boys down there trained for a couple of weeks to handle weapons."

"Humph," Tommy snorted. "Bernie, I guess this is your usual group of trained killers, trained just well enough to go in and take out a target and get themselves killed in the process, of course leaving no trail back to you?"

"Yeah, what's wrong with that?"

Tommy ignored him; he was gnawing on a toothpick and looking out the side window.

"We have a crew from Pensacola at the resort today starting to look into the phony HVAC problem that I set up. I was going to go there in the morning to devise a way to get our friend here in the case into the ductwork. Now, since our plans have changed, let's go have a look at the place and come up with a different approach."

They made a quick exit from I-95 to Route 17 then on to Tappahannock, picking up Route 360 across the Rappahannock River and on down to Burgess, where they turned on to Route 200, taking them across Tippers Bridge over the Great Wicomico River and on to the resort entrance.

The entrance to the resort off of Route 200 was through a beautifully landscaped, gated, arched stone entrance. The gates were open but a large sign was posted on the left side of the entrance advising that the resort was temporarily closed and only service vehicles should proceed. The brick drive went about 100 yards before making a sharp left turn. It was just beyond this turn and out of view to anyone who approached the entrance that five Marine MPs were stationed to check personnel and vehicles.

All members of MJ-12 carried a special Department of Defense ID that indicated that their status was the same as that of a general or flag officer. There was also documentation that they held the highest possible level of security clearance.

Bernie put down the window and handed the Marine corporal his ID.

"Corporal, one of my companies is repairing a serious problem with the resort mechanical system. We are here to look into the repairs."

Then it dawned on Bernie: if they did the usual vehicle check they would be doing a lot of explaining about the little toy sitting at Tommy's feet. Fortunately for them, the corporal was so impressed with Bernie's ID that he waved them through without the standard check.

"Shit, that was close," hissed Bernie as he flopped back onto the seat.

The limo drove to the main hotel parking area, stopped, and the two men stepped out. The presence of so many Marine MPs posted around the property was unnerving but they were able to walk the entire property without being challenged. Within thirty minutes, Tommy had seen enough to come up with a plan, and he had also seen enough Marines with M-16's. They returned to the limo and left the resort grounds.

"Call Barnett and tell him to get those Mexicans here the day after tomorrow. Let's go back the way we came. I want to check something out."

When they approached Route 360, Tommy put down the window to the driver's compartment and told the driver to stop at the real estate office up ahead. Tommy had Bernie wait in the car and he went into the office. He returned with a hand-drawn map and information on an old five-bedroom farmhouse for rent about one and a half miles from the resort.

They looked the house over and decided it would work well, returned to the real estate office where Bernie signed a short-term lease agreement and then headed for his Crystal City office. Just outside of Fredericksburg Bernie's cell rang.

"Yeah."

"It's a done deal, Bernie."

"Any problems?"

"None, everything's fine. What now?"

"Take the boat to Norfolk and enjoy yourself for a couple of days. I'll get back to you shortly." Bernie closed his phone.

"Carter won't be telling anybody about MJ-12."

Tommy didn't respond.

At an FBI facility just outside of D.C., Ralph Emerson looked up at the FBI agent standing over him. The agent nodded, took his cell phone and shut it down.

52

Breaking Ranks

In a downtown Dallas hotel suite, Roland Ellis, president of Ellis Aircraft Industries, was standing in his underwear before two men. The men were FBI agents and they were placing very small listening devices and transmitters on his body.

"Mr. Ellis, as small as these devices are, they are very powerful. We will be able to easily pick up any sound in the room from the property parking lot. You should forget about them, be completely normal, and enjoy your dinner."

"That's easy for you to say, but it's my ass that's on the line and these are powerful men who play rough when necessary."

"We understand that, and there will be two agents having dinner in the main dining room not thirty feet from the entrance to the private dining room. We'll be in constant contact with them and if there are any problems they can be in the room in seconds. You should also keep in mind, these people may be powerful businessmen but they are not mafia; they won't try anything in public even if you are detected, which you won't be."

Roland Ellis had flown into Dallas earlier in the day to have dinner with Earnest Brandywine, president of Wellford Oil and Gas; John Fine, president of Ramstead Electronics and Avionics; William Bellenger, Chairman of Bellenger Aircraft; and Donnie Springer, founder of Springer Computers.

The dinner had been called and was being hosted by Brandywine at the exclusive Clear River Resort and Spa about thirty miles southwest of Dallas. The men were all members of the MJ-12 Group and their true interest in the continued concealment of MJ-12 secrets was just as intense as Bernie's, but they, as a group of five, concealed their true feelings from the others. They considered Bernie a loose cannon. He was a person of wealth and power but someone who was well below their social class and status.

Some years before, this group of five anticipated that they would have to deal with a situation similar to the one they now faced. They held the feeling that continued secrecy was imperative so they devised a plan to address and attack just such an event. The plan would use Bernie Jarvis as their unwitting foil, and now that plan was working perfectly. This dinner meeting would establish the final action and tie up whatever loose ends still existed prior to the plan's execution.

Roland Ellis was the youngest of the group at forty-two. His grandfather had started Ellis Aircraft and Roland took over the company after his father suffered a severe heart attack and retired two years before. He and his wife had been married for eighteen years, and they had two sons and a daughter, ages sixteen, fourteen, and eleven. He loved his family deeply and considered himself a patriot. Although he strongly favored the continued concealment of MJ-12 matters, and he had gone along with the plan in the planning stage, he always knew that he could never be a part of it if it became necessary to implement it.

The group of five was called together for an emergency meeting by Brandywine when it was discovered that Admiral Simpson had bolted from the NSA and gone underground. The meeting was called to put the plan into action and Ellis was forced to take the steps that he had been dreading for so long, a meeting with the FBI.

53

The Bait

It was just a little after 7:00 AM on Thursday morning. POTUS was in the Oval Office with Vice President Stevens, Bob Hite, Gill Chambers, Barry Cummings and FBI Director James Hughes. The President was in an armchair facing the two sofas where the others sat.

"George, I had Gill brief you on the MJ-12 matter because you need to be in the loop. Now, I'm going to take a little trip that is upsetting Director Cummings and my security detail, but I think it's worth a little added risk to maintain tight security. Admiral Simpson is being housed in our secure facility at the Great River Resort. He wants to talk to me and I sure want to talk to him. That facility is in a rural area and flying in on Marine One would be detected. Instead we have decided to leave the White House in secret and drive to the resort. We are going to keep a tight lid on this—only the people in this room and the security detail will be aware of the trip. I'm not sure how Barry plans on getting me out of here but we'll arrive there at 8:00 PM, meet with the Admiral, and leave in the morning."

The vice president was nodding. "I can see why the Service doesn't like the plan, it is a risk."

"I don't think it's that much additional risk. No one will know about the trip," said POTUS.

V.P. Stevens leaned forward with his hands on his knees.

"Have you decided if you are going to disclose any of the MJ-12 program as Admiral Simpson is requesting?"

"I'm leaning in that direction, but I'll wait to make a final decision till after hearing what the admiral has to say. George, this whole matter directly involves national security and the facts have been kept from this administration and several previous administrations. The existence of extraterrestrial life is a natural fact; it is not some program that the government developed, not some secret weapon. For that reason I believe the people have a right to know; at least the very basics anyway. I'm angry that a very few made decisions that they didn't have the responsibility or right to make. That will end whether or not I disclose the subject to the public."

"Mr. President, there are many people, knowledgeable people, who think disclosure of advanced life in the universe would seriously disrupt the stability of world governments." Chambers looked at Jim Hughes and gave him just a hint of a nod.

"Bullshit, George," said POTUS, "we're not living in the '40s and '50s anymore. Over half the population thinks that extraterrestrial life is a fact. No, the people who promote that crap are the people who stand a chance of being hurt financially because of new technology that will outdate their products."

"But Mr. President, what about damage to our religious institutions, they would—" Horton held up his hand.

"George, I'm not going to argue this matter now. You'll have a chance to voice your opinion after I meet with Admiral Simpson. I brought you in here to give you a heads up on my travel plans, and to request that you be here in your West Wing office while I'm in the meeting with Admiral Simpson, just as a precaution. Now, if there is nothing more, I have an appointment in fifteen minutes."

Everyone stood, shook hands and filed out of the Oval Office. George Stevens turned left, walked down the corridor, then turned right and into his West Wing office reception area.

"Karen, would you get Brad Collins on the phone and tell him I need to see him in my EOB office at once."

"Yes sir," replied his secretary as Stevens walked into his office and closed the door.

The other men in the meeting with POTUS had gone to the Situation Room. A few minutes later POTUS walked in. Jim Hughes had been on the phone and hung up as the President came in the room.

"You got anything yet, Jim?" the President asked.

"Yes sir, the vice president just had his secretary summon Brad Collins to his EOB office."

"Well, I guess that pretty much seals it. I'm going to need guidance from Justice on this in a hurry. Also, we must keep a tight lid on it until Sunday night, so be careful whom you talk to and what you say.

"Jim, how is everything going down in Dallas? Did your boys get what they wanted?"

"I have not heard the tape yet, Mr. President, but I will have it within the next two hours and my boys say it's explosive. I've set up a meeting with the Attorney General in my office to listen to it at lunch."

"After you do that, Jim, if you and the AG could get it over here late this afternoon I would like to hear it also, and of more importance, hear input from Justice."

54

One Last Party

Jake Barnett and Bobby Lee were not happy campers. Bouncing back and forth between the Texas ranch and Washington D.C. with a baker's dozen of Mexican killers was not pleasant to begin with and now the thought of another trip back East was hateful. At least here at the ranch the Mexicans could be sent out into the scrub to train and keep fit. Back East they had to keep them out of sight in some seedy airport motel and hope they didn't tear the fucking place down.

Jake and Bobby were driving to the training area located in South Texas scrub land about two and a half miles from the hangar complex. The men had been taken out there for training on the M-136 LAW rocket.

In this part of Texas the population is sparse, and the land is sandy, relatively flat, with mesquite and brush. Deer hunters love the South Texas plains because of the large number of trophy bucks found in the area. Other wildlife such as javelina, wild pigs, rattlesnakes, coral snakes, mountain lions and scorpions are the dominant population.

The men were driving a new Chevy 2500 Silverado and Jake had his Remington Model 700 BDL on the back seat.

"Bobby, did I tell you that Bernie has his cousin Tommy Jarvis with him in Virginia?"

"Oh shit, Jake, no you didn't tell me that. The guy is a nut case, a psycho. I thought you were going to kill him when he was down here several years ago."

"I almost did. I called Bernie and told him to get him out of here before one of us ended up dead, and I didn't plan on it being me. I think Tommy is the one person, the only person, that Bernie is afraid of or at least won't cross. I'll tell you this, Bobby: if Bernie has that guy with him, a big deal is about to go down, something we don't want to know about. My plan is to deliver those men to the house they are renting and get the hell away from there as fast as possible."

"I'm with you, bud," said Bobby.

Jake spotted a nice buck in the brush about 100 yards ahead. Tapping

Bobby on the arm he pointed to the deer and Bobby slowed to a stop. Jake picked up the rifle with his left hand and eased the door open with his right.

Jake was able to get out of the truck without spooking the animal. The deer was about sixty yards away and he continued on a slow gait towards the dirt road. As the deer broke from the brush and into the open road he turned his head and spotted the truck, but before he could bolt Jake squeezed off a round that dropped the big fellow in his tracks.

It didn't take them long to clean and load him into the pickup. They had to fly the Mexicans back East tomorrow and see Bernie, but tonight they would party. Both Jake and Bobby had become fond of most of their Mexican guests and tonight they would be treated to beer, tequila, and grilled venison. Tomorrow Jake knew these men would leave, and probably never return.

55

Taking the Bait

It was 8:30 AM Thursday morning. Bernie and Tommy Jarvis were in Bernie's Crystal City office developing an outline plan for the next three days. Reviewing the HVAC plans, they had developed a workable plan to introduce the gas into the CECPC HVAC system. Now they were focused on a plan that would direct blame for the assassination towards Middle Eastern terrorists. Tommy was to leave for the resort within the hour to oversee the work his controls people were doing and at the same time look for an opportunity to place the cyanide delivery device in the HVAC system.

They were deep into the plot when Bernie's phone rang and he saw that it was Brad.

"Yeah, Brad, what's on your mind?"

"Bernie, plans are for the President to arrive at the resort at 8:00 PM Sunday, and get this, he is coming by motorcade from the White House."

"Brad, where in hell did you pick that up? If that little bitch you're bonking told you that then she's worthless as a source of information. That's just pure bullshit, Brad."

"I didn't get it from her. It came from a much higher source. It's a fact, Bernie."

Bernie had the speakerphone on and he and Tommy were looking at each other. Tommy was slowly nodding his head as the logic of such an unexpected development was starting to sink in. He pointed his finger in a circular motion at Bernie indicating that he should continue to question Brad.

"Brad, just how high up is your source?"

"Almost as high up as you can get. I've never told you about this contact before—those were his instructions—but he's up there. Bernie, I would bet my life on this information."

"You just did, Brad," Bernie said as he slammed the phone down.

Tommy's face turned beet red. "Bernie, you God damned dumb son of a bitch, what the hell did you hang up for, he was about to give us more information. You are a stupid shit for brains idiot!"

In a blur Tommy jerked the phone from the desk and threw it against the wall, lodging the base in the drywall while the receiver dangled to the floor. Bernie had seen these flare-ups before and it always unnerved him. Something or someone would set Tommy off and he became mentally unstable, striking out at anything or anyone near. When this occurred Tommy had to be handled like a vial of nitroglycerine; that is, very gently.

Bernie said, "Tommy, I'm sorry, I guess I acted too quickly, but he was on a phone in the clear and I always worry about calls in the clear."

Bernie had thought that Tommy may come after him, but that statement seemed to sink in and he could see the rage start to recede.

Tommy looked at Bernie for a few seconds then nodded, turned and walked to the bar and poured himself a glass of water. It took a few more minutes for Tommy to pull himself together, which as always was done in silence.

"Bernie, you know this changes everything. In one way it simplifies our job in a big way, but in another way it complicates it. It's easy to take out a car or cars in the open, but it also gives us a lot more territory to cover as we can't be sure of the route."

Tommy stopped talking for a few moments.

"Bernie, we need about six M-72 LAW rockets or something similar. Can you get your hands on six?"

"I think we have twelve M-136 rockets in the weapons locker at the MJ-12 compound and more back in Texas, and by chance Jake told me he has been training the men to use the rockets."

A smile crossed Tommy's face. "When are those men from Texas due to arrive?"

"Around 11:00 tomorrow morning in Richmond. I faxed Jake directions to the house and have two vans at the airport."

Tommy nodded. "Tell him to bring the rockets."

56

The Fishing Party

It was Friday morning and Ruth had just gotten out of the shower, slipped on a pair of jeans and a denim shirt, and was off to the Food Lion for weekly groceries. Walking into the great room she saw agent John Walker look over the top of the morning paper he was reading.

"Where are we off to this morning, Ms. Bennett?"

"Now look, John, I go grocery shopping every Friday morning at the Food Lion in Kilmarnock and I've yet to have any problems. I promise you that I have not had as much as a cut finger on any of these trips. Now why don't you just sit there and read the paper—" She saw that he was shaking his head from side to side with more of a smirk than a smile.

"I'm wasting my breath, aren't I?"

"Yes ma'am, I'm afraid you are. I know you wouldn't want to see me get in trouble, would you?" Ruth gave him a sneer and a little sigh for a reply.

"OK, James Bond, let's hit the bricks, but I'm driving."

"Fine with me, Ms. B. It gives me two hands to hold my weapon."

"Good God almighty," muttered Ruth as they walked out the back door.

Ted was in his office after making his morning rounds. He was having the same problem as Ruth but was somewhat more colorful in his approach to Roy Steele.

"Roy Lee, do you remember that old hound dog I had when we were kids, his name was P.J.?"

"I sure do. I remember when you started dating and would bring a girl by your house, old P.J. would come on a dead run and ram his nose right in her ass. Many a girl left your house with a dirty ring on the back of her skirt."

Ted started laughing.

"Yeah, but do you remember Claudia Sellers? She finally broke him of that trait. He did it to her and she balled up her fist and hit him right in the side of the head—almost knocked the dog out cold, but he never did it again. Anyway, Roy Lee, you remind me of P.J. the way you've been rooting up my ass for the last day and a half."

"Well, all joking aside, you know it's not going to stop until this case is wrapped up tight, even if you are a tough guy ex-SEAL."

Ted's phone rang as he was about to respond to Roy. He had a brief conversation and hung up.

"That was Bill; a helicopter will be here in thirty minutes to take him and me along with you and his security detail to the White House for a meeting with President Horton. He has no idea what this is about, do you?"

"No, but I'm honored to be included in your lofty social circles."

The helicopter was a Sikorsky VH-3D from HMX-1 and was in fact the primary bird used by POTUS. It was on time as expected and the four men entered the big Sikorsky for the quick hop across the Potomac River to the White House. By tradition, only the President and the first family arrived or left the White House by helicopter, so the fact that the President had this arrangement for Ted and Bill was in itself unusual.

Landing on the South Lawn, the men were escorted toward the White House West Wing. The President had left the Oval Office when he heard the helicopter land and greeted the men at the Rose Garden steps to the West Wing Colonnade. After a few words he escorted them into the Oval Office and handled the introductions.

"Gentlemen, I would like to introduce our arriving guests. Mr. Bill Russell, owner of the Great River Resort; Mr. Ted Carter, his partner in the resort, and the resort CEO. Also with them are agents Steele and Williams of the Secret Service protective detail. Mr. Russell and Mr. Carter, you know Director Cummings of the Service; next to him is Director James Hughes of the FBI; to their right is my chief of staff, Robert Hite, and my Director of National Intelligence Gill Chambers. Oh yes, I almost forgot, standing back there keeping a watchful eye on you fellows is the head of my protective detail, Joe Martin. Gentlemen, please take a seat and I'll get down to business."

Everyone took a seat except Steele and Williams, who joined Martin.

"Jim, why don't you handle this? It's really your show."

"Mr. Russell, Mr. Carter, what I am about to tell you is classified and under no circumstances should anything I say leave this room. I'll be honest, I have serious reservations about telling the both of you about any of this, but the President wants you advised on the matter and it's his call.

"We have just about wrapped up the murder investigation and investigations into your attempted murders. With one exception we know who was behind everything that occurred, and our investigations have uncovered an elaborate plot to assassinate President Horton.

"President Horton has told me that both of you were in the meeting with Admiral Simpson and are well briefed on the MJ-12 Group and their investigations. So I can tell you that the plot to assassinate him is to silence him and prevent disclosure of the existence of extraterrestrial life to the public. There are at least thirty people involved in the plot and probably more. Most are little fish but there are seven leaders who wield immense power and control great wealth. To insure that we establish an airtight case and net everyone involved, especially the leaders, we have devised a little plot of our own.

"I'm not going into detail now, but I will if you so wish after everything is over. What I can tell you now is that these people expect the President to arrive at your resort, or the CECPC to be exact, Sunday evening at 8:00 PM to meet with Admiral Simpson. We think this will draw them out and if they do what we think they will do we will have that airtight case against everyone.

"The reason you are being told this is that you may be able to be of assistance in some way. We can't say what because we don't know exactly what these people will try. In any case, we would like for you to be at or near the resort during that time, with of course agents Steele and Williams. We see the risk as minimal but we do strongly recommend that the ladies not be on the property from say, 6:00 to 10:00 PM Sunday." Hughes stopped and looked over at POTUS.

"Do you have any questions?"

Ted and Bill looked at each other, and Ted spoke. "Gentlemen, is this operation legal?"

POTUS leaned back in his chair and smiled at the asking of the perfect question. Jim Hughes looked at the President and nodded. They both knew that, at least in Carter, they had a man who understood.

"Mr. Carter, the Justice Department has looked at every detail of the operation and everything is well within the law. There have been numerous wire taps and intercepted calls and all have been done with court orders or proper authority."

Bill asked, "What is the risk of damage to my property?"

The President responded to that question.

"Mr. Russell, as Jim said, we don't know what those birds will try to pull, but yes, there is some possibility of damage to the resort, perhaps even substantial damage. If that were to occur you have my word that that the property would be returned to its original state quickly and without any cost to you. I would use the power of my office to see that happen."

"Thank you, Mr. President, I'm comfortable with that."

"Director Hughes, you said that 'with one exception' you knew who was behind everything that occurred. What is that one exception?"

The FBI director thought for a moment. "Mr. Carter, we have not been able to figure how the information on what you received from Billy Smart got to the main operators, and how it got to them so quickly. That is the one piece of the puzzle that we have yet to locate. Now, does anyone have any other questions?"

President Horton rose and walked over to Bill and Ted.

"Gentlemen, thank you for coming on such short notice. We felt it best to discuss this face to face. We can't afford any misunderstandings with such a delicate operation as this. I'm sure you understand that the greater number of people who know about a secret the greater the likelihood is that the secret will be revealed. However, your resort is ground zero and both of you are deeply involved in this, uh, matter. I made the decision to bring you both into the small loop of insiders who know about and set up this gambit. If you are needed in any way we won't have time to explain background so I wanted you in the loop. I ask that when you leave here that you not discuss this matter with anyone, even with each other. We must have absolute secrecy to succeed.

"Once all of this is behind us we'll get together again under more relaxed circumstances. I want to properly thank both of you for all you have done for my administration, and for your country."

There were handshakes all around as the big Sikorsky could be heard powering up in the background.

57

Set Up

The Fokker touched down in Richmond just a little after 11:00 AM. Jake Barnett drove the lead van and Bobby Lee followed in the other. The drive from Richmond International Airport to the Northumberland County farmhouse that Tommy Jarvis rented two days before would be a very careful drive. Bobby Lee said that the two vans probably had more violations of immigration and firearms laws than a small state sees in a year. Jake agreed, so the drive to the farmhouse was with great care and well within the speed limit.

Felix and his boys needed rest. The party the night before had gone on well into the early morning and the boys were in a bad way. Several had thrown up in the plane, prompting Jake to order in a cleaning crew.

The group arrived at the farm a little after 2:00 PM. Felix was told that at 5:00 AM the next morning they would start rehearsing the operation plan. Until then the boys could do as they wished, as long as they didn't leave the farm and stayed quiet. Tommy had spent most of the day before at the farm and had brought in sleeping bags and food for the Mexicans.

Jake and Bobby had to share a room with cots and a private bath. It had been Jake's intention to drop the men with Tommy, then he and Bobby would hightail it to a Richmond hotel to wait for Bernie to carry out his plan. Unfortunately, he found out that he and Bobby were to be part of Bernie's plan; also, Bernie wanted them to oversee Felix and his boys.

The day before, Tommy had spent a couple of hours at the resort and made two very important discoveries. One, it was easy for contractors and maintenance people to get temporary passes to enter the property. Two, if you had these passes and your work required an overnight stay you could rent accommodations in the hotel. Tommy got passes for both him and Bernie and rented two rooms for Saturday and Sunday nights. His three-man crew from Pensacola Controls replacing the HVAC control panel stayed in a local motel.

As closely as Bernie was being watched, for some unexplained reason his property pass and presence at the resort was not picked up by any of the feds. There had been a breakdown in his surveillance and it was thought he was still in Crystal City. For his part, he continued to remain totally ignorant of the fact that he had been under almost constant surveillance for the last week. He was moving about in a normal fashion without fear; normal, that is, for Bernie, and that actually played a role in the surveillance breakdown.

Bernie and Tommy had another factor that played to their favor. The HVAC panels had been placed in a location that did not require entry into the CECPC. That was by design so that technicians could address problems with the system without needing the top-secret clearance required to enter the CECPC and close scrutiny by security personnel. This allowed Tommy and Bernie to use the cover of overseeing the repair work without drawing unwanted attention.

The next day was a twelve-hour day as Tommy, Jake, and Bobby looked over the indoctrination of Felix and the Mexicans on how to carry out the plan. It was a simple plan, and Tommy felt a foolproof plan, at least for the four leaders. Felix and his boys were expendable, which in fact was another part of the plan. Dead men don't talk.

Tommy and Bernie had gone over it in detail with Jake and Bobby the night before. Jake didn't like being this close to the action but he and Bobby would simply be in cars scouting the motorcade and radioing updates to Bernie, Tommy, and, most importantly, Felix. Once the action started they would just keep on driving to the airport and then back to Texas.

As for Bernie and Tommy, they would watch the action from the resort. After everything quieted down they would go to bed, get a good night's rest, get up early Monday, check on their workmen, and go home. Bernie wanted to be back in his Crystal City office early Monday. Stevens knew the bottom line but had asked to be left out of the loop as far as plan details. Bernie was looking forward to calling the "Kingfish" on his secure landline and telling him exactly how he had just become POTUS.

58

Ambush at Tippers Bridge

At 5:30 PM Sunday afternoon, just in case someone might be looking, a Chevy Suburban quietly left the White House heading east towards the Suitland Parkway. The President of course was not in the Suburban; rather it contained a heavily armed five-man Secret Service Counter Assault Team. Joining this Suburban were three more identical vehicles, one of which contained another five-man Counter Assault Team and in the other two were FBI SWAT teams. The four vehicles turned on to Route 5 heading for Route 301 just north of Waldorf, Maryland.

POTUS was in the Situation Room of the White House with Director Cummings, Director Chambers, Director Hughes, Chief of Staff Bob Hite, and Agent Joe Martin. The vehicles were sending voice and picture images to the Situation Room so Cummings and Hughes had real-time contact with their team leaders.

At the Patuxent River Naval Air Test Center, two Army AH 64-D Apache Longbow helicopters equipped with Arrowhead Night Vision System had been dispatched there from the North Carolina National Guard's 1st Attack Reconnaissance Battalion of the 130th Aviation Regiment and were being readied to lift off after darkness. The birds would also transmit real-time data to the Situation Room, where the military chiefs of staff had joined the others.

Darkness was approaching as the motorcade crossed the Potomac River Bridge and entered Virginia.

Fifteen miles south, at the intersection of Route 3 and Route 301, was a 7-Eleven convenience store. Jake Barnett sat in a rented Buick next to a dumpster in the store parking lot. He watched for the motorcade and would fall in behind at a safe distance as it passed. Bobby Lee waited at the Route 17 and Route 301 intersection and would trade places with Jake as the motorcade reached that point.

The two Apaches lifted off from Pax River as the motorcade passes the Naval Surface Warfare Center at Dahlgren. Traveling south on Route 301, the group picked up Jake, who stayed back about one half mile. When they reached Route 17 they turned east towards Tappahannock, now with Bobby Lee in tow.

The Apaches were well ahead of the motorcade, searching for unusual activity along the route to the resort. The Apaches were sweeping the highway in front of the motorcade as insurance. The coverage was so good that the group in the Situation Room could see a mouse if it crossed the road in front of the Suburbans.

"What exactly do we want to happen here, folks? I'm starting to get nervous about this operation. I don't want to put any civilians at risk."

"Mr. President, I've checked this out again with Justice: to have a rock solid case we need an act that is an attempt to murder the President. We need that to get everyone caught in the same net."

The President was looking at the FBI director when he heard Bluebird One advise his team leaders that they were detecting activity around the south end of Tippers Bridge about a mile from the resort entrance. Both birds now backed off and moved away to avoid detection. Bluebird One and Two flew back to a point about one mile in front of the motorcade and started another sweep of the highway. This was done only as a precaution, as visual data from the Arrowhead System indicated a group of at least twelve people at the bridge, and it appeared most had weapons.

The county had kept a 200-foot section of the old bridge on the south side of the river and sixty feet from the side of the new bridge as a community fishing pier. However, during the demolition of the bridge the section to be used for a fishing pier had been damaged and was now condemned. The men had been hiding just under the part of the condemned section that was on land. When Bluebird One spotted the men, they were starting to disperse to the topside of the old span.

It was clear that the Apache's rotor and engine noise would prevent an undetected approach. There was a brief discussion about this problem in the Situation Room, prompting Barry Cummings to place a quick call to Ted Carter at the resort. He gave a quick outline of the situation.

"Ted, is there anything you can do to create a little noise around the marina, anything that won't put you in any line of fire?" Ted thought for a moment and then it hit him.

"Oh hell yeah, Barry, I've got an idea that I think will solve the problem. Let me run and I'll call you back shortly.

Bill had sent the *Swamp King* to Lawton's with Ruth and Bonnie aboard to sit out whatever may happen. When the call came through, Ted and Roy Lee were sitting on the patio having a beer. Now Ted jumped up, ran into the cottage, picked up his Glock, stuck it in his waistband and took off from the cottage with Roy Lee right behind him. Not knowing what was going on, Roy Lee was holding his service .357 SIG over his head as he ran.

Ted ran to the marina dock where they kept the resort ski boat. The boat was a high performance 23' open craft used to pull resort guests water skiing and parasailing. It had a huge V8 gas engine with chrome plated un-muffled exhaust risers.

Ted jumped into the boat and fired it up, pulled it out of the slip and ran it out into the creek. Roy Steele had jumped in beside him, his weapon still in his hand.

"Ted, what in hell are you doing?"

Ted had left the marina and was now running northwest up the river. He leaned over and yelled in Steele's ear. "Cummings said that they have a couple of choppers in the air and think they've spotted some bad guys around the old bridge. He wants us to try to cover the noise from the choppers and I think this boat should do it. The problem is that if I just start up the boat and let it run at the dock the bad guys will be spooked, so I'm going to make a quick circle out here in the river and hope it'll look like a normal resort activity. We make a loop, let them get used to the noise, and then go back to the dock but let the boat run."

Ted turned the ski boat around and headed back to the dock closest to the bridge. He tied the boat to the end of the dock with the stern facing the bridge and ran the engine up to 4000 RPM. The big un-muffled V8 had the same sound as a NASCAR stock car and with the high banks of Ball's Creek funneling the noise of the boat like a megaphone toward the bridge, the sound of the choppers was concealed.

Ted punched the redial on his cell and the call went directly to Cummings. He explained how he had resolved the problem, and that information was immediately relayed to the chopper pilots, who found the fix extremely amusing. The fix in fact had worked. Felix and his twelve men were startled by the boat starting and leaving the marina, but when they saw it turn left and head away from them it appeared to be just a resort joy ride. They watched the lights on the boat but their attention soon returned to the bridge as they waited for the motorcade.

It was almost 8:00 PM when the four Suburbans turned onto Route 200 at Burgess, about five minutes from the bridge. Bluebird One was hovering just above water level behind a bluff at a bend in the river. Bluebird Two had dropped down behind a wooded bluff just up Ball's Creek. Their positions were to the west and concealed from the men on the abandoned bridge section. Felix's men were looking east at the new bridge for the approach of the motorcade. The Apaches could rise, take a quick look, and drop back down and the noise from the ski boat was effectively blocking out the engine and rotor noise from the birds. The Situation Room was keeping a running tab on the motorcade and instantly relaying it to the choppers through their home base.

The motorcade was just approaching the north side of the bridge when Bluebird Two popped up for a look.

"This is Bluebird Two, we see men with what appears to be LAW weapons."

This transmission went to the Apache's home base, the Situation Room, and the motorcade, where it was received like an electric shock. The heavily armored Suburbans could handle small arms fire but not a LAW rocket. The commander in the lead Suburban simply said, "Go!" into the radio and all four shot forward. In the next few seconds, events seemed to drag on in slow motion. Poorly trained men with exotic weapons, quickly developing and changing situations, and general confusion led to an extremely dangerous environment for both sides.

Felix heard the change in the sound of the engines of the big Suburbans before he saw them pick up speed. He knew something had spooked them and that sent a shiver up his spine.

The SUVs were climbing the north side of the high-rise section. As soon as they cleared the high rise to the south and were back on the level trestle section of the bridge they would be in perfect range. Six men had M136 LAW launchers on their shoulders and all had radios and were waiting for the fire order from Felix. Felix had the radio to his mouth with his finger on the transmit button as he watched the accelerating motorcade reach the top of the high-rise section and start descending the south side. As the motorcade screamed ahead an order went out to the Apaches.

"Bluebird One and Two, take 'em out!"

This order came from the Situation Room and was anticipated. In a prearranged plan, both Bluebird One and Two shot straight up, Bluebird Two got a fix and launched a Hellfire missile at the old span. At that very instant Felix gave the order to fire, and one of his men got a LAW rocket off before the Hellfire missile hit the old wooden bridge section.

In the poorly trained and shaking hands of a frightened Mexican, the LAW rocket hit the right concrete railing well in front of the lead Suburban, blowing out a chunk of railing and a small section of bridge deck. Chunks of concrete fell on the two lead vehicles, causing only cosmetic damage. A second later the Hellfire missile struck dead center of the old span, completely taking out a thirty-foot section, creating a huge fireball and concussion that shook the ground for several miles. Felix and six of his twelve men were killed instantly; three more were thrown into the water. The remaining three had been standing near the end of the bridge and the old roadway, guarding access to the old span. The four Suburbans cleared the bridge and made a U turn on to the road that now served as access to the old span. As the vehicles pulled to a stop the three men opened fire on the two lead vehicles carrying the two counter assault teams. Team One leader was the first man out of the front SUV. With one flowing movement he was at the front of the vehicle and with his M-16 to his shoulder he fired three quick rounds, all of which struck their intended targets, ending what the headlines in the local paper called "The Ambush at Tippers Bridge."

While the ambush at the bridge was unfolding, another drama was taking place at the resort. Ted and Roy Lee Steele had returned after starting the ski boat. Reaching land and heading to the dock office, they stopped and watched the lights of the motorcade coming onto Tippers Bridge. As they watched, Roy Steele noticed one of the Apaches rise above the bluff to his west. Grabbing Ted's arm, he pointed to the bird and they both stood open mouthed as the Hellfire missile leaped off the chopper's rail and raced towards the now-exploding bridge.

As they watched, two other men came from behind the marina office behind them and stopped near the dumpster, some thirty yards away, also eager to see the action unfold. Although Ted and Steele were anxious but hopeful of the outcome, these two men, Bernie and Tommy Jarvis, were watching in horror, realizing that their plans were crumbling before their eyes.

Steele was holding his service SIG in readiness. Noting the poised gun, Tommy pulled his own weapon. When Steele saw the movement in his peripheral vision, he lowered his gun, but his reaction alerted Tommy, who aimed and fired hitting Roy Lee Steele in the chest. Instinctively, Ted pulled out his Glock and did three barrel rolls toward a hedge, drawing two more of Tommy's bullets, both of which went high and wide. Ted had come up on one knee and raised his Glock just after the first man had gotten off the second shot. Holding the grip in his right hand and cupping the butt in his left, he squeezed off a round that caught the man just under his left eye, ending Tommy Jarvis's tormented life.

At the first gunshot, Bernie had disappeared behind the marina office. When he heard the fourth shot, knew it didn't come from Tommy's gun. With his rage building over the certain collapse of their plan, Bernie wanted only to get the son of a bitch that had just fired. Now, circling around the front of the office, he saw him, still on one knee, his back to Bernie, looking towards the dumpster at the rear of the building. Bernie walked right up to the man.

"Freeze, cocksucker, and drop the gun or I'll blow your God damned head off."

Ted didn't flinch; he stayed down on one knee and slowly lowered his arm and let the Glock slip out of his hand.

"Get up and face me, you son of a bitch, who are you?"

Ted was hoping that this man was a federal officer as he slowly rose and turned to face him.

"I'm Ted Carter, the resort CEO."

The man studied Ted for a few seconds.

"I thought you were dead."

For some reason people who are under great stress may say very unusual things. In this case the man's question brought an exchange from a John Wayne movie to Ted's mind and he repeated the follow-up line.

"Not hardly!"

The man continued to look at Ted for several seconds while aiming his gun at Ted's chest, then said, "Well, you will be soon."

The shot sounded like an explosion to Ted and he tensed, expecting to feel searing pain from the bullet entering his chest. But there was no pain, nothing, and now Ted realized he'd seen no flash and no smoke from the man's gun. Ted looked at the man's face and saw that his eyes were wide open and his face registered shock. His legs started to buckle, the gun slipped out of his hand as he collapsed at Ted's feet. The man fell forward, his body twitched, and Ted saw a rapidly spreading stain over the back of his jacket.

Looking up, Ted saw a young woman holding what appeared to be Roy Lee Steele's SIG in both of her shaking hands. Her grip on the gun instantly told Ted that she had probably never fired a weapon of any kind. She lowered her arms, letting Steele's service SIG slip out of her right hand and fall to the grass. She stood motionless, looking down at the twitching body of the man she had just killed. Then, she raised her head, looked into Ted's eyes and spoke very slowly.

"My name is Pam Jarvis. I'm his daughter."

59

Netting the Fish

At 8:30 PM CDT that same evening, in a gated and guarded exclusive community north of Houston, Texas, Earnest Brandywine was in his study reading the Sunday newspaper. His butler knocked on the study door and announced that two agents with the FBI were there to see him. The agents were shown to the study and presented Brandywine their identification.

"Mr. Brandywine, we have a warrant for your arrest, sir. The charge is conspiracy to murder the President of the United States."

Brandywine was cuffed, his rights were read to him, and he was driven to the FBI field office in Houston. At approximately the same time at other locations around the country, John Fine, William Bellinger, and Donnie Springer were similarly being put under arrest.

At 9:00 PM EDT, the vice president was in his White House office as the President had requested, even though he thought it was pure idiocy. His jacket was off, his tie was loose, his feet were on his desk and he was sipping a Jack Daniels on the rocks. His wife had called fifteen minutes before just to say hi, or so she said. Her real reason was to check up on him, and that always pissed him off. The Jack was helping and he had a little cutie waiting just a few blocks away and as soon as he could get the hell away from here that would be his next stop.

There was a rap on his door and his protective detail along with agent Joe Martin came in and requested that he come with them to the Oval Office. Stevens thought the request was strange since he knew that POTUS was meeting now with Simpson at the CECPC; then it hit him, maybe Jarvis had made his move, maybe he was now the President.

He buttoned his collar, slipped his tie back in place, put on his jacket and made the short walk to the Oval Office. Joe Martin opened the door and Stevens saw POTUS sitting behind his desk. Standing in front of one of the sofas were FBI Director Jim Hughes and Attorney General Mitchell Hass. Barry Cummings and Bob Hite were standing in front of armchairs.

"Please come in, George, and have a seat."

"Mr. President, I thought you were meeting with Admiral Simpson?"

"I know you did, George. Jim, would you please take over?"

There was a small recording device on the table between the sofas.

The FBI Director said, "Mr. Vice President, listen to this if you would, sir."

Hughes pressed a button on the device and a recording started playing. It was the phone conversation between Brad Collins and Bernie Jarvis about the motorcade to the CECPC. When the tape ended, Hughes pressed the stop button and looked at the V.P.

"Sir, do you recognize those voices?"

"No, should I?"

"Well, you at least should know one; it's Brad Collins, aid to General Anderson, the President's military aid."

"Jim, why on earth should I know one of General Anderson's aides?"

"Mr. Vice President, you need to tell us that. He was in your office this past Wednesday, just after you left a meeting here in the Oval Office. Your secretary summoned him for you after you returned to your office, and he was in your office for fifteen minutes."

Stevens face was flushed and his mind was racing. How the hell was he going to get out of this mess?

"Collins, yes, now I remember. He's married to my wife's cousin. He wants to come to work in my office and I promised her that I would talk with him last week."

"Is that so? Well, he's under arrest and our information shows that he's not married. But that's really of no importance. What is important is that within thirty minutes of leaving your office he made the call you just heard. He was passing on information to Bernie Jarvis, the other voice on the phone, secret information that only you and the people in this room possessed."

A light was starting to come on in the head of George "Kingfish" Stevens, a light that was telling him that he had been set up.

"OK, look, I admit I made a mistake. In talking to him about taking a job in my office I used what we discussed here to make an example of the level of security needed to work in the West Wing. I didn't know—"

POTUS slammed his fist down on top of his desk. "God damn it, George, that's enough. My trip to the CECPC was a set-up to draw you bastards out. I met with Simpson there a week ago. At 8:00 PM this evening a motorcade that your buddies thought I would be in was attacked just before it arrived at the resort. There were two Secret Service assault teams and two FBI SWAT teams in the Suburbans, backed up by two Apache helicopters. They took out the attackers in less than a minute. We watched the whole thing from the Situation Room."

Stevens's face was ashen now and his breathing was becoming rapid. He started to sputter. "I—I didn't know what they were going to do...." He stopped when he realized what he was saying—what he was admitting to.

"I'm sure you didn't, George. You didn't need to know, didn't want to know. You didn't give a damn about disclosure; you just wanted them to succeed so you could take over this seat. Your desire to be President bordered on the fanatical. It always has, and you knew the only way you would ever be President was to somehow fill my unexpired term."

The President looked from Stevens to the floor and shook his head. "You're a sick man George."

Hughes took over from POTUS. "Sir, Bernie Jarvis is dead. Brad Collins has talked and detailed your role in furnishing information to pass on to Jarvis. Your friends Brandywine, Fine, Bellinger, and Springer are under arrest and being held by the FBI. We have a tape of their conversation at a private dinner that lays out the entire plot. They wanted to shut the President up to prevent extraterrestrial disclosure and wanted you to be President. They knew that Jarvis had become a psychopath and that if they fed him the proper information he would take out the President on his own. Just feed Jarvis information and let him do the dirty work and take the fall. Once you were in office they would have control. You would be their puppet and they would pull your strings. ET disclosure would be a moot issue. Bernie Jarvis was a psychopath and their stooge, but he was still very smart. His downfall was his mental condition. You, on the other hand, were also their stooge, but unlike Jarvis you are simply stupid."

Stevens jumped to his feet but before he could move both Joe Martin and Jim Hughes had their service weapons out.

"Mr. Vice President, please don't try anything. We will take you down if necessary."

Two more agents had entered the Oval Office. Now Martin and Stevens's own detail stood with Stevens between them.

Jim Hughes spoke again. "Mr. Vice President, you are under arrest for conspiracy to murder the President of the United States." The attorney general stepped forward, holding a binder with a sheet of paper on it.

"Please sign this document." Stevens looked at the paper; it was a simple one-sentence letter of resignation. He hesitated for a moment, and then took the pen the AG was holding and signed his name. Joe Martin on earlier orders from the President had brought in the White House photographer, who now took several photographs that would never be seen by the public.

60

Tying Up Loose Ends

Richard Dill punched off his cell phone.

"He's in intensive care and listed as critical but the doc said that barring any complications the wound should not be life threatening."

"Thank God," said Ted. "Richard, is this shit finally over?"

"I think so, Ted, but you have much higher contacts than I do, you need to talk with them. My boss got here thirty minutes ago and is over at the bridge with Director Cummings."

Dill had opened a beer and Ted was sipping a Jack and water as they stood outside on the patio. Looking east they could see the high-intensity lights that had been set up at the bridge.

"Damn it, must be five hundred people milling around up there, and my boss and Cummings are probably in the middle of a turf war over who runs the case." That was said as Hughes and Cummings walked around the corner of the cottage.

"Uh, Agent Dill, would you mind repeating what you just said?"

"Sir, you must be mistaken. I haven't said a word. Isn't that correct, Mr. Carter?"

"That's correct, not a word, a regular clam."

"Hmm, pretty cute pair we have here, Barry. OK, Dill, get your ass back to the bridge and the investigation. We need to talk with Mr. Carter."

"Yes sir, I'm gone." And he was.

"Mr. Carter, your performance was exceptional and I'm sure you also saved Steele's life. We are all in debt to you."

Ted just made a slight nod. "What I want to know is if this is finally over."

"I think we can say with certainty that yes, it's over."

"Well, gentlemen, you would do me a great favor if you would tie up some loose ends. You know I've sort of been in the middle of this saga, not by choice I may add, so I think I deserve to know at least the basics. Let's start with the story behind his daughter."

"I think that's fair. May we sit down?"

"Of course, I apologize. I'm still a little shell shocked by all of this."

"We understand, Mr. Carter."

Ted had seen the *Swamp King* return to the marina dock from Lawton's yard. Now he saw Ruth and Bill heading to the cottage. As they approached, Ted could see that Ruth was crying, and she ran the last several yards to Ted's arms. She held on to Ted and Ted held her until she regained her composure.

"Bill just told me what happened, and what almost happened to you. Oh, Ted, please tell me it's over. How much more can we take?"

"Come on, babe, let's sit down."

"Folks, please have a seat and let me get everyone a drink."

After Ted had introduced everyone, he took drink orders and went to fix them.

"Folks, Director Hughes was just telling Ted that this mess is finally over. We have everybody involved in the plot and when Ted gets back we'll give you the background."

It only took a couple of minutes before Ted returned with the drinks.

"OK, Jim, why don't you pick up the background on Pam Jarvis."

"Barry, before I do that, let me get one other person over here." Hughes placed a call and asked the person to come to the Carter cottage. In less than five minutes a grinning Mango stepped on the patio.

"I would like to introduce you folks to Manuel "Mango" de la Torre, former special agent of the C.I.A.," said Jim Hughes.

Mango was still grinning and both Ted and Bill were speechless.

Finally, Bill was the first to speak. "Just how many feds did I have on my payroll?"

Cummings said, "I know of four, Bill: Smart and Dunn, the resort engineer, and Mango."

Ted was just shaking his head but finally managed to speak. "Mango, you dirty son of a bitch, I ought to shoot you."

Barry Cummings said, "OK, folks I know we have a lot of explaining to do, so Jim, why don't you pick it up again."

"All right, let's start with Mango here."

"Please do," said Ted.

"I'll let Mango go into his personal history with you later. What I'm telling you now is what Director Rutherford told me a couple of days ago. Mango came to work for the agency about twenty years ago. His jobs have always been what he did here. That is, he would secure employment in a business involved in sensitive government work and become the on-site eyes and ears for the agency. His job here was fairly mundane, until the last few weeks."

Mango was nodding in agreement. Jim Hughes then took them step by step through the arrests of the four industrialists and their background, and the arrest of the vice president. He told them that Bernie Jarvis had dispatched two of his thugs to come here on the *High Roller* and snoop around after he had gotten some vague information that the President may be holding a secret meeting at the resort on the MJ-12 issue. These same two men murdered Smart and Dunn on Jarvis's orders. The man now in custody had confessed and told the whole story.

"So you see, folks, the murders and the attempted murders were just peripheral issues to the main issue, the plot to kill the President. I believe that Jarvis had become mentally unstable. He was so sure of himself that he was careless. Perhaps operating for years in the vacuum of secrecy that surrounded MJ-12 actually made him careless; we'll never know. Of course, if one of the five industrialists had not come forward, their part in the plot and that of the vice president may never have been discovered. They were programming him like a robot and he didn't have a clue."

"Director, you still haven't told us what role our friend here played," said Ted.

"Oh yes, so I haven't. Well, after word of the meeting leaked, Mango was getting increasing pressure from his superior at the Agency for information. That is the reason Mango was here the night of the shooting asking what you thought were unusual questions."

Mango spoke up. "Ted, this guy was on the phone to me five times a day just raising hell about more and more information." Mango motioned for Hughes to continue.

"Mango thought something didn't seem right so he came to us— Richard Dill, to be exact. Dill came to me, I went to Rutherford and then Rutherford got into it. It turns out Mango's superior was on the take from Jarvis. I don't know the particulars on how they found out but he was feeding information to Jarvis and the vice president. The vice president was feeding information back to this person who would pass it on to Jarvis. That is one way they were using Jarvis. It will probably be another month before the picture is totally clear."

Bill got up and walked to the edge of the patio. "Mango did nothing wrong, he just reported to his superior, but that's how the information got to the bad guys so quick."

"That's exactly right. That was the missing piece of the puzzle."

Bill spoke up. "Mango, what's this about 'former agent'?"

"I resigned Friday, Bill. I had enough and I hope I still have a job here."

"Mango, you have it as long as you want it."

"Well, we still haven't gotten to the story with Pam Jarvis," said Ted.

Hughes got up and walked in front of the group. "OK, here is the story on the daughter. Jarvis was in Honolulu this past Tuesday to visit a company he owns there, a very questionable company that will be investigated. Anyway, while there he paid a visit to his daughter who lives in a home Jarvis owned. He lived there until sixteen years ago, when in a drunken rage he strangled his wife and raped his sixteen-year old daughter. It's alleged he dumped his wife's body in the Pacific from his yacht but there is no proof that happened. In any case, she was never seen again. His daughter became pregnant and had a retarded child, Jarvis's daughter/granddaughter."

Hughes stopped for a moment and looked at Ted.

"Ted, the man you killed tonight, Tommy Jarvis, Bernie Jarvis's cousin, was a very sick and evil man, but the person Pam Jarvis killed was even worse."

Ted was staring at Hughes. "Go on."

"The visit from Jarvis was not pleasant, as you can imagine. Oh, he was taking care of her—the house, five million a year, care for the child and so on, but she hated him with a passion. When he showed up at her door it all came apart and she couldn't take it anymore. She called our Honolulu office and told her story. She wanted to testify against him and put him away. We knew if the story got out, he would kill her, so we brought her East to protect her. We decided that this was the best place to keep her safe and comfortable, with all the agents here and so forth. For him to also be here was a major fuck up—oh, please excuses me, ladies—on our part and that will be reviewed. Anyway, from our brief talk with her tonight she said she walked out of her cottage to see what all the commotion was about. She was going to the marina office when she spotted her father and Tommy Jarvis, so she found a place to hide. When Jarvis shot Steele, his service weapon flew out of his hand and landed at her feet, then when she saw her father preparing to shoot you, she picked up Steele's weapon and, well, saved your life."

Ted was just shaking his head. He walked to the edge of the patio and looked up towards the bridge, the lights, the people, and the activity that would go on all night. Ruth walked over to him, put her arm around his waist and laid her head on his shoulder. They both knew that the nightmare was finally over.

61

The Great River Disclosure

The arrival of the world leaders at the resort was smoother than Bill or Ted could have imagined. It became apparent that the White House was perhaps the one part of the government that functioned properly. It had been decided that security at the resort itself was so good that the use of the CECPC was not required. In doing this, the existence of the CECPC was not revealed and its viability for future use was retained. The visiting dignitaries were put up in the cottages with their support people being housed in the hotel. It was a tribute to Bill, Ted and the entire staff that they were able to adapt to this change of plans so quickly.

The meetings lasted a day and a half, and Admiral Simpson and his people played a major role in all of the sessions. There was finally a consensus that the existence of extraterrestrial life was a natural occurrence and as such no government had the right to conceal its existence. Somehow it seemed so funny, after all the years of secrecy, all the official denials, all the threats, and all the deaths; it really came down to that one simple fact.

The White House and the Justice Department were trying to keep the lid on the arrest of the vice president until after the ET disclosure. They wanted that story to be the dog that wagged the tail, not the other way around. A brief address had been written that described in scant detail the existence of ET life and the work of the MJ-12 Group. POTUS had decided to make the MJ-12 Group a part of NASA, until he found that NASA was a co-conspirator with MJ-12 in the whole ET cover-up. It was decided that MJ-12 would be changed to Majestic Operations, or MJ-Op, and come under the Director of National Intelligence. President Horton appointed a former UN ambassador with a no-nonsense reputation as director of MJ-12 operations.

Although the address was brief, it created a worldwide thunderclap, which increased greatly after the next day's Presidential news conference. The address was taped in the Grand Ballroom of the Great River Resort with all of the attending world leaders present. It aired at 8:00 PM EST, exactly one hour after the last officials had departed for their home countries.

"Good evening, I requested this time to address you concerning a matter of great importance. Over the last few weeks, I have received information on a covert government operation that has been concealed from my office, the office of my predecessors, and the Congress. The seriousness of this matter cannot be overstated since the operation in question involves matters of national security and international security. The Justice Department is in the process of investigating this operation to see what federal laws were broken and identifying any people responsible for breaking the law. We do know that several people involved in this operation were part of a serious crime and are now in federal custody.

"I'm sure you noticed that while I was talking the other heads of state sitting on the dais with me where shown and identified. I invited them here in secret to discuss this matter and determine how we should disclose the information we now possess. What I am about to tell you has the support and backing of all present. Tomorrow morning at 11:00 AM I will hold a news conference and will go into the details of this subject, but tonight I would like to give you just a brief history of the operation."

"In the late 1940s, there was a dramatic increase in the sighting of what were called 'flying saucers' and later to become known as 'unidentified flying objects' or 'UFOs.' In 1947 it was reported that a saucer crashed near Roswell, New Mexico, but the next day the Army reported that what crashed was simply a weather balloon. The truth is, the Army did recover a crashed extraterrestrial craft and proceeded to cover up the event. Shortly thereafter, President Truman authorized the establishment of a panel of scientists and military leaders to investigate this phenomenon. This panel would be called the Majestic 12 Group and would operate under the highest level of security and report to the President. Let me say here that if I had been in President Truman's shoes I would have done the same thing. In 1947 the world was shattered and just beginning to recover from the horrors of World War Two. There was instability around the globe. Our government simply could not acknowledge that alien spacecraft were flying in and out of our airspace at will and we had no means to stop them. The government couldn't acknowledge that we were being visited by extraterrestrial beings but that we didn't know where they came from or what they wanted. No, at that time we were too fragile as a people for that disclosure. There would have been certain panic."

The President went on to describe the MJ-12 Group, the power it amassed over the years, the beginning of the concealment of information from his office, and subsequent corruption brought on by the amassing of power. He stated that this would end and that it was time for disclosure and re-direction of MJ-12. He emphasized that there was nothing to fear from these visitors but gave scant detail about anything of substance.

"As you can understand, this is a complex and fascinating story that will unfold in the months and years to come, and one we will start to explore in detail tomorrow morning. Until then, I ask each of you, citizens of the United States and citizens of countries around the world, to use reason and restraint in your speculation. Think of yourself and your loved ones as being part of the fortunate few who were alive when the planet Earth grew from adolescence to maturity and became part of the citizens of the galaxy.

"Thank you and good night."

As so often happens, major events in history take on special names such as "D Day," "The Battle of the Bulge," or "9/11." In this case, the *Richmond Times-Dispatch* headline had the distinction of being credited for the name that stuck. Their headline in the next morning's edition read, "The Great River Disclosure."

There was much overheated rhetoric over the next few days about all sorts of worldwide catastrophes. The print and electronic media interviewed a never-ending string of so-called experts from scientists to kooks who predicted everything from Armageddon to a glorious new beginning. The next day's news conference proved to be a marathon session for the President, who was accompanied by Gill Chambers and Admiral Simpson. The attorney general and the FBI director were also on hand to handle the issue of the vice president. It had been decided to only reveal that VPOTUS had been implicated in illegal activities with several MJ-12 members and that an investigation was in progress. It was stated that he had resigned, left Washington, and his whereabouts would not be revealed until the investigation was completed. The attorney general was able to handle the questions about the vice president because the major interest was in the extraterrestrial matter, supported by the fact that Stevens was not well liked. The press wanted to know about little green men, not "Kingfish" Stevens. Within a week, the rhetoric died down and once again life moved on as normal, although changed forever.

President Ray Horton scheduled individual meetings with each member of MJ-12 still alive or not under arrest, requesting a thirty-page or less report from each on their particular responsibility and findings within the group. It had become clear to him that no one person had access to the complete extraterrestrial picture, and that was going to change. With Gill Chambers now in control of the MJ-Op they grilled each former MJ-12 member until a broad picture of the United States involvement into the world of extraterrestrial life was fully documented into the top secret electronic files of the Director of National Intelligence.

This process took almost three weeks, and when it was wrapped up, POTUS met with Gill Chambers and his new director of MJ-12 Operations, Ambassador Norris Shelton, along with his newly appointed senior staff, in the Cabinet Room.

Everyone stood as POTUS entered the Cabinet Room. "Take your seats, folks, and thank you for coming."

Chambers introduced Ambassador Shelton, who then introduced his senior staff. In addition, the President had a briefing document with an outline biography of each person present.

"Ambassador Shelton, Gill tells me he believes you are the best possible person to straighten out and organize this convoluted mess known as the MJ-12 Group. On the other hand, some of my advisors tell me you have the problem of always speaking your mind and doing so to the point of being abrasive. Would you care to address that matter?"

"Mr. President, the federal government is full of people who wear several faces, which is especially true of those who are here in Washington. I don't, and my work ethic is simple: I work hard and I'm honest and I expect the same from those who work for me. I don't have time to mince words and if I'm dissatisfied with something or someone I let it be known in no uncertain terms so the message will stick. I suppose this doesn't sit well with some people; so be it. The senior people I have selected to work with me, the people who sit in this room, know me well and I know them well. We'll do a job for you, I can promise, but in the process we will step on some toes, perhaps some big toes. You need to be aware of that fact and you need to be prepared for it or get someone else to do this job."

The President's people, including Bob Hite, were taken back by the bluntness of Shelton's comments but POTUS just smiled.

"Mr. Ambassador, this is not a diplomatic mission. It is a mission to straighten out the country's idiotic handling of the most important development in the history of mankind. It's going to take someone with keen intelligence, uncompromising character, tough skin and may I also add, huge balls, to undo sixty years of mishandling. I think we have the right man to lead this project. You have my support.

"Now I want to make one point clear from the beginning, for you to use as sort of a foundation to the way you structure your efforts to untangle this mess. I think the government was correct in 1947 to conceal the ET issue. We were just recovering from a horrible war, the cold war was beginning and the Soviet Union was a serious threat. We were being visited by extraterrestrial beings that could come and go and fly through our skies at will and we had no means to stop them or any knowledge of what they wanted. The citizens of this country and the citizens of the world were not yet ready for that knowledge. However, as we grew up, the secrecy should have been lifted little by little—that's where we made mistakes.

Starting now, the results of your efforts will be reviewed by the President, which, by the way, was the original intention of President Truman. Those reviews will determine what will be declassified and released to the public.

"Now, in the beginning we will be meeting often, perhaps every day. The more I read the more confused and bewildered I become. I don't mind telling you that I don't understand much of what I'm told or read. What our private contractors have been given to experiment with and research, and what they have discovered in such areas as propulsion, computer technology, anti-gravity generators, and so on are simply beyond me. What I do understand is that much of this must remain classified for national security reasons. The public had the right to know about the discovery of extraterrestrial life, I have no argument with that, but scientific discoveries resulting from contact with these beings that have the potential to affect national security or the global economy must remain classified until it is determined that declassification and public awareness is warranted. At this point I don't know where we draw the lines; that will be part of your charge to work out and bring to me."

Shelton raised his hand. "Mr. President, do we communicate with these beings?"

POTUS lowered his head and rested his chin in his right hand for a moment.

"Ambassador, I assume everyone present here is cleared for all levels of MJ-12 Op data?"

"Yes sir, they wouldn't be here if they weren't. Every one of my people here will head up a particular division and will have access to the same knowledge that I have."

"I thought that was the case, but I had to ask. OK, yes, we are in contact with them through the NSA. There are a couple of men at the NSA who have some way, some system set up with them, and are in regular contact."

POTUS sighed and looked out into the Rose Garden and was quiet for several seconds.

"Damn," he said softly as he turned back to the others. "This is the part that I admit just scares me to death. Admiral Simpson says that they have been gently pushing for worldwide disclosure of their existence for some time. They want the people of this planet to unite as one and join some sort of galactic community, although I'm sure they have another name for it. He says at some point I will need to talk with them about spearheading this effort. That, ladies and gentlemen, is a frightening proposition, and it will also be a part of your charge to develop and set up for me."

POTUS paused again as he thought; he was tapping a ballpoint pen on a leather binder on the table, a nervous habit he had when he was in deep thought. Finally he spoke.

"Now there are many roots and branches to this subject, but the area of theology is of particular importance. If you don't know already, you will soon find out as you start your research that these beings are our ancestors. As such, the basis of the various religions that we Earthlings practice came from them. This is probably the one area that needs to be brought to the public's attention as soon as possible. We want to insure that the religious underpinnings of the world remain strong.

"It is your charge, people, to structure an organization to deal with all facets of extraterrestrial life. Everything is open to you: the research facilities, the contractors, the intelligence community; and of course the old MJ-12 facilities and employees now come under your jurisdiction. Ladies and gentlemen, the people of this planet are getting ready to grow up real fast and you will be at the core"

POTUS looked around the room and saw that the enormity of the challenge facing these people had just started to sink in. The revelations were so astounding and the potential impact on national security was so great that POTUS knew it would be many years before the public could be told the full story. The existence of extraterrestrial life had finally been revealed to the public, but it would take the slow release of information over many years before the public understood the big picture, and that was the way it had to be.

Epilogue

The first of the following month, Ruth and Ted were married in a small but elegant service and reception at the resort. The President had handwritten a warm and touching note to the new couple and apologized that he and the First Lady could not attend, explaining that the Presidential presence at any wedding would turn it into a media and logistical circus. The letter was enclosed with a sterling silver serving platter with the Presidential seal in the center.

Bill was best man and Mango gave the bride away. Barry Cummings and a recovered Roy Steele represented the Secret Service and Jim Hughes from the FBI also attended. All of the resort employees had been invited, as well as members of the country club. Ted was amazed at how many club members showed up. Even Baker was there, who told Ted, "I'm only here for the free booze and food." Then moving over to Ruth he said, "I sure hope you can make him a kinder and gentler fellow. My game sucks."

After the cake was cut, Lawton and June took the newlyweds away from the reception in the newly repaired 53' Lawton for a trip up the bay to the Pax River NAS. Having friends in high places allowed Bill to get clearance to land his Citation X at the Navy's test flight center. The base commander met Ruth and Ted at the dock and escorted them to the waiting plane and the beginning of their two-week honeymoon.

A two-week honeymoon with the use of a private jet and crew allowed them to visit Paris, Rome, Naples, Athens, Barcelona, Lisbon, and then return home. Landing back at Pax River two days before Thanksgiving, they were picked up by Bill and Bonnie on the *Swamp King II* for the trip back down the bay to the resort. On the way back, Bill told them of another surprise. The four of them had been invited to Camp David to spend the night and have Thanksgiving Dinner with the President and First Lady.

The two couples were on the bridge of the 88' Broward as the boat crossed the mouth of the Potomac and approached Smith Point Light. They were all sipping champagne and watching the sun slowly sink into the western horizon as Bill slowed the big yacht near the light.

"You know, life is a funny and sometimes strange thing. It's amazing how small and seemingly insignificant occurrences can have such a great effect on a person's life. Had I not run in to look at that light some twenty years ago and picked up a crab pot, I would have never gone up the Great Wicomico River to Lawton's yard. There would not be a Great River Resort, what we've all just gone through, the good and the bad would never have happened. You two would not be returning from a wonderful honeymoon, and we would not be guests of the President at Camp David. Just an impulse and a little turn of the wheel and all of our lives changed forever."

The four touched glasses and Ruth slipped her arm around Ted's waist as they sipped champagne and watched the sun slip below the horizon on the beautiful Chesapeake Bay.

Author's Message

The Great River Disclosure is a work of fiction. The resort and the characters featured in the story are also works of fiction. The Great Wicomico River and Balls Creek are real places and exist as described in all of their beauty, as do most of the other scene locations.

There is a substantial and growing percentage of the population that believes the existence of extraterrestrial visitors is a fact and that the government, for whatever reason, is covering up their existence. More and more people of prominence in the government, the military and civilian life are coming forward and stating that they were involved in some area of this fascinating story. The existence of MJ-12 or MAJESTIC-12 documents and the briefing report for President-elect Eisenhower is a fact, although the authenticity of the documents has been questioned by some. In using this intriguing theory to drive the plot, it was my desire to stay within the mainstream of legitimate research into this phenomenon and away from the fanatical fringe. To do this, I contacted one of the most respected researchers on the subject, nuclear physicist Stanton T. Friedman. He has been researching this subject in depth for forty years and his findings are well reasoned and based on fact. Stan's input and insight were invaluable in helping me develop a work of fiction based on what many believe to be fact.

It was not my intention in writing this novel to promote or debunk the theory of the existence of extraterrestrial life, but merely to use this fascinating and controversial subject as the basis for my plot. In developing the storyline, I have taken the novelist's freedom of bending facts and theories to accommodate the plot while hopefully remaining in the arena of reasonable possibility.

Larry Holcombe
Callao, Virginia
July, 2008

Printed in the United States
219235BV00002B/1/P